Desert Noir

Desert Noir

Betty Webb

Poisoned Pen Press

Poisoned Pen Press
6962 E. First Ave. Ste 103
Scottsdale, AZ 85251
www.poisonedpenpress.com
info@poisonedpenpress.com

Printed in the United States of America

To Paul, who saved my life.

Acknowledgments

Many thanks to the Sheridan Street Irregulars: Sharon Magee, Sharon Geyer, Edward M. Dixon, Holly Newman, Denise Domning, Marcia Fine, Alexandra Soave, and Judy Starbuck. You guys saved me a ton of rewrites, and maybe a tree or two in the process.

Thanks also to Sgt. Mike Anderson and Officer Mike Whitcomb of the Scottsdale Police Department, two good men who steered me away from my most egregious errors. Any errors which remain are mine alone.

One key scene in *Desert Noir* could not have been written without the information found in Charles A. Lehman's excellent *Desert Survival Handbook* (Primer Publishers, Phoenix)—no desert traveler should leave home without it. Lena's singing of the "Corn Song" was adapted from a translation in *The Papago and Pima Indians of Arizona*, by Ruth Underhill, Ph.D. Lena's knowledge of Pima creation myth comes from a wonderful book on Pima religion, *The Short Swift Time of Gods On Earth*, by Donald Bahr, Ph.D., Juan Smith, Willam Smith Allison and Julian Hayden. A personal thanks to Dr. Bahr for clearing up conflicting information on early Pima tattooing patterns.

But the biggest portion of my gratitude is reserved for Paul, the man who saved my life.

Chapter 1

I was admiring the view from my second story window when the screaming started.

Below me, sunburned tourists, plastic champagne glasses clutched in their hands, ambled along the sidewalk while in front of the Western Heart Gallery a Mariachi band swung into a Mex-Rock version of "Mi Rancho Grande." Across the street, in flagrant cultural competition, two African tribal dancers made eight feet tall by stilts bebopped to the accompaniment of conga drums.

A typical Thursday evening in Arizona.

Typical, that is, if you lived in Old Town Scottsdale in July, when the Summer Spectacular Art Walk was in full swing and thousands of tourists from Maine, Minnesota, and Vancouver hoofed their way through the scores of art galleries that lined Old Town's streets. They drank, they grazed, they bought. Even though I'd been taught the difference between good art and bad, the cynical part of me loved watching the tourists get fleeced. Arizona could use the additional sales tax, and if the tourists had more money than taste, hey, that was their problem. For free entertainment, you couldn't beat the show. I tapped my foot in time to the congas and was getting ready to take another sip of Diet Coke when I heard a woman scream.

"Ooooaaaahiiiiieee, sheeee's d-d-ddeeeadddd!" The screams were coming from the Western Heart.

Talk about stopping the party.

Once a cop, always a cop, so I didn't waste time on puzzlement. Adrenalin spiking, I snatched my snub-nosed .38 from my carryall and thundered down the stairs, taking them two at a time, ignoring the fact that I hadn't been a cop in eight months. When I hit the landing, though, I remembered why I wasn't a cop anymore. The bullet fragments lodged in my hip hurt like hell.

"Deeeaaaad!" the woman still keened, and as I reached the street, gun waving, the tourists scattered.

"What's going on?" I yelled to no one in particular. Had something happened to my friend Clarice Kobe, owner of the Western Heart?

The screaming woman picked that moment to emerge from the gallery. She was plump, in her fifties, her manicured hands and bone-colored linen dress smeared with blood.

"She's dead!" the woman sobbed. "Dead!" Then she pitched forward onto the hot cement, shredding her sheer pastel nylons and bloodying herself even further.

As a bald, pot-bellied man stooped down and wrapped his beefy arms around her, I spotted a cellular phone dangling from his Gucci belt.

"Call 911!" I snapped, then, holding my .38 high in the air, sidled past the two and into the gallery.

Not wanting to take another bullet from the armed-and-desperate, I ducked behind a table-top fountain shaped like a pregnant dolphin. The acrid scent emanating from it hinted that it flowed with wine, not water, but this was no time for a wine tasting.

I lifted my head and shouted down into the gallery's long, narrow length, "Drop your weapon and come out with your hands up!" My voice echoed back at me over the sound of trickling wine. All else was silence. No tell-tale rustlings. No ragged breathing, other than my own.

Cautiously, I raised myself up until I could peek around the dolphin's fat belly. Track lighting illuminated row after row of paintings of doe-eyed Indian maidens and craggy-faced cowboys, the usual over-priced Western clichés Clarice's gallery was infamous for. Only one painting appeared remotely original, but not because of any talent on the artist's part. Jay Kobe, Clarice's estranged husband, had never displayed originality in his entire life, so why did this particular canvas project such impromptu energy? I squinted at it. Surrounded by a gilt frame more fitting for an Impressionist master than a contemporary hack, a solitary white horse stood on the edge of a cliff, the wind fluffing out its mane and tail until they blended into the overripe cumulus clouds behind it. Jay's horse was no scraggly, range-roving mustang. Instead, it looked like someone's pampered horse-show-circuit Arabian—with one peculiar difference.

The horse sported red spots all over its body, spots of crimson so bright even the hokiest hack would avoid them. The spots began at its withers, oozed down the shoulder to the leg and from there, onto the gray granite cliff edge. In a marvelous feat of *trompe d'oeil*, the spots then spilled out over the frame's edge and trickled down the buff-colored wall.

I lowered my eyes to the floor beneath the painting, knowing what I would find there.

"Oh, shit," I muttered when I saw her.

It was Clarice, all right, and as the woman outside had so loudly proclaimed, she was indeed dead. No one could possibly live with an eye bulging from its socket like that, or with a nose battered into mush, or with a neck twisted at such an ungainly angle.

Goddamn you, Jay! I cursed under my breath.

But before I could go hunting for Clarice's abusive husband, I had to first make absolutely sure. I lowered my gun and crept up to her body, careful to touch nothing but the artery at her neck. No pulse. Although her body was still warm, her skin looked waxy and her fingernails were pale. No rigor, though, so I estimated that she had probably been dead anywhere from two to five hours. Now I could smell the other signs of death, the released contents of the lower intestine, the emptied bladder. Poor Clarice. She had always been so fastidious.

I swallowed the bile that rose in my throat and took a last look around. The killer had been careless. Two bloody footprints led away from Clarice's body and out the blood-smeared back door to the alley. Both the footprints and the blood on the door appeared dry.

I looked back at the front door, which had been standing open ever since the poor tourist from wherever had walked in. *Something wrong about that.* I pressed my lips together and thought. What? Then I got it. The front door, as well as the back, should have been locked. On Art Walk nights, Clarice always locked both doors at five o'clock, then she and the hired help readied the gallery for the big party. They poured champagne in the fountain, set out canapés, and did all the little things necessary to keep customers inside and spending. She didn't unlock the door again until seven sharp.

Then who had opened the door this evening? Surely not the killer. He would be more concerned with getting his ass out of there than keeping the tourist traffic flowing.

But that was a problem for Scottsdale's Violent Crimes Unit, not me.

My police training standing me in good stead, I backed out of the gallery the same way I entered, not disturbing the crime scene any more than necessary. As the smell of hot concrete began to replace the scent of death, I heard sirens wailing towards me.

In a little while, I'd be able to grieve for my friend, but now I had to tell the police what I knew. At least I wouldn't have to talk to Jay, wouldn't have to look at his vicious face until we got to the courtroom, wouldn't have to slog through the reams of paperwork that were a homicide cop's lot. Thanks to the felon who'd shot me eight months earlier, I didn't have worry about any of those things.

At least, that's what I thought at the time.

Chapter 2

Jimmy Sisiwan, my partner at Desert Investigations and resident cyberhead, was tapping away at his keyboard as I staggered down the stairs from my apartment into our office, coffee mug in hand.

"Want some?" I asked. I always like to start the morning with an argument. It gets my blood moving.

"Lena, you know I don't drink coffee. As he shook his head, his shoulder-length black hair rippled across his broad shoulders. Like so many Pima Indians his age, Jimmy had been raised with a Mormon family in Utah, but had recently returned to his roots on the Salt River Pima-Maricopa Reservation.

"It's decaf."

The Pima tribal tattoos that ran in four vertical lines across his forehead twitched. His Mormon family was still in shock over his reversion to traditional Pima appearance. His biological family—tattoo-free for the past one hundred years—was simply bewildered.

"Decaf poison is still poison," he nagged, as I knew he would. "Why don't you try some of my prickly pear cactus juice? It's loaded with Vitamin C." Notwithstanding his footballer's bulk, Jimmy's voice was as light and musical as a woman's.

"I'm allergic to Vitamin C."

Ignoring Jimmy's grunt of exasperation, I took another sip of the scalding coffee, then picked up the *Scottsdale Journal* lying on his desk. Only a week since Clarice's murder and she had already been bumped to page six, although I guessed the coverage would pick up again when the trial began. Her husband had been arrested, all right. The bloody footprints found on the gallery floor matched a pair of Nikes found in the trash can behind his girlfriend's house. When Jay Kobe admitted they belonged to him, he'd been charged with Murder One. He'd already been transferred from the Scottsdale Jail to the Madison Street Jail in downtown Phoenix where—as far as I was concerned—his battering ass could rot.

Feeling my stomach churn with rage as I thought of Jay, I tried to calm myself with memories of Clarice. She'd been the first of the gallery owners to welcome me to Main Street, the only one who hadn't been initially nervous about sharing the neighborhood with a private detective lured there by the reasonable rent. While I'd been intimidated by her rich-girl beauty, her democratic personality eventually won me over. As I remembered her generous smile and outgoing manner, I caught myself frowning at something that had bothered me at her funeral. Hardly anyone had been in attendance. Had Clarice devoted so much time to her art gallery that she'd neglected her family and friends? Still, it was unusual that people hadn't turned out, given the sensational way she died.

Refusing to think about it any more, I turned back to the front page of the paper and studied today's headline. COYOTE BITES TODDLER! Underneath was a picture of a crying child, adults hovering around him in a nervous circle. The story's sub-head read, NEIGHBORS DEMAND PROTECTION!

"What the hell's all this?" I pointed to the paper.

Jimmy turned around, his mahogany eyes sad. "You know those new condos along Indian Bend Wash, just west of the new freeway?"

I nodded. The Pima Freeway, which separated Scottsdale from the Salt River Pima-Maricopa Reservation, was named in honor of Jimmy's tribe although recently, an effort had been launched to rename it the "John Wayne Highway." Since Wayne had spent much of his movie career slaughtering Indians, the Pimas—who had always been peaceful farmers—were not amused.

"Well, the freeway and that new development are poking into the coyotes' territory," Jimmy continued. "It's annoying the javelinas, too. None of the animals out there have enough to eat now so they're all starting to come into town, raid the Dumpsters."

He shook his head again. "We won't have any wildlife left at all in a year or two. Maybe just a cactus wren or something flying down from the Tonto National Forest."

I feared he was right. "Maybe, maybe not. Maybe the wildlife rescue folks can do something about it."

"You wish. You know those people in the condos are always screaming rabies."

I did wish. All too often these days coyote corpses were seen lying alongside Scottsdale's eastern border, sometimes even in the city itself. Only last month a Mercedes broadsided a young javelina as it oinked its way across the street in back of the IMAX Theater. Bit by bit, we were destroying the West.

Suddenly I didn't feel like arguing anymore. I sighed and looked out the front window past the big gold DESERT INVESTIGATIONS letters, hoping to catch a little pre-scorch sunshine. Instead, I was rewarded with the sight of a disheveled tourist propped against a lightpole coyly shaped to resemble a carriage lamp. If I wasn't mistaken, that vomit-stained rag he wore was an Armani suit.

"Pale face drink too much firewater," I said.

Jimmy laughed. "I'm surprised the cops haven't scooped him up by now." Then he returned his attention to the computer screen. He was trying to break into Seriad Inc.'s security system, all on the legal up-and-up. Since computer crime was such big business these days, large corporations paid big bucks to companies such as ours to see if we could find weaknesses in their systems. As it said on our business card, "If we can't break in, no one can." I still couldn't get over how much money we were making.

As if Jimmy's words were father to the deed, a blue-and-white wheeled around the corner with its lights flashing and stopped in front of the drunk. Two uniforms got out, raised the man up, brushed him off, and gently helped him to the squad car. They probably wouldn't arrest him, just take him back to his hotel. Jailed drunks don't shop.

I was getting ready to share this bit of social commentary with Jimmy when the office door opened and a lawyer walked in. You could tell he was a lawyer by his immaculate baby blue linen suit over an even paler blue shirt, the whole business ornamented by a burgundy bow tie. Although gray as a badger and pushing sixty as hard as he could push, the man was lean and fit with a tennis player's body. Money there, I thought. Big money.

Big Money looked at Jimmy, then at me, eyeing the two-inch scar above my right eyebrow. Geez, *two* people with messed-up faces. "Are you Lena Jones?"

"You don't have an appointment." I don't like walk-ins, no matter how much money they represent.

"I'm here on Clarice Kobe's behalf."

I blinked. Why would a dead woman need a private detective? "Mister-whoever-you-are, I've met Clarice's attorney and she didn't look anything like you."

Big Money gave me a sour look. "Is there some place we can talk in private?"

For a moment I was tempted to have Jimmy throw him out—which he could have easily done since Jimmy, like most Pimas, was a large man—but my curiosity won out over my irritation. Matching the attorney's sour look with my own, I led him into the small office set aside for client consultations, and used exactly twice since Desert Investigations opened. Gesturing him into a chair, I moved to the bleached oak desk I'd bought in a fit of temporary insanity. I took another sip of my coffee but didn't offer him any.

"On Clarice's behalf, you say?"

He raised his shoulders. "In a manner of speaking. I'm actually here on behalf of Jay Kobe, her husband."

I stood up. "You've got three seconds to clear out of this office, then I call Jimmy."

The lawyer remained seated. "Whatever problems were between them, Clarice wouldn't want her husband to go to prison for a crime he didn't commit."

"Oh, come on. She was divorcing him, as you well know, because for years he beat the holy living hell out of her. And just in case your client didn't tell you, there was a restraining order in effect against him when he killed her. And let us not forget the bloody shoes they found in his alley. His shoes." Remembering

Clarice's savaged body, it was all I could do to keep from spitting in his face.

Big Money smiled. "Now, Lena. You know better than that. Just because a man beats his wife doesn't mean he'll actually kill her."

"Tell that to Nicole Brown Simpson. And it's *Miss* Jones to you."

Another sour look, then he rustled around in his pocket, pulled out a business card and slapped it down on the desk. The card was Albert Grabel's, CEO of Seriad, Inc. On the back was a note in Grabel's handwriting which said, "Lena, Jay Kobe is my wife's nephew. Please help him."

I looked around the office, at my expensive—if tacky—furniture, all courtesy of the computer chip magnate who'd set me up in business after I took a bullet in the hip. True, I'd been shot getting his foolish, drug-addicted son out of a self-inflicted mess, but still…I was a cop and protecting fools was my job. Grabel hadn't looked at the situation that way. After the doctors released me from the hospital, he shipped me off to a fancy clinic in California. And when the head of the Violent Crimes Unit moved me to a desk job despite my protests, Grabel stepped in again and convinced me my future lay in preventing computer crime.

The fact that I was scared of my own Macintosh didn't faze Grabel. He knew somebody who wasn't, he said, an Indian genius with a tattooed face who had just spent the morning spooking the hell out of Seriad's personnel director.

I handed Grabel's card back to Big Money and sat down again. "So what's your name?"

"Hal McKinnon. *Mr.* McKinnon to you."

I smiled. "Well, Hal. Convince me that shithead didn't kill Clarice."

By the time McKinnon finished talking, I was worried. Jay was screaming frame—no surprise there—but some aspects of the case bothered me. True, Jay was an evil-tempered thug who'd beaten his wife on numerous occasions, a hearty partier with recreational drugs. And true, as a widower instead of an ex, he was now the beneficiary of Clarice's will—one hell of a motive for anybody. Clarice was worth, what? Several hundreds of thousands? A million? Motive, means, opportunity. They were all there. But didn't the whole case look a little too slick?

Unlike detective fiction, real murder cases leave loose ends dangling all over the place. McKinnon had made a pretty good point.

"Let me reiterate," he finished with a smug look. "At the time of the murder, Mr. Kobe was in bed with his girlfriend, who will probably swear to that in court. And even if she doesn't, I'm betting the toxicology tests done on him will prove he was simply too drunk to leave the house. As for those bloody Nikes, they could have been planted."

"Who by? Elvis?"

He ignored me. "And don't forget about the gallery's back door. It was halfway open, right?"

I nodded carefully, wondering where he was going with this.

"The door was smeared with blood, yet there were no fingerprints. Now, Le... uh, Miss Jones, don't you think that's odd?"

Yes I did and the thought didn't cheer me. I wanted Kobe to be guilty. Clarice's face haunted my dreams, perhaps because I hadn't done enough to save her. In the six months I'd been her neighbor on Main Street, I'd seen bruises on her face more than once. But every time I'd tried to talk to her about it, she'd changed the subject. And I'd let her.

I sighed.

"Well?" McKinnon sounded impatient.

"Well what?" Just because he said his client was innocent didn't mean *I* needed to do anything about it, Albert's note or not. If Kobe hadn't killed Clarice, it was only because he hadn't gotten around to it yet.

McKinnon leaned forward and the flush that began at his neck rose slowly to his cheeks. Now he didn't look quite so healthy, more like a heart attack waiting to happen. "I'm trying to save this man's life. You were a cop. Didn't you ever save someone's life?"

"Several times, as a matter of fact, but none of them were wife beaters."

The flush intensified. "There's a lot of money involved here. You could get a goodly chunk."

I shrugged. "I already have a car that runs, a two-year, paid-up lease on this office, and I don't collect Picasso. So exactly why would I need that, as you call it, *chunk?*"

McKinnon looked like he was about to stroke out. Then, after taking a few deep breaths, he surprised me and said, "Then let's see how this strikes you, Miss Jones. Albert Grabel told me how you got that scar on your face, and..." His flush now had nothing to do with anger. "Well, what I mean to say is, you help me and I'll help you. As I'm sure you realize, in my years as a defense attorney I've had some interesting clients. Maybe one of them knows somebody who shot a little girl in the head thirty years ago."

My scarred face must have revealed my sudden interest because McKinnon nodded and said, "Now that we've got our pissing contest out of the way, maybe you should go down to the Madison Street Jail and talk to my client."

I sighed again.

It seemed to be my day for sighs.

Chapter 3

As soon as McKinnon left, I called the Scottsdale Violent Crimes Unit and asked to be put through to Captain Kryzinski, my old boss.

"Jay Kobe? You workin' for Jay Kobe? You nuts or what?" His Brooklyn accent always thickened when he was upset. "I thought you hated that dirt bag!"

"Actually, I never met the man, so for now I can only hate him in the abstract. Will you help me or not?"

Kryzinski breathed heavy for a moment. "If you were still one of my detectives you'd already have the information you're wantin'," he snapped. "So why don't you come on back?"

I didn't want to be bothered covering old territory. "I'd like to see the case file. The lab test results, the notes from the investigating officers, the photos, everything. And I'd like to know the results of the AFIS check you ran on Jay when you booked him."

AFIS was Scottsdale's laser-based Automated Fingerprint Identification System, which was linked electronically with all other state and federal fingerprint identification systems around the country. The suspect put his fingers on a glass plate smaller than a post card, the laser scanned them, and the results came back almost instantaneously. You could book somebody for a D.U.I. and within an hour find out if they'd killed their Aunt Tilly in Winnetka—even if they'd given you a phony name and were driving under a phony license. Cops loved it. Suspects hated it.

Kryzinski grumbled. "Well, I don't got any problem lettin' you know 'bout that since that crazy Indian you're working with can find it out in a New York minute. Yeah, Kobe had form. Back seven years ago, before he became an artsy-fartsy type, he worked as a nightclub bouncer out in Bakersfield. One night he got a little too rough with a patron and put her in the hospital."

"Her?"

"Yeah, her. Some shaved-head punker with more piercings than Arizona's got snakes. She was drunk and making a total ass out of herself, but shit, he didn't have to go and do what he did. Busted her jaw, knocked out a few teeth. She came out of it okay, sued the club for a bundle. As for Muscle Man, he pulled six months."

I thought about that for a minute. A nightclub bouncer? That was a long way from the art galleries of Scottsdale. I said as much to Kryzinski.

"God works in mysterious ways. Seems while he was sitting around the correctional facility counting his toes some bleeding heart came in and started giving art lessons. Guess it was supposed to make the cons appreciate the finer things in life or somethin' like that. Turned out Kobe had a knack for painting. But you know something else?"

He gave a dark laugh, as he always did when confronted by the more twisted pathways of human nature. "When Kobe got released, he moved in with his art teacher, who apparently had been swayed by his highly sensitive nature. Two weeks after movin' in, our boy beat the crap out of her, too. What is it with these women, tell me that? When Clarice Kobe threw him out, he moved in with Alison Garwood within two fuckin' weeks. He's already knocked her up, too. Not that he let that stop him from having his heavy-fisted fun. When our guys got there the night of the murder, she was lyin' in bed with an ice pack pressed to a black eye. Face swollen the size of a football. Kobe was passed out next to her, scabs all over his knuckles. Hell, Lena, I just can't wait for this trial. Men like Kobe oughta be euthanized or somethin'."

I closed my eyes. Whatever had possessed me to take the Kobe case? The man was an unrepentant thug. It was probably a miracle he hadn't killed someone before now. Or maybe he had.

"You still there, kid?" Kryzinski sounded smug.

"I'm still here and I appreciate you giving me all that information. Now what about the rest of it? The case file?"

He didn't answer and I knew he wanted a promise I couldn't give. Instead, I threw him a bone. "Look, Captain, you let me take a look at the case file and I'll give some serious thought to coming back to the Department. How's that sound?"

He sounded perkier. "Sounds good. The VCU just ain't the same without you. But hell, kid, you know that case file's classified information. It's not supposed to leave department hands, or at least not until the prosecutin' attorney gets his shot at it."

"The case file doesn't have to leave the building. I'm a speed reader. Let me come up there, I'll be done with it before you know it."

"Ah, shit, Lena."

That's when I knew I'd won.

Chapter 4

The next day, Jay Kobe's first words attacked me as the jail guards ushered him into the urine-scented visiting room, "You could be a beautiful woman if you did something about that scar. McKinnon told me you got shot in the ass, not the face."

Still the brute. Jail hadn't settled him down at all.

"I was shot in the hip. Or as my doctor phrased it, my pelvic girdle."

He frowned. "Then what about that awful scar on your forehead"

What a guy. "I was shot for the first time when I was about four years old."

"First time?" Kobe let out his breath in a hiss. He had halitosis. Living in the Madison Street Jail will do that to you. "Jesus, who'd shoot a kid?"

For some reason, I never minded telling criminals my story, perhaps because violence was already so much a part of their own lives. A bullet wound here, a knife scar there—all were badges of honor to them. But there was another reason, too. Since violence attracted violence, there was always the chance that they knew someone who knew someone who knew someone who knew something about it. This was the way most crimes were solved.

I settled myself back into the visitor's chair. "It's nice that you're concerned, Mr. Kobe, but nobody knows who shot me or why. When I turned eighteen the social workers told me some Hispanic woman brought me to St. Joseph's Emergency Room and then took off. She didn't leave her name and nobody ever showed up to claim me. You know anybody who knows anything about a kid getting shot around thirty-two years ago?"

Kobe, who probably wasn't more than thirty-two himself, shook his head. "So that's why you don't have it fixed. You're still hoping someone will see it and recognize you."

The disappointment hurt, it always did, but I shoved it away. "Smart man. Now tell me why I should believe that you didn't murder Clarice."

Even dressed in Sheriff Joe Arpaio's black-and-white striped jail duds, Jay Kobe was still a handsome man. The hazel eyes were unclouded by guilt or allergies, the cleft in his chin rivaled that of Kirk Douglas, and his bulked-up bod proved the efficacy of free weights. His only physical imperfections were his bruised knuckles. From Clarice? Or his girlfriend?

Yes, he was a pretty boy, but like most wife-beaters, I knew he would reveal himself to be a moper, a self-described perennial victim forced into unseemly behavior by his nearest and dearest. Jay didn't let me down. As he recounted his wife's many sins— arrogance, stinginess, duplicity, and an all-around inability to recognize his many sterling qualities—his black-fringed eyes took on a wounded look.

"I'm an easygoing guy but Clarice could really press my buttons, you know? But with all her faults, I loved that woman with every inch of my being."

"Apparently you had an inch or two left over. Somebody down at VCU told me your new girlfriend is pregnant. Congratulations, stud."

Kobe's bedroom eyes narrowed and for that one unguarded moment, psychopathy radiated off him like skunk skat. "The bitch told me she was on the pill. And since you're working for me, what the fuck are you doing hanging around the police department?"

"All my best friends hang out there, remember? Jay, I hope you don't expect me to take your word for anything, not with your track record."

His eyes opened baby-wide. "I told you, Clarice knew how to push..."

"Your buttons." I yawned. "Now before I fall asleep here in Sheriff Joe's Motel, why don't you tell me your version of the events last Thursday night?"

Kobe looked like he wanted to hit me but since he knew I might help him beat a Murder One rap, he recounted the events of last Thursday. According to him, he was sleeping it off at Alison Garwood's house, Clarice having thrown him out of the house a couple of months earlier. He and his girlfriend had been partying hard all day, he admitted, and he seemed to remember bopping her one.

"Alison can really push…"

"Your buttons. Continue."

He ground his teeth. "Listen, bitch, *you're* pushing my buttons, you know that?"

I smiled sweetly. "Touch me and you'll be shitting teeth for a week."

He flinched. Like most batterers, Jay was a coward. He'd never hit a woman who might hit back.

"Come on, Jay. I'm not staying down here all day. Tell me more about the night of the murder."

"There's nothing else to tell. The cops came and dragged me out of bed about two in the morning, and after one of them found those damned Nikes in the Dumpster, that was it. I told them and told them I hadn't seen those shoes in months, but they wouldn't listen to a word I said." His fingers tapped a nervous rhythm on the wooden table and I could see that his nails were growing a little long. He was overdue for a trip to the manicurist.

"Why couldn't your girlfriend convince them you'd been with her all day?"

"Ummmm." He looked thoughtful. "Alison, um, well…"

It was obvious he wasn't going to tell me the truth, so I cut to the chase. "How's this sound? Alison was mad at you for hitting her so she told the police she was in bed with an ice pack and didn't know if you'd gone out later or not. She also told the detectives that you'd often talked about killing Clarice before the divorce went through so that you'd be able to keep all that lovely money."

I enjoyed the expression on Jay's face. He looked like he'd swallowed a scorpion and it was stinging its way back up. "She's nothing but a lying whore. Look, I admit I had problems with Clarice, but I wasn't the only one. *Everybody* did."

Here it came, the I-Didn't-Kill-Her-But-I-Know-Who-Probably-Did Tango. I raised my eyebrows and slouched lower into my chair, prepared for a long monologue.

"See, Clarice was always having trouble with her family. There was something weird going on there, especially with dear old dad, you know what I mean?"

I shook my head.

"Ah, come on, a woman like you? You've been around, you know what's what."

I shook my head again.

He looked exasperated, which was what I wanted. Exasperated people were careless people. "What I'm trying to tell you, lady, is that Mr. Stephen Hyath himself had one big skeleton in his closet where Clarice was concerned. *Capice?*"

I began to *capice* all right but needed to hear more. "I'm afraid you've lost me, Jay."

"Incest, you stupid bitch! Before things went bad between us, Clarice told me that her daddy used to crawl in bed with her when mommy dearest was too drunk to care!"

I thought about that for a moment. Even if the rumor was true, would it make any difference to the murder case? It seemed to me that if long-ago incest had been the Hyath family secret, it would have been Clarice murdering Daddy, not Daddy murdering Clarice. I said as much to Kobe but he just sneered knowingly.

"She was getting ready to take him to court."

I laughed. "C'mon. Clarice was thirty. The statute of limitations on child molest would have run out years ago. Or was she going to use Recovered Memory Syndrome as an explanation for a tardy filing? That wouldn't get her much in *this* state, because none of those judgments are holding up on appeal."

Kobe shook his head. His fingers stepped up their nervous drumming on the table. "Clarice wasn't interested in justice, just money. She was going after her father in civil court to the tune of thirty million dollars. I doubt if old man Hyath was crazy about the idea of forfeiting any of his millions. He'd rather see her dead. That whole fucking family worships money."

"And you don't?"

The fingers stopped drumming and clenched into a fist. He began to rise from his chair but made the mistake of looking into my eyes. What he saw there stopped him. He sat back down slowly and forced his hand open again. His nostrils flared and I could hear the hot, fast breath whizzing through them.

I couldn't remember disliking anyone so much on first meeting, not even the serial child molester I'd once caught in the act. But I remembered McKinnon's promise to help me out with my own problem.

"OK. I'll interview Clarice's father, see what he has to say. But somehow I just can't see him rending his Brooks Brothers suit, throwing ashes upon his head, and confessing to me that he feels guilty about diddling his daughter."

Kobe frowned. "Jesus, you're vulgar."

I tried not to laugh at this pot calling the kettle black. "Got any more likely suspects?"

"Well, there was that Indian artist giving Clarice trouble over his stuff being kicked out of the gallery. Apache guy, mean looking. From up on the San Carlos rez."

An incestuous father and a mean Apache. What next? The case was starting to resemble *As the World Turns*.

Kobe was oblivious to my skepticism. "And I remember her getting into some kind of legal boondoggle with somebody over at the new Museum of Western Art she and the family built. It had to do with some old Mexican broad who got displaced when eminent domain gobbled up her neighborhood. Anyway, the old bitch up and died and for some reason, her family blamed Clarice."

Some old Mexican broad.

From what I could remember about the eminent domain case, the court fight had gotten pretty ugly, with the Hispanics screaming discrimination and the Hyaths screaming progress. As usual, progress—backed by serious money—won. The fact that an elderly Hispanic widow had been bulldozed along with her home had meant little to anyone other than her family. But that was Arizona for you. Anglos loved the state's Hispanic heritage: Hispanic food, Hispanic beer, Hispanic art, Hispanic clothes,

Hispanic architecture. In fact, Anglos loved everything Hispanic except the Hispanics themselves.

"Well, you've given me a few things to look into, Jay, so I'll see what I can do," I said, shoving my chair away from the table. "I'll get back to you."

"That's it?" My indifference appeared to shock him, or maybe he was just used to having a bigger impact on women.

Whereas I didn't even kiss him goodbye.

Chapter 5

Although I'd timed my jail visit for early morning, the temperature had already climbed past 110 degrees by the time I reached my car—a refitted hot pink 1945 Jeep I'd bought four years earlier from a desert touring company. I still hadn't bothered to repaint it or even remove the chipped steer horn decorating the hood, so as I ground gears through downtown Phoenix, derisive hoots from pedestrians accompanied me. Ignoring the tasteless rabble, I swung a hard left at the pseudo space age grandeur of Pioneer Park, where triangular-shaped "sails" hovered over large round globes tacked onto improbably curved pieces of metal. What *was* the architect thinking?

I then shot down Central Avenue past the Westward Ho Hotel. The grand old building had once housed Marilyn Monroe when she filmed *The Misfits,* but since those days of glory it had degenerated into a welfare hotel, which was the true story of the West. Forget Marilyn and Roy Rogers and the Riders of the Purple Sage. The West has become a place where luxury sedans run down coyotes and arrogant architects look upon shaman-haunted vistas as nothing more than empty lots suitable for building monuments to their own egos. Every time I drive along this raped section of the Valley of the Sun, my trigger finger starts to itch.

But back to the business at hand.

What had I learned so far? Although the Violent Crimes Unit had a strong case against Kobe, McKinnon could still have a field day with the loopholes. The shoes looked good for the prosecution, but after the Simpson case, cops were no longer sanguine about the holiness of DNA and other material evidence. What if Kobe's girlfriend decided to alibi him after all? What if she swore upon her father's grave that Kobe was snoring next to her all night? She had no police record herself and might make an unfortunately credible witness.

I tried to think like a prosecutor. If Kobe'd been with Alison all evening, he could have hired someone to punch out Clarice's lights. Still, hiring a hit man to beat your wife to death sounded pretty lame, even for Kobe. Hit men ran to .22 caliber bullets strategically aimed above the ear, not battered faces and broken necks. They were professionals carrying out business contracts and usually held no particular animosity towards their victims. Hit men were dispassionate when carrying out their duties. If not, they became victims themselves.

By the time I drove the eight miles east from downtown Phoenix to the Scottsdale city limits and the Jeep shot between the two cave-pocked sandstone buttes which straddled McDowell Boulevard, I'd decided to find out more about Clarice herself. I needed to know if there was anyone besides her husband who hated her enough to beat her to death.

Jimmy no longer hovered over his beloved computer when I got back to the office. Instead, he was relaxing in a deep leather chair, sipping a tall glass of bright pink cactus juice.

"I'm in," he announced with satisfaction. "Took me less than two hours. A child could do it."

Not this child. But as Jimmy launched into an explanation of how he'd hacked past Seriad's security and slashed his way through their encryption system, he did make it seem easy—if you shared his IQ of one-sixty-four. While he droned on I walked over to the small refrigerator in the corner and dumped several cubes of ice into a tall glass. In a nod to clean living, I filled it up with caffeine-free Diet Coke.

I waved away the rest of Jimmy's techno-babble as I felt the happy bubbles dance their way down my parched throat. A healthy burp followed. "You know I don't understand a word you're saying."

"If you would just try…"

"I have tried and it makes my head hurt. Now, about that other matter we've been working on. What have you come up with?"

The smug look left his face. "Lena, please understand that computers aren't God in a box. They have to have input. Garbage in, garbage out, right? But it's also true that nothing in, nothing out. You don't have the name of the woman who left you at the hospital. All you've got here is a date and a vague description. Hispanic, about twenty, long black hair in a braid, cotton print dress, sandals. That's it. I've hacked my way through every single hospital file and police report in the state for the two weeks surrounding that date but I just can't come up with anything. It's like you appeared out of thin air."

Or from out of state. After all, the woman told the receiving nurse she'd found me lying by the roadway.

"OK. For a minute, let's forget the woman who took me to the hospital. What about my mother? Where is she? Where did she come from? I think you should check whatever missing persons reports you can find, say, in Nevada or Utah, California, or even New Mexico. Or any state where a woman or little girl turned up missing."

A woman. Why hadn't I asked Jimmy to find a *man* and a woman—two parents, not one? Was it because my subconscious knew something my conscious mind refused to face?

Jimmy gave me a sad look before he answered. "It was the early Sixties, Lena. A lot of young women, many of them with children, went missing around then. Young men, too."

"Then let's narrow the search to women who went missing within a thousand-mile radius of Arizona."

He smiled with perfectly straight teeth courtesy of his Mormon adoptive parents. "I'm already on it. Did you think I wouldn't be?"

I blushed. Nobody had to convince Jimmy of the importance of identity. Although he knew who his biological parents were, we were both engaged in the same pursuit—chasing down the ghosts of memory. Who were we—really? Was Jimmy a Pima or a Mormon or a combination of both? Who was I? A victim of child abuse or the lone survivor of a family tragedy? As Jimmy had explained during our first meeting when I asked about his unusual tribal tattoo, "You can't know where you're going until you know where you've been."

The rest of the day was filled with the usual tasks. I followed up on another of Albert Grabel's referrals and secured a contract from a restaurant chain. The Golden Apple's profits had dipped severely in recent months and they had grown suspicious of a certain manager. The personnel director, hamstrung by state and federal employee's-rights law, could only give me the manager's name, birth date, and social security number. She told me to do my thing and not to let her know what that thing was. What she didn't know about couldn't be testified to in court.

Within three hours, Jimmy had generated a five-page computer print-out listing every address where the man ever lived, the names and histories of his three ex-wives, his ex-neighbors' telephone numbers, his educational background (he had not graduated from college as his application stated—he'd been expelled for cheating during his sophomore year), his entire work history (which included seven jobs he had not listed), a bankruptcy, overdue credit card balances amounting to more than twelve thousand dollars, two convictions in Florida for petty theft, and one conviction in South Carolina for embezzlement. Jimmy even discovered that the man had also amassed a considerable on-line gambling debt.

After a few phone calls to make certain the manager we were investigating was the man on the print-outs, I knew we'd found the source of the Golden Apple's problem. What they would do with this information was their business but past experience convinced me they wouldn't prosecute. They'd just fire him and write on his personnel record that he was "not eligible for re-hire." The man would then move on to the next job and the next embezzlement.

I smiled at Jimmy. "Brilliant. Now let's wait until tomorrow before we call the Golden Apple. No point in letting them know how easy this is."

He smiled back. "A child could do it."

"That's what you keep saying."

The next job, an insurance investigation, would take a little longer. Copper State Insurance wanted to know if the woman claiming crippling injuries in a car accident was faking. A cursory glance at the print-out of her recent credit card statements hinted at just that. Of course, there might be a perfectly good explanation why a wheelchair-bound woman living alone might need rock-climbing gear. A gift for a boyfriend, maybe? I studied the print-out closer and discovered the shoes were a size six.

Jimmy went home just after five and I locked up and went upstairs to my overhead apartment, taking my .38 with me. Dusk was more than two hours away, but instead of closing my apartment door behind me, I raised my gun, flipped on the overheads, and slipped carefully through the two rooms, peering behind the shower curtain, into the kitchen pantry, and even into the bedroom's long, dark closet. Inspection finished, I went back to the front door, closed it firmly, and dead-bolted the lock. I'd learned to inspect my living quarters at the age of ten when I'd come home from school to what I thought was an empty house, only to discover that my foster father—my third in as many years—had hidden himself in my closet and I'd locked myself in with him.

I never made that mistake again.

Finally feeling safe, I nuked some ramen noodles and ate them while I watched the rape and pillage on CNN. It always comforted me to know that things were much worse elsewhere. By the time the sports segment came on, a black bar had appeared at the top and bottom of the thirteen-inch screen. Letterboxed football? I got off the couch and thumped the TV a good one, but the black remained. I switched it off. Now I needed new everything.

I looked around at my beige living room. When I say beige, I mean it. Courtesy of the former tenant—a tax preparer who left everything but his clothes—the carpet was beige, the sagging sofa was beige, the occasional chair was beige, the dinette was beige, and the walls were beige. Even the plastic faux pine coffee table was beige. The only spots of color in the entire apartment were the few items I'd brought with me—the Two Gray Hills Navajo rug hanging over the couch, a yellow-and-black striped clown kachina doll lounging on the window sill, and the black satin toss pillow with red embroidered lettering that said, "Welcome to the Philippines." I'd stolen it from my fourth foster home because they were nice people and I wanted something to remember them by.

Or was that the fifth foster home? Over the years, I'd lost count.

The living room held several other items which differentiated it from a Motel 6—an old phonograph turntable and next to it, a rack of vintage blues albums I'd begun collecting in my early days at Arizona State University. I owned the usual, of course— Robert Johnson, Muddy Waters, John Lee Hooker, Willie Dixon, Howlin' Wolf. But I'd also accumulated an admirable collection of the less famed blues masters—Lightnin' Slim, Jimmy Anderson, Lazy Lester, Whispering Smith, Elmore James, Big Joe Turner, Mississippi Fred McDowell.

I put some Leadbelly on the turntable. As he moaned "Where Did You Sleep Last Night?" I wondered for the hundredth time why this music moved me so. I was white, had lived in Arizona all my remembered life, and I'd never traveled east of Texas. Yet the plaintive songs of these old Black men from the Mississippi Delta filled me with a familiar ache nothing else could. Had I heard this music as a child?

My ramen finished, I tossed the Styrofoam cup into the beige trash can. While Leadbelly wailed his suspicions, I went into the bedroom to change into a T-shirt, shorts, and running shoes. After strapping a pedometer around my ankle, I went back to the kitchen, filled an insulated bottle with ice water, and tucked the water and my .38 into the special fanny pack I kept on the counter. Then I let Leadbelly rest and went out the door.

At a jog slow enough to prevent further injury to my hip, I headed west on Main Street, then south on Sixty-Eighth Street, and west again on Thomas to Sixty-Fourth. By the time I crossed McDowell Road and headed past the shadows of the giant double buttes at the entrance to Papago Park, I was slippery with sweat but no longer cared. Serotonin hummed along my brain synapses, making me as high as a red-tailed hawk on a windy day.

Papago Park was a thousand-acre oasis of sage and sand sur-rounded by an urban ocean of concrete. Home to the Phoenix

Zoo and the Desert Botanical Gardens, its natural beauty was somewhat blemished by the hiking and biking trails that criss-crossed over the site of the old Hohokam Indian village long since reduced to rubble. Over the years pot hunters—those thieves of time—had stolen everything of value and the only artifacts left were a petroglyph here, a crumbling wall there. The Hohokam were gone now and their descendants, the Pima, had been pushed onto the reservations to the east and south.

Now the park itself was being threatened by city planners who wanted to replace the desert with soccer fields and tungsten lighting. This bothered Scottsdale's Anglos more than it did the Pima, because the Pima had always believed impermanence was the way of the world. *Everything* changes, they claimed, even the gods.

After Elder Brother wrestled power away from Earth Doctor, the disgruntled creator of First World took refuge in the Underground. Some Pima believed the entrance to the Underground was located in a cave in the Superstition Mountains thirty miles to the east. But on evenings like this, when I thought I could hear the echo of a medicine man's wooden flute in the wind that whispered down the buttes, I sided with those Pima who believed the entrance to the Underworld was right here in the park.

And now the city fathers wanted to pave it shut.

Some day, the Pima warned, when the outrages against the land became too extreme to be born, Earth Doctor would re-emerge from his hiding place and wash away Second World like he did the first, with a mighty flood. The fact that we weren't already swimming never ceased to amaze me.

Even though the temperature in the park still topped one hundred degrees, today my usual route was congested with joggers. A southerly breeze carried discordant traffic noise up from Van Buren Boulevard. Annoyed, I broke away from the crowd and jogged past the big cave called Hole-in-the-Rock towards Hunt's Tomb, the gleaming pyramid that housed the body of a former Arizona governor. When I reached the base of the butte where the tomb sat, I stopped to catch my breath and gulp some water. Thirst quenched, I jogged across the through-park highway, then west up the slope to the giant twin buttes. Slowing to a walk, I picked my way across the loose rock as I climbed higher in elevation until I reached the old amphitheater nestled between the buttes. Utterly winded, I sat down on the stone steps and chugged some more water. Now I needed to climb higher. Paying no attention to the jagged rocks that tore at my hands, I scrambled to the top of an outcropping that rose above the amphitheater. As far as I was concerned, this was the best seat in the park.

The skyscrapers of Phoenix lay to my west, sizzling under the first intimations of a gaudy sunset. To the northeast lay the luxurious homes of Scottsdale. East of Scottsdale's city limits sprawled the corn and cotton fields and dusty rancherias of the Salt River Pima-Maricopa Indian Reservation. I squinted my eyes, but in the glimmering dusk, I couldn't quite see Jimmy's house, let alone the traditional dome-shaped limb-and-brush hut he'd built and where he sometimes communed with the old Pima gods. Beyond the rez rose the pale lavender peaks of the Superstition Mountains where, as legend claimed, the Lost Dutchman Gold Mine awaited rediscovery.

And where—perhaps—Earth Doctor plotted his revenge.

The butte behind me blocked out most of the street noise from Van Buren Boulevard, while in front of me the thick streams of traffic along McDowell had begun to thin. I was as alone as I was going to be.

As I waited for the sun to do its sunset thing, I thought about Clarice. Her open-handed friendship had come as a surprise because I'd originally suspected she was too much of a Scottsdale snoot for a blue-collar cop like me. She said *iither* while I said *eether, potaato* while I said *potayto.* But she stopped by Desert Investigations at least twice a week bearing gifts of exotic coffee beans, bouquets of flowers from her garden, and baskets of scented potpourri. I expressed bemusement at these unearned gifts, but she had simply explained that she had been overjoyed to find another non-painter who could tell the difference between a gouache and a casein wash. When I had admitted I'd gained my knowledge of art from a long-ago foster parent, she hadn't looked down on me as had so many others. Instead, she'd been intrigued.

For all Clarice's beauty and sophistication, I had detected vulnerability in her eyes and along with it, a surprising lack of the surety that her privileged background should have guaranteed. Once I started noticing the bruises that sometimes marred her face, I'd wondered what childhood damage she'd suffered that bore such strange fruit.

Takes one to know one, doesn't it?

And I wondered once more about her husband. Was Jay Kobe really innocent of Clarice's death? Or was I more impressed by a firm chin and a pair of black-fringed hazel eyes that I wanted to admit?

I decided not to think about Clarice or Jay for a while. Instead, I would just concentrate on the present. Be here now, as the hippies used to say. And in the Here and in the Now, life was growing more beautiful by the minute. As the sun dropped out of the sky and slid behind the Phoenix skyline, streaks of fuschia and gold shot out past rose-tinged cumulus clouds. I waited a few more minutes until the light was just right, then began my daily ritual.

I stood up and spread my arms out in front of me. The dying sun kissed them and the golden hairs along my forearms began to glow with bright colors stolen from the sky.

For a moment I simply stood there, smiling. Then I turned to the east and focused on the flame-touched Pima cornfields and began to chant the "Corn Song" Jimmy taught me.

On Tecalote fields, the corn was growing green.
Growing green.
I came down to the land and I saw.
I saw the tassels waving in the wind.
And I sang for joy.

As I sang the old words, something rustled behind me. Raising my hand towards the zipper on my fanny pack, cursing myself for not having my gun at the ready, I turned slowly, only to see a coyote slip between two creosote bushes. His face—an unusual pale blond—tilted querulously, as if he had been listening to my off-key serenade. Did something deep in his blood recognize the old Pima song? A closer look proved that he was no casual music critic, just a weary hunter commuting home with a limp gopher dangling between his teeth instead of a briefcase.

Oops. Cancel that sexist metaphor. As the coyote trotted nonchalantly past me, I saw the swollen teats hanging from her belly. *Mama,* not Daddy, was headed home to the kiddies.

I stopped my song when the coyote, without even looking, dashed onto McDowell Road at the same time a huge Winnebago came barreling through the gap between the buttes. The driver must have seen her—the setting sun was at his back, after all—but he didn't even slow down. By the time the coyote was halfway to the traffic island the RV was upon her.

I quit breathing and steeled myself for the thump.

But I heard nothing but the whine of snow tires as the overloaded Winnebago rushed past. The coyote had made it to the traffic island where she sat looking at me.

I'd swear she was laughing.

I didn't do much jogging on the way home. My hip ached and I remembered Dr. Elfride's warning: "You can exercise, Lena, just don't get compulsive about it."

Hadn't anybody told him Compulsive was my middle name?

Hot and tired, I limped my way up Main Street, glad it wasn't a Thursday and another damned Art Walk night when I'd have to drag myself past the gawkers. But I was in luck. Although I could hear the ever-present hum of traffic from nearby Scottsdale Road, all was quiet on the Desert Investigations front. Only one car, a silver Taurus that probably belonged to one of the gallery owners, remained parked in front of the building next to mine. Carriage lamps glimmered in the dusk and a few soft-throated doves cooed lullabies. The best of all possible worlds.

I smiled again, my second smile in less than an hour. Life was good.

But I stopped smiling when the man in the silver Taurus leaned out his window and shot me.

Chapter 6

When I woke up, both my shoulder and my head were killing me. And I was surrounded by men.

Looming over me was Captain Kryzinski, his round face so drawn and grim he looked like a dried apple. He hated it when scumbags shot his cops. The fact that I wasn't "his cop" anymore had never really registered. Standing next to him was Dr. Elfride, his lean, monkish face looking most unmonkishly pissed-off. Some tattletale must have told him I'd been jogging. And there was Jimmy, looked more worried than I had ever seen him.

A strong animal odor filled the private hospital room. I lifted my sore head from the pillow and tried to peer over Captain Kryzinski's chunky shoulder. "Somebody let a horse in here?"

A rustling, then a parting of masculine heads and shoulders as another face appeared above me. "She must be feeling better," Dusty said. His taut, Clint Eastwood face was out of sync with his edgy voice. "She's stopped whining and started bitching."

"That's what's always intrigued me about you, Dusty," I said sweetly. "You always know the right thing to say to a woman. So why didn't you bother to shower before coming to see me?"

Kryzinski turned pink as his ridiculous suit. Like so many Eastern transplants to Arizona, he tried too hard to fit in, regularly squeezing his bagel-shaped body into slim-cut Western suits. Most of the detectives in the Violent Crimes Unit found his ludicrous appearance endearing but they still weren't above humming a few bars of "Rhinestone Cowboy" as he waddled down the hall.

"Now, c'mon, Lena, why you talking to Dusty like that?" he frowned. "When we called him and told him you'd been shot, he burned some serious rubber getting down here. Picked himself up another speeding ticket, not that he needs it, him already being a lifetime member of the Speeder's Hall of Fame and all. Now here you are remarking that he didn't slow down long enough to take a shower. Jesus, Lena, show some respect."

Dusty turned a wry face to Kryzinski. "Haven't you learned by now not to get embroiled in our domestic disputes?" With that, he strode back to the armchair in the corner and collapsed into it, draping his long, Levi-clad legs across the arm in a pose of the utmost boredom. At least he'd taken off his spurs.

Jimmy choked back a laugh. Then I noticed that he was holding a dozen yellow roses in his hand. How unlike Jimmy, who usually preferred to leave blossoms on their vines. "We've been pretty worried about you, Lena," he said. "What happened?"

Kryzinski broke in. "Yeah, that's my question. What happened? By the time the EMTs got to you, the shooter was long gone. But we're gonna get him, don't you worry, and when we do, I'll personally put his balls on spin cycle."

"Make sure you read him his Miranda first." I winced as my head gave an almighty throb. It hurt almost as bad as my shoulder. "The perp was some guy in a silver Taurus, but don't ask me for his license number because I was too busy passing out to write the damned thing down. And, no, I didn't see his face, either. It was in shadow, and I think..." I stopped for a moment, trying to remember exactly what I had seen, not what I *thought* I had seen— two entirely different things. "He may have been wearing a mask but there was so much shadow on him I can't be sure. Before I could get a good look, I heard a noise, the gunshot, I guess, and that was it. I don't even remember falling. How long have I been here?"

Kryzinski looked at his watch, which had a picture of a palomino on its face, the horse's tail doing service as the second hand. "About an hour. You lucked out all the way around. One of them gallery owners was stayin' late doing inventory or some other artsy crap and heard the shot. He ran out, saw you layin' there, and screamed so loud the shooter took off. Then he called 911 and when the EMTs came along, he'd already stopped the bleeding. Took his shirt off and pressed it against the wound. Smart, huh? The EMTs say you were semi-conscious and swearing like a Marine by the time you rolled into Emergency."

I smiled, gratified by my machismo. "So who was my Good Samaritan?"

Jimmy grinned. "Cliffie."

Regardless of how much it hurt, I had to laugh. "*Cliffie?* And he actually let himself get dirty?" Cliff Barbianzi owned Damon and Pythias, the gallery next door to Clarice's which specialized in gay art. Cliffie was so well known for his ultra-chic lifestyle that *GQ* magazine had even featured him in a recent article titled "Fashion Plates of the New West. "

Jimmy's grin broadened. "He got dirt, blood, hair, spit—you name it—all over him. He was a real mess. Oh, and he gave me these flowers for you, took them right out of his front window display since all the flower shops were closed. Told me to tell you he'd have come down here himself but he wanted to wash down the front of our building before you got home. He didn't want you to have to see the, uh, mess."

A lump formed in my throat at the thought of the immaculate Cliffie down on his hands and knees scrubbing away my blood. I'd never thought of him as being a particularly close friend but I guess you never know about these things until your blood's splattered all over the sidewalk.

At that point, Dr. Elfride elbowed everyone aside and scowled down at me. "Want to know the damage? Not that I think you give a rat's ass."

I swallowed the lump and said, "Make my day." A snort of laughter from Dusty's corner.

Dr. Elfride's mouth twitched, too. "The bullet passed through the fleshy part of your right shoulder, completely missing the bone, the artery, and most of the muscle mass. The Emergency Room docs picked out the bits of clothing imbedded in the wound and closed you up with six stitches, so you won't have much of a scar at all. The only reason you lost consciousness was because your head hit the sidewalk when you fell. Now, Lena, about what you were doing before the bullets started flyin'. The ER doc told me he took a pedometer off you and it registered twelve-point-three miles. Can it be true that a patient I've told *not* to, I repeat, told *not* to exercise too vigorously, is actually jogging twelve miles a day? In this heat?"

More snorting from the corner.

I shrugged and a tiny demon prodded my shoulder with a pitchfork. "You told me to exercise, that it would be good for my hip."

Dr. Elfride opened his mouth, left it open so long that I worried a horsefly from Dusty's direction might wing in, then closed it again. "I give up," he said, then stalked towards the door. Before he opened it, he glared back.

"You're going to do what you want no matter what I say, so you might as well run the friggin' Phoenix Marathon." He made sure he slammed the door on his way out.

Kryzinski ignored him. "Bet you a steak dinner at Monti's this is connected to the Kobe killing."

I thought about that. On first consideration, such a connection seemed unlikely, but what other reason could there be? The embezzling restaurant manager didn't know he was being investigated, ditto with the possibly fraudulent insurance claimant. And Scottsdale wasn't exactly a major venue for drive-by shootings. Then whodunit? The only truly violent person I'd rubbed up against in the past few weeks had been Jay Kobe, but he was still in jail—or at least he had been at 10 a.m. this morning.

Which begged the question. "Uh, by any chance did Jay Kobe make bail today?"

Kryzinski's round face flushed in anger. "Damn right he did. His lawyer went down there this afternoon with the bail bondsman and the fuck was back on the street by three. Probably already beat his girlfriend up again, too. These batterers, they can't get enough of that shit. Gets them hard, y'know? But hell, Lena, I'm worried we're in trouble with this case. You need to come down to the station and see what came in from the crime lab this morning. The prosecutor's gettin' worried."

So Kobe was on the loose. The last time I'd seen him he'd wanted to punch me out, but still, since I was supposed to be on his side, I thought it doubtful he'd actually take a gun to me. Fists were more his style—he liked that close, interpersonal contact. Feeling pretty pissed at McKinnon for not keeping me up to date about Kobe's whereabouts, I decided to have a talk with him first thing in the morning.

Kryzinski was no happier than I. "Shit, Lena. You resign from the force because you're sick of getting shot and look what's going down. You might as well come back. Get shot on company time."

We were back to our old argument. "I *didn't* resign from the force because I was sick of being shot. I resigned because I was sick of sitting at that stupid desk you put me at."

"I *didn't* put..."

"The hell you didn't!"

"Children, children! Don't fight." Dusty uncoiled himself from the chair and approached my bed. Giving Kryzinski a neutral look, he said, "Let's leave the who-pissed-off-who-first argument for another time." Then he turned his attention to me. "And you. You need to get some rest instead of picking at old scabs, so why don't we all clear out of here so you can sleep? Dr. Elfride told me that if you keep improving, he'll release you tomorrow."

"Tomorrow hell. I'm going home tonight." With that, I struggled out of the stiff hospital sheets, taking care that the split-back hospital gown was closed. No point in shocking my visitors. When my feet touched the floor, a wave of dizziness swept over me but I fought my way through it and staggered towards the closet.

"Hey, kid, you can't..." Seeing the look on my face, Kryzinski shut up.

Jimmy knew better than to say anything. He did heave a great sigh, though.

Dusty strolled after me like I was a recalcitrant calf and slid the closet door closed. "I brought you some fresh clothes. The others are all messed up."

"We're impounding them as evidence," Kryzinski managed, his turquoise-studded bola tie bouncing with anger. "I don't plan on letting this fuck get away with shootin' one of my officers."

I started to say, "I'm not one of your officers anymore," but didn't, because as far as he was concerned, I still was.

Dusty drove carefully—for him. He wrestled his wide pickup truck through Scottsdale's narrow side streets, somehow managing to avoid the omnipresent bicyclists and inline skaters enjoying the relative cool of the evening. He was so considerate that he didn't even nag me about checking out of the hospital against Dr. Elfride's orders. He did, however, lay down the law in another respect.

"I'm staying over, just in case you start seeing two of everything," he announced, in a don't-you-dare-talk-back tone. "The horses can take care of themselves tonight."

I shrugged before I remembered my shoulder. The pain almost made me drop Cliffie's yellow roses. "Did you bring your gun?" Because of the permissive Arizona gun laws, just about every man, woman and child in the state was packing, and Dusty was no exception.

"What do you think?"

"I think you're a regular Boy Scout."

"You're a perceptive woman. Sometimes."

I smiled.

I'd met Dusty just before I was transferred to the Violent Crimes Unit, when I stopped him as his truck sped along Frank Lloyd Wright Boulevard, going—as my radar gun affirmed—thirty-seven miles above the speed limit. I flashed my blue lights and he pulled over immediately. As I wrote out a ticket to Grant "Dusty" Norris, his politeness impressed me almost as much as his handsome face.

"Anybody ever tell you that you look like Clint Eastwood?" I asked, handing the ticket through the truck's rolled-down window.

"Only several hundred people," he said, receiving the summons with as much grace as if it had been an invitation to a White House dinner. I noticed that he wasn't wearing a wedding ring.

Since cops aren't supposed to put the moves on their *clients*—as Scottsdale cops are encouraged to term them—that would normally have been that. But a week later my fifteen-year-old Toyota gasped its last on a lonely stretch of the Beeline Highway about thirty miles northeast of Scottsdale, stranding me in 116-degree heat. Like all sensible desert dwellers, I carried several water containers in the trunk, but the radiator was the least of my car's woes. I exited the car and stood in its shade, sipping water and feeling pretty sorry for myself when a familiar-looking truck pulled off the road behind me. I leaned back in the car, grabbed my gun from the glove compartment, and unsnapped its holster. Just in case.

I didn't know whether to be pleased or alarmed when last week's Clint Eastwood double stepped from the truck and started towards me. "Anything I can help you with, ma'am?"

When he recognized me, those amazing blues eyes narrowed, and for a moment, a frisson of fear crawled up my spine. Something told me this man could be dangerous. My hand had already begun easing the .38 out of its holster when he finally grinned and said, "They say revenge is a dish best served cold but it's too damned hot out here for any of that, don't you think, Officer? What say I give you a lift to the nearest gas station and then we figure out what we're going to do with each other? If anything."

All fear gone, I grinned back.

Four years later, I knew little more about Dusty than I'd learned that day and the shame was that I didn't care. With knowledge came intimacy, something I'd never been very good at. Foster homes aren't the greatest places for learning how to love—or even how to like. Just when I began to settle into any particular family, to trust them—to *like* them—something would happen, necessitating a move to another family. After hundreds of tear-filled nights, I finally learned not to get attached to anyone.

So I was content with our relationship as it stood, with Dusty living on the dude ranch where he was head wrangler and me living above my detective agency. Dusty preferred it that way, too, which sometimes made me curious. I knew quite well why I had trouble getting close to people, but what was Dusty's story?

An interesting question, to be sure, but not one I needed to answer now. I needed to know who killed Clarice. Gut instinct told me my own shooter was connected to the Kobe case, but I'd only agreed to take the case the day before it had happened. To my knowledge, the only people who knew of my involvement were Albert Grabel, Kobe himself, and Kobe's attorney. Then again, Kobe's release on bond meant that he'd been out and about and probably shooting off his mouth in every bar in town.

"Shit!" Dusty swerved the truck suddenly to the left.

I snapped out of my reverie. "What?"

"Goddamn skater almost ran into me."

I turned around and in the glow of a streetlight, saw a woman dressed in a Day-Glo bikini with matching kneepads flipping us the bird. "Probably some goddamn Californian," I said.

"Goddamn Californians are ruining this town."

I said the most optimistic thing I could think of. "But the statistics show that for every three Californians who move out here, two go back."

"Leaving one more son of a bitch every half block to make us miserable."

For the past decade, Scottsdale—founded after the Civil War by Winfield Scott, a U.S. Army chaplain, and which had once called itself "The West's most Western town"—had been overrun by Californians fleeing earthquakes, New Yorkers fleeing crime, and Chicagoans fleeing snow. The city had grown from 130,000 to 180,000 residents in just six years, and while the influx was good for the tax base, Scottsdale now suffered from streets too narrow for the increased traffic. Not a day went by that some rancher didn't sideswipe some underdressed immigrant on rollerblades.

Nobody liked it, but there wasn't a thing we could do about it. In twenty years, I figured, the Valley of the Sun would look just like Los Angeles.

And smell like it, too.

That night the pain in my shoulder kept me awake so I lay staring at the ceiling, thinking about Clarice and all the other battered women I'd come in contact with in my years with the Violent Crimes Unit. Each year, an estimated one-and-a-half million women were severely beaten by their husbands, and everyone in VCU believed that Scottsdale had more than its share of these dysfunctional couples. We'd arrest the batterers and refer the women to shelters, but nine times out of ten the next day the scarred and beaten women would be down at the jail bailing out their men. The psychologists told us it was because the women could see no way out of their situation, but while that theory might explain some victims, it didn't explain Clarice. She was a childless, educated beauty with money of her own. She didn't need to be dependent upon anybody else's paycheck, she owned a house worth a half million, and she could get any man she wanted.

Why had she wound up with Jay?

A sudden rumbling pulled me from my reverie. I rolled over and nudged Dusty, to whom insomnia was a stranger. "You're snoring, babe."

"Mmph." He gave me a few minutes' reprieve, then started up again.

Careful not to wake him, I pressed my hand against his cheek and caressed it slowly, surprised as always by how soft his weathered skin actually felt. He turned his face into my hand and, eyes still closed, kissed my palm. I moved my hand away.

I didn't love him. I didn't.

I was still safe.

Chapter 7

Dusty was gone by the time I crawled out of bed, but he'd filled a vase with water and arranged Cliffie's yellow roses in it.

My head still hurt, but not as fiercely. I showered carefully, keeping my bandaged shoulder out of the spray, dressed in jeans and a loose T-shirt, then limped downstairs to the office.

Jimmy greeted me with a disapproving glare. "You should stay in bed. There's nothing going on down here I can't handle."

I ignored him. "The Violent Crimes Unit ran an AFIS check on Jay Kobe and came up with a few things I want you to follow up. See if he owes money, stuff like that."

"Great minds think alike. The print-out's already on your desk."

"Remind me to give you a raise."

The glare vanished as he laughed. "You can't give me a raise. We're equal partners, remember?"

I smiled, even though my shoulder was screaming at me. "You talk to the Golden Apple yet about that light-fingered manager?"

"They're very pleased, didn't even ask about the bill."

Which I knew would be considerable. "They might make a few comments when they receive it. How about our little insurance claimant?"

He was silent for a moment then said in an oddly even voice, "I think one of us ought to run some surveillance on her with a video camera. Those credit charges don't prove a thing on their own."

"You looking to get out of the office?"

Another long silence. Then, "If I do, will you promise to take it easy?"

"Sure," I lied, anxious for him to leave so I could do some work without him nagging at me. "Just remember what I told you the last time we discussed surveillance. Don't ever, ever let her get a look at you or it's all over. With your size, long hair, and tribal tatts, you don't exactly blend in with the scenery."

Jimmy agreed to rent a nondescript car and conduct the first day's surveillance parked down the street, with his hair tucked under a baseball cap and his tattoos hidden by cosmetics. We both knew that the woman wouldn't be foolish enough to sashay down the sidewalk in broad daylight but she might drop her guard at night. If so, Jimmy would be waiting. If she didn't...

Well, surveillance cameras weren't exactly unknown in my profession. Nothing a little breaking and entering couldn't take care of, although I'd have to wait until my shoulder wasn't quite so stiff. I wasn't about to send Jimmy in there to do my dirty work. He needed a police record like I needed another bullet wound.

As soon as Jimmy took off for the car rental agency, I settled down to read his print-out on Jay Kobe. What I found had me boiling.

After battering his art teacher girlfriend in Bakersfield, Kobe had split town and moved to Scottsdale, where he'd joined a private S&M club on the Scottsdale/Phoenix border. After a couple of incidents that shocked even their kinky clientele, he'd been asked to hand in his membership card. He was also deeply in debt and from the names and amounts Jimmy had managed to find, his drug problem appeared to be escalating.

Ah, give us your tired, your poor, your huddled masses yearning to be free, your hopped-up crackheads... No wonder we Arizonans owned so many guns: We were scared to death.

More disgusted than ever, I picked up the phone and called Jay's lawyer. "Thanks for letting me know Kobe was out of jail," I snapped, after his harried-sounding secretary finally put me through.

"Couldn't," McKinnon said.

"Why the hell not?"

"Because I drove straight from the jail yesterday into a court hearing and by the time it let out, the day was shot so I went home. I don't make courtesy phone calls from home."

Courtesy phone calls. I should have paid more attention to my instincts when McKinnon first entered my office. He might wear expensive suits, but morally he was a sleaze. "Your day was shot, hum? Well, so was I."

For a few seconds I could almost hear the rats running through his maze-like brain, then he asked cautiously, "Meaning?"

"Meaning that somebody shot me last night, Mr. McKinnon. It might have been your client."

There was another lawyerly pause while he thought about this. Then he said, "I'm sorry you were shot, Miss Jones, but the wound couldn't have been too bad or you wouldn't be on the phone talking to me right now. Am I right in guessing that you're calling from your office?" After I grunted in the affirmative, he continued, "I'd like to remind you that Mr. Kobe is your client, too. Why would he want to harm someone who is helping him?"

"We didn't exactly hit it off yesterday."

"Jay seldom hits it off with anyone. He's not the most personable man in the world. Artists seldom are."

A memory flashed into my mind of Madeline, one of my foster mothers, wiping paint off her hands with a turpentine-stained rag. Turning towards me, she caressed my cheek with a soft hand. "Did you know that you're such a beautiful little girl I'm having trouble painting you? Say, I've got an idea! If you frown a little harder, you'll give me some nice easy frown lines to paint."

When my standard morose expression disappeared into giggles, she caressed my cheek again. "Thank you, dear. Laugh lines are easy to paint, too."

Remembering all this, I said to McKinnon, "Most artists I've known are perfectly decent people. Kobe's the exception."

He didn't say anything for a while, and for a moment, I thought he might have walked away from the phone. But then he surprised me. "You know, Lena, I don't think we're going to have any trouble getting the charges against Mr. Kobe dropped, so why don't you just send me your bill."

"Hal, that's the smartest thing I've ever heard you say."

Interesting. One day after begging me to take the case McKinnon was backing away. Was he trying to protect me?

Or was he afraid of what I might find out?

I spent the rest of the day just sitting around, more or less following my doctor's orders. After call-forwarding the phone to my apartment, I went upstairs and read a few pages from the new Stephen King, listened to some barnstorming Chicago blues by KoKo Taylor, then put together a scratch salad from the browning lettuce in the refrigerator.

By 2 p.m. I was bored enough to ignore my shoulder's complaints, and hobbled down the stairs and through the ghastly heat to the Damon and Pythias Gallery. The last time I'd seen Cliff Barbianzi—at least to remember—was at Clarice's funeral. Although I was certain he'd been close to her, his face had betrayed nothing.

Just as I'd hoped, Cliffie sat enthroned behind his Louis Quatorze desk, as elegantly attired as the Sun King himself. The hand-tailored dark suit might not be very "Arizona" but it whispered money and good breeding, as did the diamond and platinum tie tack which kept his rep tie from running off. The Sun King, however, would probably have disapproved of an art gallery devoted to male nudes; Louis XIV preferred women. Cliffie looked up when I entered and a look of horror spread across his crinkled baby's face.

"Lena! You're supposed to be in the hospital!" Although in his sixties, Cliffie was one of the handsomest men I knew. With his cherubic face and silvery hair, he looked like an impish elderly angel just one good deed away from getting his wings.

I eased myself carefully into an exquisite needlepoint chair. "Don't nag, Cliffie. It makes my head hurt. Why don't you offer me a drink instead?" I looked hopefully towards the small back room where I knew he kept a small refrigerator stocked with strawberry smoothies and Beck's. "I need the vitamin C."

He gave me a bemused look but without another word, got up and walked to the back room, returning shortly with a Beck's for himself and a smoothie for me. He knew that I never touched alcohol, although he didn't know the reason—that not knowing my genetic background, I was afraid to indulge in anything that might be even remotely habit-forming. For all I knew, my parents were both alcoholics. Or drug addicts. Or maybe even a nasty combination of both.

"*L'chaim,* dear heart," he said, as he tilted his Beck's towards me.

"*L'chaim* to you, too." The smoothie was delicious. We sipped in quiet communion for a moment, then I cleared my throat and said, "Cliffie, I want to thank you for everything you did last night. Not everybody would have come running like that when the shooter was still around."

Cliffie wiped a thin line of froth from his delicate upper lip. "You're not 'somebody.' You're my friend."

Refusing to get emotional, I took a deep breath and continued. "And thanks for the flowers, and thanks especially for cleaning up the, uh, mess. That really went above and beyond."

He smiled so sweetly I could almost hear angel's voices. "Dear heart, as tough as you might like to act, I know you would have done the same."

Emotion threatened me again but I managed to fight it off. "Naw, I wouldn't. I'm not a cop anymore."

His smile returned. "Being or not being a cop has nothing to do with it. You're just a very nice person, Lena, no matter how you try to disguise it underneath that prickly exterior of yours. You care when other people feel pain, probably because you've felt so much in your own life."

Damn the man. If he kept on like this, I'd be a slobbering wreck. It was time to get the subject off me. "Uh, if you're through playing psychiatrist now, Cliffie, I want to ask you a few questions about Clarice."

He frowned. "You're working on the case?"

"Yep. Jay Kobe hired me." I didn't tell him McKinnon had issued my marching orders earlier that day, orders I had no intention of obeying.

"What do you want to know?" Was it my imagination, or did his voice sound wary?

"I was wondering how she spent her last day in the gallery, who you saw going in, going out, what time she locked up to get the gallery ready for Art Walk. That kind of stuff."

"*That* kind of stuff is what I've already told the police, as you should certainly know if you're still as close as I think you are to that strange little man, what's his name, Kryzoutski?"

"Kryzinski. I'll tell him you said that."

"Those *clothes,* my dear! What in the world could he possibly think he's doing?"

"I imagine he thinks he looks like Bat Masterson, Cliffie, and please quit changing the subject. Just tell me how Clarice spent her last day in the gallery."

He sighed theatrically. "Well, as I told Kryzinski's minions, I have my own gallery to run so I don't exactly keep an eye on the Western Heart all day long. But from what I did notice, not much seemed to be going on over there that day. Just the usual. The only strange thing I can think of was that Clarice told Gabriella, her assistant, to leave around four o'clock. That she'd get the gallery ready for Art Walk all by herself."

According to Cliffie, and as he had already stated in the police report, Gabriella had opened the gallery at ten that morning and Clarice had drifted in sometime around two o'clock. This much had already been confirmed by Gabriella's own statement. Yes, Cliffie had thought it odd when he'd seen Gabriella leaving a couple of hours later, but at the time, he'd taken it for granted that she was just stepping out for a minute. He didn't find out she hadn't returned until the police questioned him the evening of the murder.

"Doesn't getting the galleries ready for Art Walk take a lot of work?" I asked.

"Sure. There's the cleaning, the straightening, the champagne or wine to uncork, the hors d'oeuvres to make and set out. That's why Javier helps me out every Thursday."

Javier was Cliffie's companion and sometimes-assistant, and his hors d'oeuvres were the talk of the Walk. Even people who didn't care much for the art in Damon and Pythias gravitated to the gallery to nosh on his thinly sliced salmon crisps garnished with capers and chopped onion. Some hung around long enough to grow fond of the oil paintings of naked men, and some, finally swayed by the artistic integrity of the paintings, even bought them.

A memory nudged at me. "When I found the body, someone had already put wine in the fountain but hadn't set out the hors d'oeuvres yet."

Cliffie shrugged. "I guess she was killed before she got to it. Gabriella came by the day after the murder—she was upset, as I'm sure you realize—and while we were talking, she told me Clarice definitely said she would take care of them herself."

The police report hadn't mentioned any food in the refrigerator, just white wine. Since Clarice surely hadn't planned on making a last-minute trip to the store, the only thing I could deduce from her behavior was that she wanted Gabriella out of the gallery.

But why? Because she had an appointment to meet her murderer?

Since I was also curious about something else, I let the case of the missing hors d'oeuvres slide for the time being. "Cliffie, when that tourist found her body, the front door was open. But according to the medical examiner's report, she'd been killed about two hours earlier, when the front door should have been locked. You know anything about that?"

Cliffie shook his head. "It's a mystery to me, too."

I was getting all kinds of pertinent information here. I tried again. "How about this. Do you know anything about some Apache artist that Clarice was supposed to be having trouble with?"

His eyes lit up and he took another sip of Beck's. "Ah, yes. The infamous George Haozous."

"What was the trouble between them?"

He spread his hands in a helpless gesture. "The usual trouble between an artist and a gallery owner. Clarice told George that she wasn't going to carry his work anymore. It wasn't commercial enough and she'd decided to concentrate on the big sellers like Jay Kobe." Here he made a small moue of distaste. "If you can call that poseur an artist."

"But Kobe's stuff sells, right?"

Cliffie nodded. "Oh, yes. It sells. Snowbirds from Minnesota just love that crap—all those noble savages, bosomy Indian maidens, true grit cowboys. Gag me with a palette knife, dear heart. Clarice couldn't keep his paintings on her walls long enough to even raise the prices. Whatever else she might have been, she had a good head for business."

Whatever else?

Before I could ask him what he meant, he continued, "George Haozous's work doesn't sell well. The irony is that it's hard-edged realism, which as you know usually flies off the walls around here. And he's very, very good, a modern master, actually. I haven't seen colors like that since Titian. The problem is with George's subject matter."

"Which is?"

"Dead Indians."

I wasn't certain I heard him right. "Did you say *dead* Indians?"

A wry smile. "You heard me right. Dead Indians. *Very* dead Indians. Indians with their heads hacked off by U.S. Cavalry sabers, Indians with their insides splattered all over the prairie from settlers' shotgun blasts, Indians with…"

"Okay, okay. I get the picture." As an ex-cop, I had no problem imagining carnage. "But you say they're good?"

"They're brilliant, dear. In a just world, Jay Kobe would be picking up litter in Indian Bend Park and George Haozous and his family would be living in a mansion on top of Camelback Mountain. Even Clarice recognized how brilliant George was, but after hanging one of his more strikingly, ah, *gory* works in her gallery, she received so many complaints she had to take it down. That's when the two of them had that terrible fight. I'm surprised you didn't hear it over at your place. Half the street did. It was the talk of Scottsdale for a while."

I raised my eyebrows. "Since when is a gallery brawl a big enough deal to become the talk of Scottsdale? Artists are always getting their feelings hurt."

He smiled mischievously. "It's not every day that an artist threatens to *kill* a gallery owner, dear. I think George's exact words were, 'I ought to take a tomahawk to your head, bitch.'"

Chapter 8

The next morning I felt better, so as soon as I finished my shower, I got on the phone to set up a couple of appointments. Jay Kobe wasn't answering, but that didn't worry me. He was a party hearty guy and was probably sleeping in. Fine with me. It would be interesting to see the expression on his face when I showed up unannounced and accused him of shooting me.

Since it was only nine o'clock, the temperature was just in the nineties, but I knew this respite wouldn't last. Heading out to the Jeep, I glanced up at the sky. It remained an uncluttered azure but the air held an ominous heaviness that hinted of the upcoming monsoon season. What most newcomers to the desert didn't realize was that beginning in the last part of July and continuing until late August, the Valley played host to a horrendous series of thunderstorms. Lightning flashed, winds raged, rain blew sideways. Trees collapsed, roofs took flight, streets flooded. The usually dry Salt River bed raged at flood pitch, and every year, some kayaking fool drowned in it. I checked the Jeep's storage compartment to make certain its bikini top was still stashed away.

How did a thug like Jay Kobe keep attracting moneyed women?

Once past the congestion of Indian School Road, I sped north up Hayden along the miles-long strip of greenbelt that comprised a pond-dotted park. Inline skaters—the Arizona natives wearing hand-tooled leather holsters—crowded the bicycle lanes. At one point, a gaggle of white geese attempted to waddle across one side of the busy street to the other. Miraculously, the geese made it but the sound of screeching brakes and the smell of burned rubber filled the air. I glared behind me when a burgundy-colored Lexus wearing Indiana license plates stopped short a hair from my Jeep's bumper.

Kobe's girlfriend lived near Indian Bend Wash, not far from the new development where the coyote had bitten a toddler. The accepted wisdom in Scottsdale was that houses increased twenty thousand dollars in value for every mile you traveled north from the city limits at McDowell Road until you reached the three-million-plus estates at the extreme northeast of the Valley. Judging from her location, I figured that Alison Garwood's house probably weighed in at the three-and-a-half to four hundred thousand dollar mark. But as I drove down the eucalyptus-shaded streets in her neighborhood, I nudged the estimate upwards because many of the huge, rambling homes were clearly closer to the half-million dollar mark. This made me wonder how Kobe's girlfriend made her money. Was she one of those successful yuppies that Scottsdale seemed to breed like rabbits, or was she just another California transplant who'd made out big in that state's hideously inflated real estate market?

As I turned onto Via Del Loma Maria, to my surprise, I saw a coyote loping east along the sidewalk towards the Pima Reservation with what appeared to be the remains of a Big Mac in its mouth. Two smiling bicyclists had stopped to watch the show. Neither made a move to rescue the Big Mac.

Alison Garwood's house was on the corner and as I drew the Jeep to the curb, a woman wearing a turquoise silk warm-up suit waved cheerfully at me. She pointed to the running coyote. "Aren't they wonderful?" An Eastern accent.

The coyote was moving too fast for me to get a good look at him. "Wonderful, maybe, but a lot of people are afraid of coyotes and it's just a matter of time before some self-styled Wyatt Earp decides to use one for target practice."

She stopped scraping at the mauve-colored gravel decorating her yard's "desert" landscaping, and leaned on the rake. She was slender, about fifty, with short auburn hair that revealed the ministrations of an expensive hairdresser. She had kind eyes.

"No one around here would ever hurt a coyote. We love them. They're one of the reasons why my husband and I moved here from New Jersey. There's nothing left back there but criminals and concrete."

It would be the same in Scottsdale soon, but there was no point in disillusioning her. "Well, be careful. Some of those coyotes are getting pretty bold. I read in the paper the other day where one actually bit some kid."

She shook her head. "That wouldn't have been one of *our* coyotes. *Our* coyotes are harmless. Why, we can even feed them by hand."

Which is exactly why the coyotes were becoming bold enough to bite children. As evidenced by the way the woman seemed to believe that wildlife could be tamed and owned—*our* coyotes— she probably also fed the bears bologna sandwiches in Yellowstone Park, then got her feelings hurt when one tried to bite off her leg. Deciding to skip my usual lecture on proper wildlife management, I gave her a friendly wave and headed up the walk.

Up close, Alison's house looked like it belonged somewhere else—like in a cheaper neighborhood. True desert landscaping (cactus, sage and dirt) was littered with old newspapers. A Babe Ruth candy wrapper had impaled itself on one of the spines of a dying prickly pear. As I climbed the short steps to the Territorial's front door, I noticed that part of the tan adobe siding had begun to flake off and that the huge oak door stood in desperate need of repair. Holes had been gouged around the latch, almost as if someone had forgotten his keys and tried to let himself in with an ice pick. At the large picture window, the vertical blinds were missing a few slats, allowing anyone who so desired to look inside. I peered through one of the gaps and didn't like what I saw.

I pulled my head away and started banging against the door. "Jay? Alison? Either of you in there?"

Not caring that I had aroused the curiosity of the woman across the street, I leaned my ear against the door. After a few minutes and some more banging, I heard groans from inside, some shuffling, then the door squeaked open and a bloodshot hazel eye peered out. "What the hell are you doing here, Jones? Don't you believe in calling first?"

"I skipped Business Etiquette 101."

I pushed my way through the door to find a scene that looked like a major staging area for World War II. Vivid red stains marred the matching champagne sofa and carpet. A rosewood occasional table tilted drunkenly on shattered legs and a once-magnificent Victorian golden oak armoire looked like it had been used for target practice. Empty wine and beer bottles were scattered everywhere. Paintings hung crookedly on wine-splattered walls, their canvases slashed. Alison's house looked like an upscale furniture store after a riot.

I'd seen houses displaying this type of destruction before, but they'd usually been crack houses in South Phoenix. Scottsdale was better at keeping this sort of thing under wraps, mainly because its citizens could afford better lawyers.

Kobe didn't look any more upbeat than the house's décor. Deep scratches marred his handsome face and his cheek sported a vivid purple bruise.

It made me wonder what his girlfriend looked like.

I didn't have to wonder long. A slender blond woman wrapped in a dirty silk bathrobe limped slowly from the next room. As the sunlight streamed through the missing slats of the blinds and illuminated her, I had to repress a gasp. The woman's face looked like raw meat. The gap in her front teeth told me she'd lost whatever battle had been fought here. I couldn't tell if she'd ever been pretty.

After clearing my throat, I said, "Look, I'm sorry for the intrusion but something happened last night and I need to ask you both some questions."

"So what happened?" Kobe didn't even bother to apologize for his girlfriend's appearance.

"Have ssssome coffee?" Alison mumbled, the missing tooth leaking a sibilant hiss.

Not wanting to bother her any more than she'd already been bothered, I shook my head, but Kobe looked at her and growled, "What the fuck you think?"

She nodded and limped off into the kitchen. Without being invited, I sat down on an undamaged section of the sofa. Almost immediately, I heard a grinding noise then caught the scent of freshly ground coffee beans. All the elegant comforts of Scottsdale life. Kobe dropped into a wine-splattered chair across from me and neither of us said a word until Alison returned with two steaming mugs. Mine said, "Have a nice day!" His said, "No. 1 Stud Muffin!"

"You usssse cream? Ssssugar?" she asked, already half-turned towards the kitchen.

Trying hard to keep from hauling my .38 out of my carryall and plugging Kobe between the eyes, I shook my head. Jesus, why didn't the woman find help?

Duties accomplished, Alison wrapped the bathrobe more tightly around her and started to limp back into the bedroom, but I stopped her.

"Miss Garwood, I need to talk to you, too." I had to clear my throat. Something seemed to be in it.

She looked timidly at Kobe. When he shrugged, she lowered herself down on the sofa as creakily as an old woman.

I cleared my throat again. "Look, someone shot me a couple of nights ago and I think it might be connected to the Clarice Kobe case. Do you know anything about that?"

Kobe smirked but Alison's face paled, if ground beef can be said to pale. "Sssomeone ssshot you? That'sss terrible!"

Maybe not as terrible as some other things I could think of—such as living with a monster—but I said, "Yes, terrible. Now, who besides you two knew that I was working on the case?"

Kobe barked a short laugh. "Oh, several guys down at the jail. Then after I was released I called Clarice's father and told him what I thought of him, told him I was siccing you on his ass. And I think I mentioned it at the party we had the afternoon I got out." He looked across at Alison. "Did you tell anybody, hon?"

"Jussst my hair ssstylisst," Alison answered. Well, this explained the one undamaged area of her person. Her hair was movie-star blond, shoulder length and parted to the side like Kim Basinger's in *L.A. Confidential,* and it glowed like an angel's halo. Alison was probably gorgeous when she wasn't banged up.

Great. Between them they'd told Clarice's possibly incestuous father. The guys at the jail. The revelers at the party. Alison's hairdresser and whoever else had been eavesdropping. Altogether, the two had probably told half the population of Scottsdale that I had taken on the case.

"So where'd you get shot this time?" Kobe was grinning.

I knew better than to let him needle me. "In the shoulder. It was just a flesh wound so I don't think we're looking for any Olympic marksman here. You know anybody who carries a gun?"

Kobe's grin exploded into a laugh. "In Arizona? Shit, just about everybody's packing, including half the kids in kindergarten. As for me, I've got a new .45 in the night stand but it hasn't been fired recently. Wanna see?"

I shook my head. The bullet casing retrieved from the sidewalk had been a .38. If Jay owned a .38, he wouldn't show it to me without a search warrant.

Then Alison spoke up. "Clariccce had a gun, a pearl-handled Derringer. Her brother hasss a gun, too, but I'm not sssure what kind. And probably her sssisssster Ssserena has one. Come to think of it, Clariccce'sss father hasss a wonderful gun collection, very, very valuable. He even hasss one of Doc Holliday'sss old riflesss, sssupposedly the one he usssed at the OK Corral. He wasss kind enough to ssshow it to me when I wasss redecorating his housss."

"You were Mr. Hyath's decorator?" This explained her own relative financial comfort. Decorators to the rich never went hungry in Scottsdale.

She nodded, then winced and lifted a fluttery hand to an area of her neck covered by her long, blond hair. Not all the damage done by batterers shows, I remembered. "That'sss how I met Jay. He wasss up there taking hisss paintingsss when I wasss ssshowing Mr. Hyath sssome fabric sssamplesss."

Jay frowned. "Those people don't know good art when it's all around them. The minute Stephen Hyath found out that Clarice and I were, ah, having our trouble, he made me take my paintings out of his house. I even had to return the money he'd paid me for them, the cheap son of a bitch."

Alison threw Kobe a trembling smile which made her lower lip bleed. "When I met Jay up there it wasss love at firsssst sssight."

Jay didn't smile back.

My finger itched to make contact with the trigger on my .38. "Look, I'm going to have to ask you both some unpleasant questions about the day Clarice was murdered. I need to know exactly where you two were at exactly what time, and what you were doing. And please don't lie to me. If you're really innocent, Jay…" Here I looked right into his drink-bleared eyes. "…the truth can only help you."

He gave me a faint smile. He enjoyed being helped. "I was right here, with Alison, just like I told you. We started partying and then we got into a fight. Alison gets pretty edgy when she's drinking. Isn't that right, honey?"

She nodded weakly, her hand at her neck again.

"Alison? Are you sure that's true? You told the police you weren't certain if Jay left the house or not."

She opened her battered mouth to answer but before she could, Kobe rose from his chair and joined her on the stained couch. As he slipped his muscular arm around her shoulder and gave her a hug, I thought I saw her wince. "Now, honey, you tell Ms. Jones that I was too drunk to leave and that it's the God's honest truth."

Alison wouldn't meet my eyes. "It'sss the God'sss honessst truth."

On a scale of one to ten, I scored the interview somewhere at a two, giving them the higher rating simply because they were both conscious. But Alison was too terrified of Kobe to answer truthfully and Kobe, although no rocket scientist, wasn't dumb enough to let her see me alone. That could still be arranged, though. The next time I saw her—alone—I'd give her the address of the nearest battered women's shelter.

Clarice's parents lived three-quarters of the way up Camelback Mountain, which afforded them a magnificent view of the Valley of the Sun. While present zoning restrictions protected the remaining part of the mountain, for all intents and purposes, the once-magnificent peak was already ruined. As the heat rose in waves from the desert floor below, the ostentatious mansions clinging to the steep hillside appeared to wiggle in the sun. They looked like gyrating hookers at a Sierra Club dance. The man responsible for most of this vandalism was Stephen Hyath, the most successful developer in Arizona. The rumor on the street was that he had long since stopped being a mere millionaire and had joined the rarified ranks of billionaires.

The mountain had been raped for its view. Halfway up Camelback I pulled the Jeep off to the side in front of an authentic-looking adobe house that could have been there since Arizona's old Territorial days, and walked to the edge of the road. This was the opposite of the view that I had enjoyed during my run in Papago Park. From there, I'd looked to the north, but from Camelback Mountain, the view was to the south and much more encompassing. As the smell of gasoline and sage rose to meet me from the hot city basin, I marveled again at the sere but threatened beauty of the Valley of the Sun.

In 1870, while Arizona was still the Arizona Territory, only two hundred and forty people lived down there. Now there were almost three million of us—more than half the entire state's population—crowded into the Valley. The wear and tear was beginning to show in pollution of almost Los Angeles proportions.

While much of the Valley's development paid homage to the territory's Hispanic and Indian heritage, too much of it had been imported from the East with the ever-increasing influx of new residents. As I gazed straight down at the Minnesota-lushness of the Arcadia district, I saw emerald lawns accented by turquoise pools, mulberry and olive trees busy skyrocketing the Valley's already alarming pollen count. Allergy sufferers, beware. To the west, Central Phoenix was trying its best to mimic the skyline of New York, pushing up skyscrapers with abandon, blocking the view of the stunning lavender mountains that completely ringed the Valley. Meanwhile, the western edge of the Valley had begun to resemble the industrial Midwest, continuously spewing industrial fumes into the once-pristine sky.

Only Scottsdale still seemed to have a chance at maintaining the Valley's Western heritage, but even there, I counted too many Taco Bell-clone houses, too much alien Midwestern landscaping, too many golf courses sucking up the ever-dwindling waters of the aquifer.

In an almost straight shot down the mountain, I could see Scottsdale's showcase resort, the old Hacienda Palms. Unlike the newer resorts, the Hacienda offered its guests only a nine-hole golf course, but it was considered one of the most beautiful short courses in the world, with swan-filled lagoons, trickling brooks, and deep, meandering greens. I was still admiring it when I heard footsteps behind me.

"This is a private road." A female voice.

I turned around and saw a tiny, white-haired woman who appeared to be in her late eighties and couldn't have weighed more than ninety pounds. The gun in her hand was almost as big as she was, a long-barreled Colt the size of a small dog. It was cocked and ready for action. The button on her white blouse said, *Neighborhood Watch*.

At least the gun was pointed at the ground.

Forcing a smile, I said, "I was on my way up the mountain and thought I'd stop and admire the view."

That didn't cut any ice with her. "If you want to gawk go on over to Squaw Peak. That's public property, this isn't."

"I've got an appointment to see the Hyaths," I said, not taking my eyes off that big gun.

Her frown intensified as she looked up the mountain. "Trash. That's what those people are. Trash." Then she looked back at me. "Get on up there then but don't dawdle on your way down. I'll be watching you."

I gave her a wary salute. "I'm sure you will."

She stood there, gun still cocked, while I climbed back into the Jeep and headed on up the mountain.

As I neared the Hyath mansion, the reason for the old lady's hostility towards them became quickly apparent. I grimaced with distaste as I wrestled my Jeep up a narrow switchback and the white marble monstrosity the Hyaths called home came into view. It was a lunatic riff on a Norman castle, with elevated walkways, narrow archers' windows hacked out of the marble, and a pseudo-drawbridge perched above a pseudo-moat. Spires and towers thrust themselves in every direction, as if to provide first defense for the mansion's long, crenellated roof. What the hell were these people expecting—an attack by mounted Saracens?

Shuddering, I coasted the Jeep to a stop behind the Rolls-Royce Silver Shadow someone, probably the chauffeur, was polishing.

"You that detective they're expecting?" he asked. A closer inspection showed that the man was that current Scottsdale status symbol, a chauffeur/bodyguard combo. He was young and tough-looking, with biceps the size of my thighs. Not that he needed them. Strapped to his hip was a hand-tooled holster, and peeking out of it was an evil-looking Glock, a clone of my old Scottsdale PD service revolver.

Should I tell him I approved of his taste in guns? Instead, I just smiled. "Yes."

"They're waiting for you out by the pool. I unlocked the gate for you." He pointed along a tiled walkway.

As I turned, he added, "Watch yourself in there."

When I looked back, he was tenderly stroking the Rolls' fender, as if he hadn't said anything.

On that optimistic note, I headed down the walk, ducking around an overly aggressive bougainvillea bush whose thorns seemed intent on ripping my clothes off. Once past the bougain-villea, I had to turn sideways to edge between the cholla cacti that crowded the area, spines a-bristling. Why did rich people have such mean plants?

As I let myself in the gate, the pungent odor of chlorine smacked me in the face. The Hyaths certainly weren't taking any chances with that nasty old desert bacteria. What I saw when I rounded the corner of the house made me gag.

Not content to merely own a pseudo-castle, at the back of the house the Hyaths had installed a tropical lagoon, complete with waterfall. A twenty-foot "mountain" composed of artificial gran-ite rose above the bright turquoise water, spewing a silvery cascade. A hummingbird darted around the summit, a confused expres-sion on its face. The bright red blossoms it kept poking its beak into were obviously artificial. At the side of the pool, two real banana palms bent solicitously over a gray-haired couple seated about eight feet apart on matching chaise lounges, shielding their patrician skin from the desert rays.

The Hyaths pretended not to notice I was there.

"I'm Lena Jones. I take it you're the Hyaths?"

Neither smiled, although Mr. Hyath eventually deigned to look in my direction. He had been cold over the phone, which wasn't unreasonable since for all he knew I was still in the employ of the man accused of murdering his daughter. I hadn't exactly been expecting an enthusiastic welcome. But this... I'd gotten warmer receptions raiding dogfights.

Hyath looked to be in his early sixties. Although not actually handsome, he was slim and elegant with softly waved gray hair that could have been styled that very morning. His eyes were the color of his upscale pool but much less inviting.

Clarice's mother was a surprise. Rich women were usually face-lifted and bone-thin, but Eleanor Hyath's face was lined and puffy, with dewlaps that could rival a basset hound's hanging from her flat cheeks. Her body fared even worse. No designer swimsuit could disguise the rolls of fat around her waist or hide the cellulite on her thighs. Her stubby, un-manicured fingers were yellow with nicotine. One lit cigarette dangled from her mouth while another smoldered in the overflowing ashtray that sat on the wide, littered table. Unlike her husband's seal-sleek mane, her own gray hair stood out in straw-dry clumps all over her head, looking like it hadn't been washed or combed in days. A reaction to grief? As I drew closer, I could tell that she was drunk.

"Nice job you've got, working for a murderer," Eleanor Hyath slurred, her voice husky from booze and too many cigarettes.

I eased myself onto a nearby deck chair, not that I'd been invited. Common courtesy was not the Hyath's currency. "Look, as it stands right now, there may not be a good enough case against Kobe to convict him of your daughter's murder, so the police are proceeding cautiously. I'm sure you don't want him to go to trial and then get off, because he'd never be able to be tried for the same crime again. Not even if he eventually came right out and confessed."

She looked at me for a moment, trying to focus. She finally managed it. "Why not?"

Her husband gave her a look iced with contempt. "Because of double jeopardy, Eleanor. In this country once someone's been found innocent they can't be tried again, not even if they confess to the crime at some later date."

Then he looked up at me and my own day got colder. "Regardless of all that, Miss Jones, I find this visit in the worst of taste. But since I agreed to see you, just ask us what you need to then do us the favor of going back to wherever you've come from."

Such as the rock he so obviously thought I lived under? "I'd like to speak to each of you separately."

"No."

This promised to be an interesting experience. I was about to ask a man if he'd had sexual relations with his daughter, while his drunken wife sat there listening to the whole thing. But, hey, it couldn't happen to a nicer couple.

I tried not to let my satisfaction show. "In that case, here we go, Mr. Hyath. Jay Kobe told me Clarice was getting ready to sue you for the pain and suffering your incestuous relations caused her when she was a child. He told me she'd already talked with an attorney and they were about to file in civil court."

He gave me a bleak look. "That's certainly an interesting story, but rest assured, Miss Jones, Clarice wouldn't have collected a dime."

His wife didn't react at all and for a moment, I wondered if she'd heard. She simply took the half-smoked cigarette out of her mouth, flicked it into the pool, and lit another one.

"Goddamn!" Hyath uncoiled from the chaise and plucked the sodden cigarette out of the pool. "Eleanor, must you be so disgusting?"

Eleanor just kept puffing away.

I was baffled by their reactions. "Is that all you've got to say about such a horrendous allegation?"

The cigarette incident overwith, Hyath calmed himself again. "What else is there to say? You'll either believe that story or you won't, regardless of any protestations I may make. But I would like to warn you that if you spread this story around you'll be facing a lawsuit of your own for slander. Now, is there anything else, Miss Jones?"

I swallowed my anger. "I'd like to get an idea of what Clarice was like. Who her friends were. Her enemies."

Eleanor pulled the cigarette from her mouth and picked at a strand of tobacco hanging from her lip. "So you think my daughter had enemies."

Her husband looked at her briefly, then away again.

"Everyone has enemies," I said to Eleanor. "Especially when they're as beautiful and accomplished as your daughter."

She sat up, barked a laugh and for a moment her eyes lost their dazed look. "Beautiful? Not before the cosmetic surgeons fixed her, she wasn't. She had her father's nose and my cheekbones. Believe me, without the magic of the scalpel she wouldn't have won any beauty contests. Men wouldn't have looked at her twice." Then she settled back against the chaise, her cheeks glowing with spite.

Clarice had enemies, all right. Her mother, for starters. I thought again about Kobe's allegations of incest and how I had wondered what kind of mother would countenance such a situation. Now I knew.

"Who were Clarice's friends?"

A smirk. "She didn't have any."

Now Stephen Hyath came to life. "Eleanor—"

She turned to him and snapped, "You call that art crowd trash she ran with friends?"

He shrugged. "She liked them. They liked her."

Eleanor sneered. "Oh, *like.*"

I wanted to drown her. Instead, I cleared my throat and directed my next question to him. Clarice's mother was a lost cause. "Perhaps you could give me the contact numbers for Clarice's friends. Maybe she was open with them about whatever problems she was having."

His face was expressionless. "Problems? With what?"

"Something that made her dead, Mr. Hyath." Jesus, wasn't anybody grieving for Clarice?

Eleanor flicked another cigarette into the pool. Hyath leaned over the long table that separated him and his wife and punched at the beeper next to the ashtray. Seconds later, a wary-looking Hispanic maid joined us.

"Clean that up." Hyath pointed to the cigarette now decomposing in the pool. Then he pointed to his wife. "And when you're through, clean *her* up. She smells."

Grabbing the beeper, he stood up and gestured for me to follow him. "I'll give you a list of Clarice's friends, but after that, I don't want you to bother us again. Now come with me."

I hurried after him, eager to escape from the human train wreck by the pool.

The interior of the house was even worse than the exterior, with no taste anywhere in evidence, just obscene amounts of money. Black marble tiled a living room the size of a football field. It was accented by rugs flayed from the bodies of zebras and polar bears, and in one horrifying instance, a Bengal tiger. A sheer glass coffee table in front of the white leather sofas was held up by two severed elephant's feet.

Somebody here had an unhealthy obsession with violence and death. Then I remembered who decorated the house.

Alison.

Not quite as grotesque as the dead endangered species—but trying hard—was a gallery off the main living room which housed a collection of pseudo-classical sculpture. I saw a copy of the Venus de Milo *sans* arms, the Athena Nike *sans* head, and scattered busts of almost a dozen Roman senators *sans* their entire bodies. It struck me that both rooms were decorated with pieces of bodies, not whole ones. Was this the way the Hyaths viewed people—as nothing more than a miscellaneous collection of body parts?

"Nice house," I lied.

"It should be for what it cost me."

After a long hike though a hall lined by a gun collection that could have dwarfed the Arizona National Guard's armory, we finally arrived at two massive bronze doors that opened onto a cavern-like den.

"I've got her old address book in here," he said.

Alison apparently hadn't waved her magic decorating wand in here. The dark brown carpeting that softened the floor was made even darker by wood paneling that looked like it had been ravaged from some primeval forest. More guns were mounted on the wall here, and they gleamed menacingly in the gloom. As I squinted around, Hyath switched on a desk lamp so dimly bulbed that I couldn't help but wonder if all this darkness mirrored his heart.

The only saving grace in the room was the large oil portrait of Clarice that hung on the wall facing the desk. Unlike the dismembered bodies in the living room and gallery, all of Clarice had been captured by the artist's expert brush. She posed proudly in the desert sunlight, her dark hair offset by a pale pink dress, and matching tights and shoes. She was complete, glowing. She appeared to be around nine years old, with a hopeful, unshadowed face. Was this the age when her father started molesting her?

Hyath rustled through a desk drawer and finally came up with an address book. "This was Clarice's," he said, tossing it to me.

"Do you want me to return it?"

"What for?"

As a memento of your daughter, I thought. But voicing that sentiment was probably pointless. When it came to sentiment, the Hyaths were definitely twisted. "Fine. One more thing. Um, I've heard that Clarice lived on income from a family trust. Is that true? I know she didn't make all her money from the Western Heart Gallery alone."

At first it looked like he wasn't going to answer my question, but then he glanced across the room at Clarice's portrait and his cold face softened. "Yes, there's a trust, but each of my children is also an equal partner in Hyath Construction. I signed it over to them six years ago."

I blinked in surprise. I'd always thought Hyath Construction was solely owned by Stephen Hyath. I couldn't help but wonder why he'd given it to his children.

Out of guilt, perhaps?

"And it's remained a successful company, hasn't it?"

When he finally turned from the portrait, his eyes were wintry again. "Being good at business runs in the family. Now, I'm afraid you need to leave. I'm a busy man." He pressed the button on the beeper. The maid wasted no time in responding. She had a towel draped over her arm. Presumably she was in the process of scrubbing Eleanor down.

"Inez, please escort Miss Jones out. Tell Randall to make certain she leaves the property."

Inez nodded and led me outside where Randall the chauffeur/ bodyguard stood waiting for me beside the now-gleaming Rolls. "I have to follow you down the hill, make sure you're gone." At least he looked apologetic.

"Fine with me. But before I go may I ask you something?"

He shook his head. "Sorry. I need this job."

"You just answered my question."

I drove away, overcome with loathing for the Hyaths and their home, until it occurred to me that my parents—if I ever found them—might prove to be even worse.

Chapter 9

After my visit to the Hyaths, the Scottsdale Police Department seemed like Disneyland, even taking into account the two drunken teenagers sprawled on a curved bench inside the door. One had peed himself, the other had a nosebleed.

"Hi ya, Lena," said Sgt. Vic Falcone, a transplant from Chicago, who was the lucky man assigned to the front desk today. He'd been at my side the day I took the bullet that ended my police career and had kept his hand pressed against my severed artery until the EMTs arrived. They told me later that he'd been crying almost as hard as I'd been bleeding.

Now he frowned. "What's this I hear you been out gettin' shot again?"

"That story's been greatly exaggerated, Vic. Just a graze, just a graze."

The frown didn't let up. "You need to be more careful with yourself."

"My middle name—Careful." I grinned, trying to lighten the mood. Like Kryzinski, Falcone had always been a nag.

The grin worked and he mirrored my expression. "Other than that, how's tricks?"

"A lot more lucrative since I stopped working Van Buren," I answered. The reference to Phoenix's notorious Hooker's Row earned the laugh I'd been fishing for. "Say, is Kryzinski in? He told me to stop by."

Vic waggled his eyebrows at me. "Doing house calls now, are ya?"

I waggled back and twitched an imaginary cigar. We were both big Marx Brothers fans.

He bared coffee-stained teeth in appreciation. "We miss ya around here. Them new broads on patrol ain't half as pretty as you."

I laughed. "I'll bet you say that to all the girls, you sexist pig, you."

Now he twitched his own imaginary cigar. "Only the blonds, Lena. Hey, ya know where Kryzinski's office is. One of the rookies'll take you up. I gotta babysit for the Katzenjammer Kids here 'til their parents arrive."

I blew him a kiss as a fresh-faced rookie trying to look scary used his pass to open the electronically locked door to the inner sanctum. He led me down the hall to the elevator, our footsteps whispering along the expensive blue-gray carpet. As in the rest of the city's municipal buildings, the police department's architect had spared no expense in creating a tasteful work environment. In fact, a casual visitor to the building would swear he was in an insurance office until he came to the glassed-in case that held the collection of guns, rifles, and assault weapons we'd confiscated during raids. There were enough in the display to stock a small army.

The rookie rode with me up to Kryzinski's lair without saying a word. I didn't think it was because he was unfriendly, just that his voice was still changing and he was afraid it would crack. They seemed to be hiring them younger and younger these days.

The elevator stopped and as he ushered me down the hushed hallway past the communications room, old friends of mine from the Violent Crimes Unit rushed from their pods, demanding to know why I was walking around so soon after being shot. I had to tell my story again and couldn't help grinning as I noticed the rookie's face begin to pale. He probably hadn't yet dealt with anything other than Iowa grannies running stop signs in their Winnebagos. But his time would come, and I felt a moment's pity for him.

After I satisfied everyone's curiosity, we continued our progress to the glassed-in office at the back of the VCU, where I was finally able to wave goodbye to my guide. Glancing through the glass, I saw Kryzinski hunched over his laptop. He was wearing a tan Western suit with chocolate piping, a black string tie completing his ensemble. Since he bulged slightly less than usual, I surmised that he was beginning to buy his clothes in larger sizes or that the Police Chief had finally convinced him to go on a diet. As I watched, Kryzinski hurled an oath at the laptop's monitor. It didn't deign to talk back.

"I love a man who loves his computer. It really makes me hot."

With a start, Kryzinski looked up from the laptop. His expression would have scared Geronimo. "Jesus Christ, Lena, you out walking the streets again?"

"That's funny. I just had the same conversation with Falcone. You cops have such dirty minds."

The scowl deepened. "Quit fartin' around and do yourself a favor. Go back home and get some rest. You just been shot, for Christ's sake."

I eased through the door. Regardless of the laptops that sat on every Scottsdale police officer's desk, Kryzinski's office was always a mess, with piles of paperwork accumulated on every conceivable surface—the desk, the chairs, the scarred lamp table, even the floor. The inspectors from Rural Metro Fire Department were always threatening to ticket him.

"You told me to come down here, see what you guys have found out."

"I didn't mean today and you damned well know it." He breathed heavily for a few beats then sighed, "Oh, hell, since you're already here, you might as well pull up a chair. I got things to tell you but remember, kid, you didn't hear it from me."

Which meant don't let the Police Chief find out.

I removed a pile of papers from the battered old lounge chair he'd had shipped all the way from Brooklyn and sat down. As I settled in the chair, a puff of dust rose around me, making me cough.

"See?" Kryzinski snapped, pointing a stubby finger at my chest. "You're still weak. You're wobblin', too."

"It's the chair. One leg's shorter than the other, has been for years. And if you'd clean up around here every now and then, my cough would go away, too. Now quit your nagging and tell me what the Medical Examiner said."

He rummaged through the mess on his desk, and finally found a fat manila envelope. "We're still waitin' for the complete toxicology results but already we got somethin' pretty juicy." He held the envelope out to me. "You're not gonna believe it."

I read through the report, at first noticing nothing out of the ordinary. The ugly crime scene photos told me nothing I hadn't already known, but the preliminary coroner's report detailed the violence done to Clarice's body. She had suffered such severe skull fractures that bits of bone punctured her brain, yet those injuries hadn't killed her. The actual cause of death had been the bloody clog of teeth and pieces of tongue lodged in her airway, asphyxiating her as she lay helpless on the floor. While she choked to death, the attack continued, this time with an object that matched the configuration of a tire iron.

I looked up at Kryzinski. "This guy really wanted to make sure she was dead, didn't he?"

Kryzinski nodded. "No shit. Keep readin'."

On the second page I found the strangest thing I'd ever come across on any homicide investigation. "What the hell's this? They found traces of latex on her face?"

Kryzinski nodded, making his string tie flap up and down. "Maybe she was beaten to death by a lead-filled condom."

"Or maybe her killer was wearing latex gloves."

"You tryin' to take the fun out of this? Anyway, now you see why the case against Kobe ain't lookin' real tight. Firstly, Kobe wouldn't have to be worryin' about leaving his fingerprints in the gallery 'cause there was plenty of reason for his fingerprints to be there. Place was crawlin' with his crappy paintings. Secondly, that asshole was too drunk to even piss straight let alone do everything the perp did. When we arrested him that night his blood alcohol level was .193.

"Just between you and me and the lamppost, kid, I can't see Kobe staggerin' out of his girlfriend's house, drivin' all the way over to the gallery without gettin' snagged by some hotshot patrol officer, then puttin' on latex gloves, then beatin' his wife senseless, then switchin' over to a tire iron to finish the job, *then* sneakin' out of there in broad daylight without anybody seeing him. Sound like any drunk you ever ran into? Shit, when Kobe's lawyer laid all that out for the judge, he dropped bail from one million to a measly ten thou and Kobe only had to come up with a tenth of that. Hell, half the homeless in Scottsdale got that much hidden in their favorite Dumpster."

I sat back, but the chair rocked wildly and I had to lean forward again until it found its equilibrium. "You're right. This is all a little too cagey for some drunk. I guess that means my former client is off the hook. Now isn't that nice?"

Kryzinski snorted. "Not to be too optimistic or anything but maybe the guy is smarter than we think. Try this on for size. Maybe he rigged all this bizarre shit, including being drunk. Maybe he was hopin' we'd take him to trial and he'd get off. Once acquitted..."

I finished for him. "...he can't be tried again." At times like this, I really missed working with Kryzinski. He was nobody's fool, which is why he'd been hired away from NYPD and why the Police Chief—an Überyuppie from Yale—put up with his atrocious English and bizarre manner of dress. Kryzinski might not be pretty but he always got the job done.

The two of us sat there in silence for a few moments, examining his theory. Then I said, "I don't know, Kryzinski, it all sounds too Agatha Christie to me. There's no way Kobe has the smarts or the self-discipline to rig up anything that sophisticated. Maybe there's some new suspects you'd like to tell me about? Just for old time's sake, you understand."

He gave me a sour look. "We shot our wad with Kobe. Now we start over again."

I met his eyes. "Then I'll do what I can. One nice thing about going private is that you're not handicapped by police procedure or any hand-tying legalities."

His sour look lightened. "You break the law, I don't wanna know about it. But you come up with anything, you're gonna share it, right? You scratch my back and I'll scratch yours?"

"Of course."

The chair gave another lurch beneath me and for one horrible moment, the room began to spin. I only managed to remain upright by hanging onto the chair arm.

Kryzinski jumped up and rushed towards me, grabbing my shoulder with a surprisingly gentle hand. "Hey, Lena! You all right?"

My vision cleared and I waved him away. "Just a little tired. Maybe you're right. I probably need to take it a easy for the next few days."

On the way back to the office, I decided to ask Jimmy to type up McKinnon's bill. I'd probably feel better knowing that I'd washed my hands of a particularly ugly piece of dirt named Jay Kobe. McKinnon didn't have to know that ridding myself of his client wouldn't end my involvement in the case. Clarice hadn't deserved to be beaten to death like that. No one did.

And I hadn't deserved being shot.

But when I arrived back to Desert Investigations, my shoulder was screaming with so much pain that I didn't even go into the office. Instead, I staggered up the stairs to my apartment, popped a Darvon and collapsed across the bed. I slept soundly but not well, seeing Clarice's battered face in each of my dreams. In one of them—the worst—Clarice aimed a gun at me, and then the ragged hole that had once been her mouth cried, "I'll shoot her, I'll shoot her! Just leave me alone!"

I heard an explosion, felt a streak of fire blaze across my forehead…

Then I fell into the night.

I woke up shivering and stared up at the ceiling, where the reflected headlights from cars driving along Main Street played across the textured surface. For a while, I watched the abstract patterns they made, then—my shoulder throbbing again—staggered into the bathroom and swallowed another Darvon.

It didn't work. I lay there staring at the ceiling for the rest of the night.

Chapter 10

Life—and Desert Investigations—trundled on.

My morning copy of the *Scottsdale Journal* informed me that a coyote finally bit the hand that fed it on Via Del Loma Maria, and that the city's Animal Control officers were patrolling the area in full force armed with tranquilizer guns. As the mayor reassured an assembly of wildlife lovers, the Animal Control officers planned to merely stun the offending coyote, then set it free in a distant location. Even the folks who lodged the original complaint against the toddler-biting coyote had grown alarmed at the uproar they'd caused.

While Scottsdale city officials struggled mightily to save the life of a coyote, human lives were being lost elsewhere.

Two hundred miles to the north, a tourist posing for a picture on the edge of the Grand Canyon slipped and fell, bouncing off rock ledge after rock ledge until his body came to rest more than five hundred feet below his horrified friends. To the east, a party of hikers and their guide had been caught by a flash flood in one of the many narrow canyons that etched the desert floor. Eleven were dead, three more were missing and presumed dead.

Closer to home, two Pima teenagers riding their all-terrain vehicles near the dry Salt River on the rez saw what at first appeared to be a pile of rags tossed behind a mesquite tree. Closer inspection revealed the rags to be decomposed human remains.

Although Arizona never tops anybody's list of America's most violent states, it's easy to get killed out here. Just a superficial list of our lethal wildlife includes rattlesnakes, scorpions, brown recluse spiders, and bad-tempered javelinas with tusks that could make shish-kebab out of you. Then there is the Arizona landscape itself. If our canyons and mountains don't get you, the desert is more than willing to pick up the slack. Too many tourists, overcome by the landscape's natural beauty, lose all common sense and wander off into the desert without enough water—which is one quart per hour in high summer. Take along less and *your* body might eventually be found moldering under a mesquite.

Depressed, I threw the paper aside. Jimmy, however, acted as if he was on the top of the world.

His fifth night on stakeout had netted him the Big One—an infrared videotape of the wheelchair-bound accident victim heading out her front door just before dawn, climbing gear slung over her back. He'd followed her to the Peralta Trailhead, located at the base of the Superstition Mountains, where he'd videotaped her climbing a rock face so steep it earned even his admiration.

"Whatever else she is, she's got guts," he said, handing me the videotape. His saddle-colored face glowed with the pride of a job well done.

I picked up the phone to call Copper State Insurance, but while I listened to the ring, said, "It's nice that you can find some admirable qualities in her, but remember, your cute little mountain-climbing grifter is one of the reasons insurance rates are so high."

"How did you know she was cute?"

Men. "I guessed."

Still looking puzzled, Jimmy returned to his computer. In the past week, we had picked up four more new accounts, and Jimmy was now trying to break into an investment banking firm's security system. For once, though, the company's encryption system had him stymied.

After delivering the good news to Copper State Insurance, I busied myself with the other accounts—two more insurance investigations, and a missing person's case. The mistress of the CEO of a big department store chain had disappeared, taking with her the man's wife's diamond necklace, which he had allowed her to "borrow." He wanted me to find her and the necklace before his wife realized it was missing. Which is another way the

rich are different from you and me. How can the average woman
not notice her diamond necklace is missing?

No new leads emerged in the Clarice Kobe murder case, but I
was unwilling to drop it simply because Jay Kobe was no longer
my client. I missed waving at her in the morning as she unlocked
her gallery door, waving to her again in the evening as she locked
up. I missed her who-gives-a-shit smile, her caustic bon mots. I
missed guessing whether she was wearing a Versace or a Zandra
Rhodes. Minor things, yes, but I was learning that it was often
these small gestures and my automatic and unthinking responses
to them that contributed so much to the comfort of my life.

My shoulder still throbbed, albeit less viciously—especially
now that Arizona's monsoon season had arrived. As I reviewed
my notes on the Kobe case, a roll of thunder announced the arrival
of another storm front making its way up from Mexico. I figured
we had about one week left before the rains began in earnest
and—God help us—the humidity began to match Mississippi's.

Slapping the Kobe file shut, I said, "Hold down the fort,
Jimmy. I'm driving up to the San Carlos Reservation before the
weather gets too bad."

He turned around, a surprised look on his face. "Why do you
want to mess around with those Apaches? Or are you planning to
hit the casinos?"

Throughout the nineteenth century, Jimmy's tribe, along with
all the other Arizona tribes, had been continually harassed by the
Apaches. Before Geronimo surrendered to General Miles in 1886,
the Apaches raided and terrorized the Pima, the Maricopa, the
Navajo, and the Tohono O'odham—not to mention the Anglos
and the Mexicans who lived along the border of the old Arizona
Territory. But, as I reminded Jimmy, the Apaches hadn't been on
the warpath for years. They'd found another way of getting their
revenge on the Anglo settlers who took their land—casino gaming.

Ever since the Arizona legislature okayed casino gambling on
the reservations, the Apaches had operated some of the finest
casinos east of Las Vegas. In some cases affixed to high country
ski resorts, the Apache casinos were elegant watering holes where
instead of losing your scalp, you could lose your shirt. But I was
no gambler. Gambling was another pastime, along with drinking

and smoking, that I'd always been afraid to try. Who knew what kind of addiction-prone DNA rattled around in my genes?

Jimmy was familiar with my fears, so I set his mind at rest. "Chill, Kemosabe. I'm just going up there to talk to George Haozous."

This appeared to alarm him even more. "Not the artist?"

"The very one. Apparently he had a big fight with Clarice just before she got killed."

Jimmy frowned. "You'd better be careful. I don't like what we've heard about him. That fight with Clarice…"

"Relax. I just want to check him out. There's probably nothing to the story, just somebody getting mad and saying things they didn't mean, that kind of thing."

He was still frowning when I left the office.

The San Carlos Apache Reservation is situated on a high plateau only ninety miles east of Scottsdale, but it could be another country. When I left Route 60 at Globe and turned onto Route 70, I left behind me the dramatic tree-lined Salt River canyons and climbed onto an endless vista of scrub-sprinkled wasteland sizzling mercilessly underneath a hard blue sky.

My pink Jeep blasted past the luxurious Apache Gold Casino, but as I took the turnoff onto West 9, the injustice of the old Indian treaties became apparent. For more than a century the Apaches been forced to live on the largesse of the American government. This proud tribe of hunters and raiders had been confined to a landscape so barren, so battered by never-ceasing winds and spring floods, that growing crops or even running cattle was next to impossible. And jobs? Don't make me laugh. There was no industry within sixty miles of San Carlos. And no banks, no offices, no fast food outlets, no supermarkets, and no lawyers within twenty-five miles. No buses or taxis, either.

How well the government's "program" worked was evident by the tumbledown shacks I passed as I drove along Highway 6 as it meandered its way around rain-washed gullies and eroding hillocks. Most of the shacks weren't wired for electricity, so their residents had built brush-roofed ramadas to sleep in during the 100-plus degree summer nights. How they could sleep with the desert wind howling around them, I'd never know.

But lately, life for the Apaches was looking up. Here and there among the hardscrabble homes a few new stucco houses testified to the increased standard of living the casinos were bringing the tribe.

As I drove into the small village of San Carlos itself, I spotted a group of fierce-looking Apache teenagers hunched against the wind near the Project Head Start building. Ignoring their stares, I eased the Jeep down the bumpy road and into the parking lot of the Reservation Police headquarters. Inside the building, two uniformed officers who had been conversing in Apache switched immediately to English.

"Can I help you?" the taller one said in a softly accented voice. He easily topped six feet and his mahogany skin reflected the ravages of years of burning sun and hard wind. Like other Apaches I had met, his short-cropped raven hair was thick and glossy, a hairdresser's dream. Male pattern baldness was unknown among the tribe.

"I'm looking for George Haozous," I said, showing him my private investigator's license. While he studied it, I checked out the name patch on his breast pocket. Ronald Gudizeh.

Officer Gudizeh's eyes narrowed at me. "You realize that you have no authority here, Miss Jones."

"When it comes right down to it, I really don't have any authority anywhere and I'm well aware of that, Officer. But I would like to question Mr. Haozous about a murder that took place in Scottsdale a couple of weeks ago."

The other officer, an older man with a huge barrel chest, said, "The Clarice Kobe case."

I must have let my surprise show because Gudizeh said, "Oh, we get the newspapers up here on the rez, too, Miss Jones."

"I didn't mean..."

His face relaxed into a smile. "I'm sure you didn't. This your first time up on the rez?"

Suitably chagrined, I said, "All I need is directions to his house. If he wants to talk to me, fine. If not, that'll be fine, too."

The shorter man laughed. "We'll see if you still feel that calm about things after you've met him. George is..." He turned to Gudizeh. "How would you describe George's temperament?"

Officer Gudizeh grinned. "Irascible. That's how I'd describe it, Pete."

"Good word. Appropriate, too."

In the end, it was Pete who told me how to get to George Haozous's house, but as I started towards the exit, Officer Gudizeh called after me, "Before he slams the door in your face, tell him Pete and Ronald sent you over. It might at least get you a slower door-slam."

I thanked them both and left. Returning to the parking lot, I found my Jeep surrounded by the same teenagers I'd noticed earlier in front of the Project Head Start building.

"Well, *I* think it's cool," one of them, a boy of about fourteen, said. His shining, shoulder-length hair was held back by a multi-colored sweatband that proclaimed in Day-Glo letters, ROCKY POINT, MEXICO.

"But pink? Jeeps are righteous wheels, not Barbie cars." This from a girl who looked enough like the boy to be his older sister.

When I approached them they stepped back, but a tall, thin boy wearing jeans baggy enough to stuff two like-sized teenagers into said to me, "The steer horns are great but maybe you should consider another color?"

"I keep intending to repaint it," I said, climbing into the Jeep. "I just haven't gotten around to it yet. So you think the steer horns should stay?"

"Most definitely." He grinned, and I was once again struck by how a mere smile could transform such fierce faces.

"Then I'll keep them." If the steer horns were cool enough for the Apaches, they were cool enough for me. I put the Jeep in gear and pulled slowly out of the parking lot, careful not to throw more dust onto the kids than had already been blown onto them by the unrelenting wind.

George wasn't home, his wife said as she peered out the door of their double-wide trailer. She was a pleasant-looking woman, a little too plump, maybe, but she carried an air of alert friendliness about her. Unlike many artists wives I had known, she appeared neither downtrodden nor arrogant with reflected glory. Behind her, three glossy-haired children constructed a medieval castle out of Legos while a fat white kitten batted stray Legos back and forth.

"It's important," I told her. "I drove all the way up from Scottsdale to talk to him."

She smiled kindly. "You should have called first. Anyway, George is over at the studio and he doesn't like to see anybody when he's painting. Why don't you just make an appointment with me and I'll see that he keeps it. He's got to drive down to Phoenix some time next week."

I wasn't about to let the two-hour drive go for nothing, so I asked her where his studio was located. She gave me a wry, you'll-be-sorry look and pointed across the road at what appeared to be a small barn. "But I'm warning you, nobody with any sense interrupts that man while he's painting. I did once, about five years ago, and it was the first and the last time."

Still, she grinned when she said it so I took comfort in the thought that Haozous's ill temper might be more rumor than reality. Thanking her for the warning, I turned around and raised my hand to shield my eyes from the blowing dust, then angled across the road to the barn. As I neared it, the barn revealed an entire wall of glass, the north side, probably, where the light, although less intense, was steadier. Steeling myself against whatever invective might be hurled my way, I knocked politely at the door.

No response. I knocked again. And again.

Finally, a male voice screamed at me in Apache. You didn't have to speak the language to know he was cursing.

Another knock brought more curses, then heavy-booted footsteps. Finally the door flew open and I stood face to face with George Haozous.

When not enraged and splattered with paint, Haozous was probably a very handsome man, even in a tribe known for its physical beauty. Black hair flowed well past his shoulders, providing a dramatic frame for a sienna face gifted with extraordinarily high cheekbones. His sharp, even features appeared to have been sculpted by an artist even more talented than himself and his chocolate-colored eyes were simply magnificent. Da Vinci must have had eyes like those.

"What the hell you staring at, Blondie?"

I blinked, realizing that Haozous had switched from Apache to English and that yes, I was being very rude. Lowering my eyes for a minute, I took my ID out of my carryall and flashed it at him.

"Lena Jones. Private Investigator."

Silence for a moment, then the anger left his face. If I hadn't known better, I'd swear he was about to laugh. "You mean like Kojak and Rockford?"

"Like the woman who ID'ed the Unabomber."

Haozous' eyes found the scar above my eyebrow and rested there for a moment. Then he said, "You might as well come in, then, Miss Jones, before you annoy the neighbors."

I looked around, not seeing any neighbors, just a few dying mesquite trees. But I accepted his invitation and stepped into the studio.

Artists' studios were nothing new to me. Madeline, my foster mother, had taken me with her when visiting other artist friends, so I was prepared for the chaos, the clutter, the acrid assault of turps and linseed oil. What I hadn't been prepared for was the astonishing beauty of Haozous's paintings. As I had been warned, their subject matter was grim in the extreme, and Haozous, who had obviously taken a page or two from El Greco's sketchbook, had perfected a manner of elongating his subject's extremities which only added to the horror. Elderly Indians' bones snapped under trampling cavalry horses. The bodies of disemboweled warriors sprawled across the corpses of their comrades. Shining-haired women lay spread-eagled in the classic rape position, while above them, leering U.S. Army soldiers prepared for an assault of another kind. The babies… No. I couldn't look at the babies.

But, my god, the colors!

Under Haozous's brush, that hard, unforgiving sky which had haunted me since I entered the reservation became a soft, shimmering azure, and the barren desert had been transformed into a kaleidoscope of umbers, golds, crimsons, and greens. The Indians' skin, lit by a chiaroscuro sun, glowed with the genius of the Renaissance. It was all so gloriously unreal, scenes of the utmost horror transformed into beauty by the palette of a true master.

"How much?"

Now it was Haozous' turn to blink. "What do you mean, how much?"

I pointed to the most horrible, the most exquisite. The painting I craved portrayed the U.S. Cavalry galloping through a village of unprotected wickiups from which women and children ran in panic. One little girl of about four already lay dead on the ground, a bullet through her forehead. Or maybe she wasn't really dead. Maybe after the cavalry left, she would awaken and creep off into the underbrush, to be eventually found by an old shaman who would nurse her back to health. And maybe then she would grow up strong and fierce and...

I realized I was projecting my own childhood horrors onto the painting, but I didn't care. I couldn't take my eyes off it. "How much for that one?" I asked.

He laughed. *"That* one? Miss Jones, you must be crazy."

"How much?" I wasn't going to leave there without that painting, not even if it had been painted by a murderer.

Haozous looked at the painting, then back at me, once more noting my scar. He threw out a figure. I threw one back. We haggled for a while, finally settling on an amount which irritated us both. That accomplished, I made arrangements for him to deliver the painting to my apartment when he made his next trip to Phoenix, because the immense thing sure as hell wouldn't fit into the Jeep. As I dipped into my carryall for my checkbook, I asked, "What's the title?"

"Apache Sunset. It's based on an actual historical event."

Hopefully, none of my ancestors had been along for that merciless attack on women and children, but I had no way of knowing, did I? I might have been descended from the very Army colonel who had planned the attack on a peaceful village. Hell, for all I knew, I could have been descended from General George Armstrong Custer himself.

Now that our business was out of the way, I finally got down to the reason for my visit. "Mr. Haozous, I need to ask you about Clarice Kobe."

He gave me a dazzling smile. "Now that you're one of my collectors you can call me George."

"Did you kill her, George?"

The smile faded as he narrowed his eyes. "You do know that you have no authority up here, don't you?"

"So Pete and Ronald took care to remind me."

His narrow expression didn't waver, but he gestured at the floor. "As long as that's understood, why don't you have a seat. We'll talk." He squatted down on his haunches, looking for all the world like Geronimo at a peace parley.

With my bad hip, I couldn't squat, and my shoulder was still too sore to provide me any kind of balance, so I simply sat down on the cement floor. For all the heat outside, it remained cool, and for a brief moment, I wondered if George and his family slept in here at night. Then I remembered the electric lines leading to his trailer and the gust of cool air that had rushed at me when George's wife opened the trailer door.

Without the least appearance of nervousness, George said, "Cliff probably told you about my fight with Clarice."

I nodded and scrooched around on the floor, trying to find a more comfortable position. For the first time I wished that I had more padding back there. "He told me that you threatened to kill her."

He didn't even blink. "I meant it at the time. Clarice Kobe and her ilk are everything that's wrong with the art world today, the reason gifted artists starve while phonies like her no-talent husband rake in the big bucks. It's disgusting and I told her so. She said I didn't know what I was talking about and I said the same thing back to her, told her I was the one with the art school degree and she was nothing but a rich man's dilettante, college-dropout daughter. Pissed her off, that did."

I'll bet. "How did the death threat come into it?"

He shrugged with shoulders that must have been a yard wide. "It was when she told me that we Indians don't understand our own history and therefore have no business painting it, that true art requires the more *universal* perspective of the White Man. That was when I threatened to bop her on the head with my oh so *un*-universal tomahawk. Scared the shit out of her." He smiled at the memory.

"Do you own a tomahawk?"

"Get real." He was still smiling.

"Well, somebody bopped her on the head with something. She's dead now, so I guess you have your revenge."

"I hope you're not expecting me to feel sorry about it because I don't."

I hate it when people minimize violence, so as a matter of principle I gave Haozous a detailed description of the state of Clarice's body when I found it. To my considerable gratification, he started looking sick.

"That's not right," he said, shaking his head. "To do something like that to such a pretty woman. That's not right at all. I thought she just got shot or something."

"Just got shot or something? A gun shot would make it right?" I waved back at his paintings, at the gory craters gouged out of human flesh by Winchesters. "Was that right, then, the ones who *just* got shot?"

Now Haozous looked distinctly uncomfortable. "It's just an expression."

"So's 'The only good Indian's a dead Indian.'"

He sighed. "You can climb down off your soapbox now, Lena. I get the point. Want the truth? I would never have harmed Clarice, even though she was everything I accused her of being. She was just a dilettante. She didn't have a creative bone in her body nor the eye to recognize real creativity when she saw it. Maybe *you* liked her, but I'm telling you there was something lacking in that woman, a lack of substance, a lack of heart."

This last observation startled me because it meshed with something I had once found myself thinking about Clarice. I'd been at one of her artists' receptions when I'd overheard her discussing the new Museum of Western Art being built over the rubble of the last remaining Hispanic neighborhood in Scottsdale. Centuries-old adobes had been replaced by a sprawling monstrosity of steel, glass, and snot-green fiberglass panels. Every time I drove by it I wanted to puke.

"Those Mexes weren't doing anything with the property anyway," I'd heard Clarice say. "So why are they whining now?"

A lack of heart.

Still, Clarice had been murdered in a particularly ugly fashion, and her casual racism didn't excuse it. "If you didn't kill her, George, who did?"

He got up gracefully and walked over to the painting he'd been working on before my arrival. "I have no idea who killed her. Why should I? I was up here on the rez when she died. My wife will vouch for that."

"Anybody other than your wife?"

Face expressionless, he looked over his shoulder at me. "Look, I haven't set foot in either Phoenix or Scottsdale in about three weeks. I've been too busy painting." Then he returned to work on his canvas.

I didn't believe him. He was holding something back.

I looked around again at the paintings in the room, at the depictions of hacked limbs, crushed skulls, flayed hides. Just how deep did George Haozous's fascination with violence actually run? He was an intelligent man, an educated man, yet he lived on this bleak reservation as if he was hiding out from something—or someone. I made a mental note to have Jimmy check him out.

I struggled off the floor, nowhere as gracefully as Haozous. The dampness of the concrete had settled into my hip, making me limp after him like some elderly woman with osteoporosis. The top part of my body wasn't doing any too well, either, because ever since I'd hit the floor, my bullet wound had been nibbling at me with tiny, sharp teeth.

"George, do you know anybody else Clarice might have pissed off?" There was no point in letting him know his story had more than a few holes in it—including his so-called alibi.

He looked at me again, his face composed, his eyes guarded. "Why don't you try that family of hers? Those are some pretty weird people."

"I've already talked to her mother and father."

He picked up his palette and studied the painting, where an Apache woman was bent over the decapitated body of a child. Her mouth opened in a bottomless well of grief.

His continued silence told me that the interview was over, so I shouldered my carryall and limped towards the door. Just before I stepped out into the glaring sunlight, Haozous called after me,

"Try talking to her brother. Or her sister. *That* one's even crazier than Clarice, if such a thing is possible."

When I looked back, he was painting furiously, his brush almost digging into the canvas.

Chapter 11

By the time I had completed the journey back down 60 and turned off Loop 202 at the Scottsdale city limits, the fat black clouds I'd noticed earlier in the day had completed their voyage from the Mexican border. Lightning blazed across the darkening indigo sky. Like a fool, I'd forgotten to put up the Bikini top on my Jeep and raindrops the size of dimes slapped me on the head. Easing off 202 at Thomas Road, I drove carefully along the drenched side streets, using my left hand as an umbrella, trying to both steer and shift gears with my right. How I ever reached the parking lot behind Desert Investigations without getting into an accident, I'll never know.

Smelling like a wet dog, I climbed the stairs to my apartment, gun in hand. I unlocked the door, conducted my usual look-in-all-the-closets drill, then put some Slim Harpo on the turntable. His enraged mutters on "I Need Money" followed me all the way to the bathroom, where I stripped and stepped into the shower. I didn't even mind that the hot water heater was broken again—the cold water felt good on my skin. I soaped myself down several times, washed my hair, and was just toweling off when the phone rang.

I told Slim to hush up and rushed to answer it, hoping that it might be Dusty. It was.

"Hey, good-lookin'. The campfire sing-along's been called on account of rain, so how'd you like some company?"

Slim switched to "My Little Queen Bee," making my smile grow even wider. "Sounds fine to me, Cowboy. I just got out of the shower."

"I'm taking it that's a hint?"

"Unlike Catherine the Great, I'm not too crazy about sleeping with horses. Or men that smell like them."

I heard him laugh. "I'll check if the horse trough is free. If it is, you're in luck."

"And if it's not, Cowboy, you're *out* of luck."

An hour later, Dusty arrived, smelling like Brut and looking more handsome and weather-beaten than ever. He toted a grocery bag full of Pete's Wicked Ale and strawberry smoothies, with which he proceeded to stuff the refrigerator. Not even waiting for him to finish, I grabbed a smoothie.

He finished putting the drinks away, then stood there for a moment, watching me guzzle. "I figured you needed your vitamins, you being so sick and laid up and all."

I wiped the strawberry mustache off my upper lip. "Sick and laid up. Right. So sick I can't even fool around."

He expelled a theatrical sigh. "Looks like I've wasted my drive."

"And the strawberry smoothie."

"Guess I'd better go, then." He made a big to-do out of putting his rain-slicked duster back on.

"Um, before you go…"

I put my smoothie down on the counter and started peeling off the duster. I continued to peel until he was down to his briefs. "My, my," I whispered into his ear. "Aren't you hard and fit."

"In a manner of speaking, yes." With that, he slipped his arms around me, picked me up, and started for the bedroom.

I nuzzled my face against his chest. "Hey, Cowboy, haven't you forgotten something?"

"You mean the condoms? Honey, I've got a month's supply on me."

"Hell, no. I meant my smoothie."

Regardless of Dusty's comforting presence—or perhaps because of it—my usual insomnia kicked in around 1:00 a.m. As I lay in my dark bedroom staring at the ceiling, I reviewed what I'd learned about Clarice.

She had been a complicated woman, more so than I originally thought. Possibly sexually abused—no, make that *probably* sexually abused—as a child, Clarice had grown up to be a woman of many contradictory parts: a sophisticated (if not tasteful) art dealer, a financial opportunist, a battered wife, a bigot. Would I still have counted her among my friends if I had known as much about her when she was alive? If it came down to that, was friendship nothing more than a coalition among like-minded people?

At some point during the night, I must have fallen asleep, because Dusty woke me at 4:30 as he was crawling out of bed. "Got to feed the horses," he whispered, giving me a perfunctory peck on the cheek.

I reached up and rubbed his naked chest. "Give them a kiss for me."

He winked. "Woman, don't you know by now that I don't kiss horses?"

The rain had stopped by morning. The *Scottsdale Journal* told me that a lightning strike on the transformers on Hayden Road had knocked out power to about twenty-five thousand customers, but other than that, the Valley had gotten off easy. The big storms were yet to come. Turning the page, I saw that a Satanist inmate at the state prison in Florence had lost his Supreme Court fight to keep his goat's head, black candles, and other religious artifacts in his cell. In another story, Sheriff Joe Arpaio had run into trouble with Amnesty International; seems they thought serving green bologna at the jail was cruel and unusual punishment. On the wildlife front, a javelina had wandered in off the Pima Reservation and been captured in the front of Baby Kay's Cajun Kitchen. Fortunately for the javelina, the cook hadn't caught it—the Scottsdale cops had, and they simply drove it back to the rez.

While I was still laughing over the newspaper, Jimmy arrived complaining about the washed-out roads on the rez, but after a glass of cactus juice he settled down and he ran a quick check on George Haozous. What he found surprised neither of us.

Haozous had been arrested several times, each time for assault. The worst incident happened in 1993 when he'd served a short stint in the Madison Street Jail for beating up a bouncer at a

Phoenix bar. Nothing since then. Presumably, after the barroom incident he'd taken an anger management course—or joined A.A.

Jimmy handed me the print-out. "Told you those Apaches were rough guys."

"That's a racist statement."

He shrugged. "It's not racist when you say it about your own people."

"You're Pima. George is Apache. Not exactly the same, is it?"

He gave me a sly smile. "Pimas are non-violent, always have been. You can't say that about the Apaches."

I thought about Geronimo, Cochise, and Naiche, all the old gang that raised hell across the Arizona territory. "They were just defending their own," I finally said.

"Yeah, like the Crips and the Bloods. You sound like one of those knee-jerk liberals."

"And you sound like a nineteenth-century Mormon."

Now that both of us were offended, I studied Haozous's rap sheet, taking careful note of how severe some of those beatings had been and what triggered them. Then I noticed something that set my mind at ease.

"Jimmy, all of these assaults were against men."

"So?" Not appreciating my reference to his Mormon upbringing, he was still sulking.

And I was still feeling guilty because I knew what a good job the Mormons had done with him. I gentled my voice as I said, "I don't see any mention here of Haozous ever hitting a woman."

"He probably beats his wife. And like most wives, she doesn't turn him in."

I remembered Haozous's wife, her unmarked, friendly face peering out the trailer door, her almost humorous attitude towards her husband's temper. She hadn't acted like any battering victim I'd ever encountered.

But then, neither had Clarice.

"Point taken," I said to Jimmy. Then I sat down at my desk and thought for a while.

While I still needed to talk to Clarice's brother and sister, I remained dissatisfied with my interview with her parents. There seemed to be no point in talking to Stephen Hyath again—he was as close as a clam with lockjaw—but I had a sneaking suspicion that his wife, if I got her alone and sober, might be more forthcoming. Eleanor Kobe hated her daughter, and I knew from experience that hatred loosened the tongue even more than love. She had no desire to protect her daughter's reputation, no reason to lie for her. I made a mental note to find out about Stephen Hyath's schedule and then try the house again. I doubted that Eleanor went out much. Before I made the trip back up the mountain to Castle Hyath, though, I needed to talk to Clarice's sister and brother, whoever and wherever they were.

A quick call to the Violent Crimes Unit resulted in the information I needed. Confirming what Stephen Hyath had told me, Kryzinski said that Serena Hyath-Allesandro was a partner in Hyath Construction, but that neither Clarice nor Serena bothered much with the day-to-day running of the business. Didn't want to get their manicured hands dirty, he snickered. Where Clarice had concentrated on her gallery, Serena was written up in the society columns because of her affiliation with the Arizona Kidney Foundation, the Arizona Heart Institute, the Arizona Opera League, and the Scottsdale Symphony Guild. She had, however, been relatively inactive in those organizations for the past year and there had been rumors of health problems.

"I know the way your twisted little mind works, kid, but we've already checked out bubba and sis," Kryzinski said. "Ain't none of the Hyaths ever been arrested for anythin'. Sterling citizens, bless their black hearts."

I took down the telephone numbers and addresses Kryzinski gave me, delivered a big, smacking kiss over the phone, and hung up. Then I dialed Serena Hyath-Allesandro's number.

To my surprise, she immediately agreed to see me. I left Jimmy sulking over his keyboard and went out to the Jeep.

Last night's monsoon hadn't done too much damage and only a few stray palm fronds littered the parking lot. As I drove along Scottsdale Road towards the Boulders, the exclusive golf resort near which Clarice's sister lived, I could see that the storm hadn't been quite so benign north of Old Town Scottsdale. At several points, Scottsdale Road lay submerged under several feet of water and traffic had been diverted onto side streets where huge eucalyptus trees lay felled by the wind. L.L. Bean-clad residents hauled debris out of muddy pools, while others took chainsaws to collapsed palms. Judging from some of the arguments I overheard between the casually clad L.L. Bean contingent and some more formally dressed men, the insurance adjusters were out in full force—and they didn't want to fork over one thin dime.

I had good memories of this section of the Valley. After one of my foster fathers had been sent to prison for raping me, I'd been turned over to a Baptist minister and his family. Every Friday night, weather permitting, we had driven out into the desert somewhere around here where we'd pitched a roomy tent and built a big bonfire. The pastor had read Scripture to us as we roasted marshmallows over the fire, and while I'd eventually rebelled against the family's hyper-religiosity, I'd enjoyed the close contact with nature. Besides Scripture, the family had taught me the desert was my friend—if I remembered to respect it.

As I drove along, I was gratified to see that the desert had changed little since those relatively happy days. Brittle-brush and catclaw clung to gently sloping ridges. Purple salsify and vetch added bright spots of color. The sky was alive with life. Yellow warblers and cardinals winged their way through the sentinel saguaros, while above them, a kestrel glided along the updrafts.

Perhaps the desert had taken to its heels further south, but up here it remained triumphant.

The temperature had risen to 108 degrees and it was as humid as a swamp when I pulled up near the top of the ridge that harbored Serena Hyath-Allesandro's luxurious spread. I was happy to see the still-intact cottonwood trees lining the driveway that led to her Territorial adobe. Although the house was obviously not a true 1880's Territorial—increasingly rare in the Valley—I didn't mind these copies as much as I minded the pseudo-Mediterranean stuccos that plagued the Arizona landscape. At least the Territorials were a part of the Southwest's heritage. And god knows, those three-feet-thick adobe walls could keep out the heat *and* the monsoon's humidity.

The only untraditional touches on the property were the sign out front which warned, "Protected by Winchester Security

Services," the closed steel shutters blocking the windows, and the steel-fortified front door desperately pretending to be oak. It didn't fool me.

The steel door swung open as I started up the paved tile walk and a vicious-looking Doberman pinscher peered out.

"Good dog," I said, stopping in the middle of the walk.

Good dog's upper lip lifted away, exposing pointy teeth. His growl sounded like a bear with catarrh.

"Back, Hans," a reedy female voice whispered, as I saw a long-fingered hand snatch at his collar. "It's nobody."

I didn't know if that made me feel better or worse.

"Mrs. Hyath-Allesandro?" I called. I was still yards from the door, not certain if I wanted to get any closer. Hans still stood framed in the doorway, lip curled. Now he was drooling.

Then Hans disappeared as a dark-haired woman looked out. "Please call me Serena. And I take it you're Lena Jones." Her voice was hardly more than a whisper.

I told her she took it right and advanced up the walkway, ready to sprint back to the Jeep at the first sign of a pointy black nose.

"Hans won't bite you now." She continued to whisper, as if talking too loud might attract undue attention. Opening the door wider, she ushered me in, and together we clattered across the Saltillo tiles into a room as vast and dark as a cavern. The shutters were closed here, too, obscuring whatever view might have existed outside the three glass walls. "Once I've tugged at his collar he goes off guard until I alert him again."

Comforting. Especially since Hans heeled at her side, not taking his eyes off me. Like most Germans, he probably liked blondes—for lunch.

As my eyes adjusted to the dim light, I could see her better. She was tall, almost six feet, alarmingly thin, and her yellowish skin was little more than a covering for a ragtag collection of bones. Her brittle black hair reminded me of that I'd once seen on a chemotherapy patient, and dandruff flaked the shoulders of the dark sundress that hung on her like a blanket on a clothesline. Cancer? AIDS? Anorexia?

From a certain angle, I could see an echo of Clarice, but only that. Where Clarice's face had been a perfect, smooth oval, Serena's was sharp and angular, with jutting cheekbones creating smudge-colored shadows below. The large, razor-sharp nose that jutted above her thin lips bore testimony to Eleanor Kobe's catty remark about Clarice's plastic surgery. Serena had obviously elected to stay clear of the knife. She wasn't an attractive woman, but at least the pink-rimmed eyes that stared out at me from the dark hollows in her caved-in face revealed that she'd been crying. Over Clarice, I hoped. It was about time someone in her family grieved for her.

Serena ordered Hans into a corner, where he sat watching me, eyes alert. "You wanted to talk to me about my sister, right?"

Almost repeating the hand gesture she'd used with her dog, she motioned me towards the large, putty-colored suede sectional that wrapped around a living room the size of the Phoenix Suns' basketball court. Maybe she'd been able to afford it all by skimping on her electric bill. Besides being dark, the room was uncomfortably hot. Three-foot-thick walls or not, it *was* over 100 degrees outside.

"Um, it's awful dark in here and since I want to take some notes do you think you might…?"

She frowned, and for a moment I thought she might refuse to open the shutters or even turn on a light, but she surprised me and moved across the room to the windows. She pressed a button and the shutters slid up, revealing a view that took my breath away.

Thousands of acres of virgin desert rolled unimpeded towards the saw-toothed ridge of the McDowell Mountains. The rain had also cleared away the smog and the McDowells glimmered in a Cezanne-like pastiche of lavenders and mauves.

"That's all government-protected land," Serena said proudly, noting my awed expression. "Nobody can build on it."

An ironic boast, coming from a member of the family which was almost single-handedly responsible for destroying any remaining desert within the Phoenix and Scottsdale city limits. But then again, it was doubtful if Serena looked at it that way. She probably used the word most developers used when they defended their actions—they didn't destroy the desert, they "improved" it.

"I'm cold," she complained, although the room was even warmer with the shutters open. "Wait here until I get a sweater. Don't make any sudden moves, because Hans is very alert." With those comforting words she abandoned me to Hans' mercies, but not before I spotted the marks running up the insides of her arms. They weren't as bad as the needle tracks I'd seen on some heroin addicts, but they were getting there.

Keeping a watchful eye on Hans, I settled myself onto the deep sofa, which was as comfortable as it was beautiful. The living room was the antithesis of her parents'—all suede, glass, and tile. There were no knickknacks lying around, no wall hangings, no sculpture, no paintings, no books, no photographs. The room was stripped to the bare bone, like the woman who lived in it.

She finally returned wearing a white cashmere sweater and carrying a silver tray weighted down with a pitcher of tea, two Bass Ales, two Diet Cokes, and two empty glasses. "I've given the maid the day off, so I'm fending for myself. I hope I've brought something you like. If you want coffee, I can go back and make you some."

I wanted the tea but told her I preferred the Diet Coke instead, afraid that if she picked up the heavy-looking pitcher, her skeletal wrist would snap.

Coke poured and her hostess duties satisfactorily performed, Serena appeared to relax. "You wanted to know about Clarice," she whispered, finally raising her eyes to mine.

The sunlight streaming in from the newly opened shutters fell on my face and for the first time she could see me clearly. She gasped, a reaction I was not unfamiliar with. Then to my surprise, she leaned forward, and with a trembling forefinger, gently traced the scar on my forehead.

"Did it hurt? I... I have the name of a plastic surgeon who is wonderful with this sort of scar tissue. If you don't have the money to get it taken care of, I'm the head of a foundation which can cover the cost. Please let me help."

Despite my usual cynicism, I was touched. I'd met women like her before. They could be bleeding from a dozen wounds, but the old scars of others caused them greater pain. It was easy to make fun of such do-gooders, but the fact remained that unlike certain other human beings I could mention, they at least *did* have hearts.

"Don't worry. I'm fine with it," I said, pushing her hand away from my face as carefully as I could. "Honestly."

Her lower lip trembled and for a moment, I thought she would weep at her inability to help me. Instead, she collected herself and said, "I'm sorry. My manners... Please. What do you want to know about my sister?"

Considering her condition, the question was a cruelty, but it needed to be asked. "Do you think Jay Kobe killed her?"

Serena shuddered, then in a voice strengthened by anger, she answered, "Of course I do. Who else would kill her? I always told her she was a fool for staying with him."

When I pointed out that Clarice had finally left Jay, she nodded. "I'm on the board of Safe Haven, a home for battered women, and I can tell you that most women killed by their abusers are killed when they try to leave."

I granted her that but pointed out that Clarice had left Jay months earlier and there had been no indication that he had ever stalked her. Instead, he had simply moved in with his girlfriend and transferred his heavy-handed affections to her.

"It doesn't matter," Serena said, throwing a look towards Hans, who thumped his stubby tail at her in gratitude. "These controlling men, they can't let go."

Behind her, framed in the huge glass expanse, a hawk plummeted out of the sky. There was a flurry of dust on the desert floor, then the hawk rose again with something struggling desperately in its talons.

The gooseflesh popped out on my arms as I wished the hawk had given its prey a quicker death. "You ever have any problems with controlling men, Serena?"

She shuddered again, then her face closed off. "What makes you think that?"

"Just a thought." I switched to what was obviously a more comfortable topic: Clarice's death. "Kobe's out on bail, you know. And he says he has an alibi."

Her bitter laugh made Hans prick up his ears. "Men like that always have alibis."

That made me wonder about her own marriage. Something was destroying this woman from the inside out. But her vulnerability gave me an idea. I'd test a theory on her that I had developed over the past few days.

"Um, Serena, Jay's alibi still looks pretty good, but I've been wondering about something. Let's say, just for the sake of argument, that I wanted to kill a woman but was afraid I'd fall under suspicion. It would be nice and handy, wouldn't it, if my intended victim was known to have an abusive husband?" I didn't mention the traces of latex the police lab had found on Clarice's face or the indication that there had been another murder weapon besides the killer's fists.

An expression of disbelief replaced the vulnerability. "That sounds like something out of a cheap detective novel."

"Sometimes life *is* like a cheap detective novel. Can you think of anyone else—besides Jay—who would benefit from Clarice's death?"

Tears finally sprang to her eyes. When one spilled out and trickled down her gaunt cheek, she didn't even bother to wipe it away. "The divorce wasn't final so Jay gets her money and the house. What better benefit could there be?"

I thought about that for a while, then decided there was no point in not asking the question. "How well do, uh, *did* you all get along?"

Now she wiped the tear away and gave me a trembling smile. "We got along like brothers and sisters."

"Well, I'm an only child, so tell me how that is."

The smile faded, became wistful. "You've met my parents?"

I nodded.

"Then you know how…" She paused, took a few deep breaths, then began again, so quietly that I had to lean forward to hear her. "We… Uh, the three of us didn't have the easiest childhood. Like a lot of children from, well I guess you'd call them *dysfunctional* families, we, uh, tended to band together against our parents. Not anything overt, you understand. We just thought we needed…" She stopped and took another deep breath. "Protection."

Judging from the house's over-the-top security system, Serena thought she still needed it. But I'd never thought of Clarice as the paranoid type. "You think Clarice needed protection?"

Serena looked over at Hans, who scrambled to his feet. "Sit," she whispered to him. Disappointed, he sat back down. "I thought she needed less protection than my brother or myself, but I was wrong, wasn't I?"

For a few moments she stared out at the beautiful, savage desert and seemed to draw strength from that. Then she turned back to me.

"Since you're investigating my sister's death, I'm sure you've already found out about the civil suit she had pending against my father. It… it surprised me because the odd thing was, even with the inces… um, abuse, Clarice seemed to be so close to him, even after she got married. But as for her relationship with Mother… Well, that's a different story. Mother was always very hard on my sister, especially when she was drinking, which just before Clarice's marriage was pretty much all the time. I think maybe that's one of the reasons Clarice rushed into marriage with Jay. As for Evan and me, well, we rushed into marriage for other reasons. Mainly Father. He was always pretty physical with us."

I wasn't sure what I had heard. "Serena, are you telling me that your father used to beat you and your brother?" I was surprised because emotional abuse, not the physical variety, was the usual torture of choice among the wealthy. And Stephen Hyath hadn't seemed like a violent man. But what child abuser or serial killer ever did? Didn't they frequently turn out to be the quiet ones? The pillars of their communities?

Serena's smile was sad. "Oh, yes. Father believed in 'discipline.' He said it built character."

That's usually the way these things go, isn't it? With the most characterless people being the most vocal on the subject.

While I was thinking about that, Serena got up, again causing great excitement on Hans' part, walked over to a bleached oak credenza, and took out a ring of keys.

"You have to do something to help my sister. These are the keys to her house," she said, returning to the sofa. "I want you to go over there and look for something, anything, that will get Jay locked up again. He killed my sister. I'm certain of it."

What did she think I was going to find? A crudely drawn map of the Western Heart Gallery, complete with instructions on how to inflict the most damage on a woman's body? But I took the keys anyway. If nothing else, the house might reveal more clues to Clarice's nature. It was a prime directive of any homicide investigation—know the victim and you'll know the killer. The past few days had already proved how little I'd known about the woman I'd considered a friend.

Her hand trembling again, Serena wrote down the address, handed it to me and said, "Please be careful while you're in there. I don't want you to get hurt. I remember Clarice complaining that one of the support beams in the dining room was sagging. That dust storm we had about a month ago blew off some of the roof tiles and I'm afraid the rain last night just made matters worse. My brother said he'll get everything fixed as soon as he has time but... Well, he's taking her death hard."

I thanked her and put the keys and address in my carryall. I didn't want to ask the next question but I did anyway. "Do you think it's possible that your father could have...?" I couldn't finish.

"Killed Clarice?"

Serena looked out onto the desert again. Her sweater fell away from her shoulders, allowing me another view of the needle tracks in her pipe stem arms. "Miss Jones, I believe my father is capable of anything."

Chapter 12

After my interview with Serena Hyath-Allesandro, I needed something to take my mind off dysfunctional families, so I continued north another few miles to the town of Carefree, then turned east on the Carefree Highway until I came to the gravel road which led to the Happy Trails Dude Ranch. Dusty never minded my dropping by. Neither did his boss, Slim Papadopolus, who looked up from the Appaloosa he was shoeing to give me a friendly wave as I drove through the gates.

"You need to be selling that Jeep to me, Lena," he called. "I sure do like that pretty color."

"You and Barbie," I said back, braking carefully beside him so as not to spook the horse.

"That Barbie, she's a fine-looking gal." Slim, whose Athens-born parents had named him Odysseus, smiled up at me. "Almost as fine as you."

I tipped an imaginary hat. "Thank you, kind sir. You get any storm damage out here?"

He put the horse's hoof down, patted its spotted rump, then stood up and stretched so hard I could hear his bones pop. With his thin, dark face, and startling gray eyes separated by a classic Grecian nose, Slim was a handsome man—as long as you preferred men no more than five feet, three inches tall. Not an unusual height for an ex-jockey.

"Not much storm damage at all, just a few shingles off the roofs, that sort of thing. We've been busy all morning nailing them back on."

I looked around. Fewer guests than usual strolled the grounds, which probably meant the rest of them were out on a trail ride somewhere. Several ranch hands were still perched on top of the main house, hammering nails into errant shingles, while below them, a few overdressed guests lolled on the veranda in rocking chairs, sipping martinis and chatting. Horses milled aimlessly in the three corrals, dogs chased each other around the water trough, while over behind the stables, a flock of chickens and two Canadian geese scratched for worms. It all looked as peaceful as a new Eden, but few of the dudes would ever know how much work and money it took to maintain that rough-hewn serenity. To keep the place going, Dusty and the other ranch hands worked a sixty-hour week and got paid for forty. Not that any of them ever complained. They'd rather be overworked and underpaid on the ranch than underworked and overpaid in the city.

"Dusty out on the trail?" I asked Slim.

He nodded. "Yep. You're welcome to saddle up and join him, just as long as you promise not to get all kissy-face in front of the guests."

Slim Papadopolus was no fool. He'd long ago figured out that Dusty's good looks were one of the main reasons so many of the female tourists returned to the ranch year after year. He didn't want any of them to know Dusty had a regular girlfriend, if that's what I could call myself. I promised to keep my horny hands off his head wrangler, then parked the Jeep in the shade of a mesquite. With growing anticipation, I strolled over to the corral. Lady, the sleek bay mare I usually rode, was still there, so I threw a halter on her, then led her over to the tack room. She enjoyed the quick brushing I gave her and patiently tolerated the intrusion of the hoof pick as I scraped a pebble from between her near front hoof and its iron shoe. Horsekeeping details finished, I eased a clean blanket and a saddle onto her, cinched her snugly, then slid a snaffle bit into her soft, moist mouth.

"Let's go find Dusty, Lady," I said as we set off out of the yard and into the rugged Tonto National Forest. Lady waggled her ears back and forth, giving every indication of understanding.

I've always talked to horses. There's something about being on a horse's broad back which is akin to lying stretched out on a psychiatrist's couch, only cheaper. Safer, too, if you've heard some of the stories I've heard about psychiatrists. Over the years, I've told a whole herd of four-legged shrinks about my various foster homes, those tough first months on the police force, my search for my mother, and most recently, my concern that I cared more for Dusty than I thought wise. The horses didn't find my fear of emotional entanglements peculiar at all. They never talked back, never judged. They just plodded along peacefully, flicking their ears.

After I got through telling Lady about the Kobe investigation, I finally fell silent, content to listen to Lady's fluttery snorts and the peep-peep-peep of cactus wrens. This was the Sonoran Desert at its most enjoyable, after a rain, when the air was clear and sharp, and many of its citizens splashed happily in shallow puddles. As we reached the place where the trail forked, I drew gently on Lady's reins and she halted. Because of the danger of flash floods, I figured Dusty would steer clear of the gully bottoms, so Lady and I took the fork that led along the ridge of hills to the north.

As we climbed in elevation, the desert spread out below like a sage-colored carpet. Because horses have such a strong scent, my presence went undetected by the top-knotted Gambel's quail that scuttled across the road in front of us, but not by the pair of coyote in the underbrush who matched us stride for stride, all the while throwing us slanty-eyed looks of suspicion.

The coyotes continued to pace us until we reached the ruins of the Hohokam village overlooking the valley. Then they threw us a final look and trotted up a narrow wildlife trail towards the village. Perhaps Earth Doctor was calling them, perhaps not. When I looked up past the ruins, I saw several buzzards spiraling down from the sky. Something was dead up here and coyotes were nothing if not scavengers. They enjoyed a tasty, desert-warmed corpse as much as did their fine-feathered friends.

The body was probably that of an animal, but on the odd chance it was human (the desert, after all, was the preferred dumping ground for all kinds of killers, human and otherwise), I touched my heels to Lady's flank and we moved briskly up the hillside to the ruins. The Hohokam had built carefully, and the small, eight-hundred-year-old village remained mostly intact.

Most of the rock walls stood upright, still winning their battle with the elements. The roofs, however, probably constructed of limbs and grass, had long ago collapsed.

Not wanting to risk bumping into the remaining walls, I dismounted just outside the village and dropped Lady's reins to the ground. As with most Western horses, she'd been taught to ground-tie, and I knew she'd remain there until I found the source of the vulture's feast.

Listening for the mutterings of the old gods, I followed the old walkway between the buildings, twisting and turning in the shadows. But Earth Doctor was silent, perhaps still sulking in his cave beneath the asphalt of Papago Park. His nemesis, Elder Brother, said nothing either. The ruins were inhabited only by memory and the flute-like notes of the wind.

When I emerged from the ghostly corridors and into the light, I found myself on the edge of a steep embankment looking over the north side of the valley. On a ledge below me the vultures were gathered around the remains of some large animal—an antelope or a deer, I hoped. But so many of the broad-winged birds were ripping at its flesh that I couldn't identify the species. Finally, though, the two coyotes reached the carcass and began snapping and lunging until most of the birds were driven away. Before they bent to their own feast, I managed to identify four spindly legs ending in black hooves.

No lost child, then. No missing Alzheimer's patient.

Sighing with relief—I was sick of finding dead bodies—I left the desert to its own and returned to my horse.

The rest of the ride was so enjoyable that I almost forgot the original reason I'd traveled out here, but eventually, as Lady and I loped along the top of a small butte, I spotted a long line of horses snaking up the side of the next hill. I eased Lady back down to a trot, then, settling my feet into the stirrups and rising in the saddle to spare her back, extended her gait so that we covered the ground more quickly than most horses could at a lope.

It didn't take us long to reach them. Before we drew up to the last horse in line, I reined Lady in, not wanting to spook any of the dudes' horses. Then I squeezed my knees gently so that we passed first the wrangler bringing up the rear, then the long line of dudes. Dusty was, as usual, the leader of the pack, and when we drew even with him, he gave me a congratulatory grin.

"Hunted me down again, huh?"

"Yep. Throw down your six-gun and surrender, varmint. I'm a-takin' ya in."

He laughed, then motioned to the dudes in back of him. "I'd love to talk, but…"

"Say no more." I wheeled Lady around and we found a gap in the line. We eased in there and for the rest of the ride, pretended that we didn't know Dusty from Adam.

I'd reached them almost at the turnaround point, so within an hour we were back at Happy Trails. As I had hoped, the pièce de résistance of the day was an outdoor barbecue dinner, complete with wine or, in my case, Diet Coke. After stuffing ourselves, we sat around the campfire under a star-spangled sky, singing corny cowboy songs which—truth be told—sounded pretty good right then.

As we sang, I tried not to notice the expensive-looking redhead who attached herself to Dusty like a long-separated Siamese twin. Once though, Dusty caught me staring at her and grinned.

After the singing stopped, Slim recited some cowboy poetry about gunslingers and unruly ponies, poems he once told me he had written in the jockey's dressing room at Sarasota and Hollywood Park. As usual, Slim had attracted his own fan club. This time, it looked like he was about to get lucky with a brunette at least a foot taller than he.

But hey, Slim wasn't prejudiced.

The party ended with glasses of champagne for everyone but me, and the sleepy dudes trooped back to the main house.

Dusty looked like he wanted to tell me something, but the redhead had attached herself to him like a tick.

Not that it bothered me at all. Nope. Not at all.

I just left Dusty to deal with the bitch and ground the Jeep's gears all the way back to Scottsdale.

Chapter 13

Before Desert Investigations opened the next morning, I scurried out to Barnes & Noble and picked up a beautifully illustrated book on the history of the Pima Indians. It was waiting for Jimmy when he arrived at the office carrying a bouquet of yellow roses in a cut glass vase.

"You were so excited about Cliffie's flowers I thought maybe yellow roses were your favorites," he mumbled, depositing them on my desk.

We managed wobbly smiles at each other, then started work.

I'm not always very good at this friendship thing. Friendship is a skill most people learn as children, playing with the kids next door or during recess at school. But I'd never been able to stay in one foster home long enough to make friends before moving on to the next, and after a few gut-wrenching moves, I simply stopped trying. Yes, a lot of those moves were my fault. Like a lot of foster home kids, I'd developed behavior problems. Foster parents tended to get excited when they discovered that their foster child slept with a knife under her pillow, not to mention the family-wide hysteria when the artist's husband found the little .22 pistol I'd liberated from her closet.

Such discoveries always necessitated a move, leaving fragile new friendships behind. And after a while, most of us "difficult" foster kids simply stopped trying. Now that no one could make me pack my luggage without my consent, though, I cultivated—however clumsily—every offer of friendship that came my way.

Thus, the odd packet of gift coffee for Clarice. Thus, books for Jimmy.

And judging from the roses on my desk, Jimmy had his own friendship issues to deal with. After all, calling me a "knee-jerk liberal" hadn't been *that* bad an insult.

I've been called worse.

I was halfway through my morning paper (child-biting coyotes still on the loose, no more Grand Canyon deaths, no more moldering corpses found on the rez, just an armed robbery at Bank One by a guy wearing a gorilla mask) when the phone rang. I picked it up and answered in what I hoped was my best new-client-impressing voice. "Desert Investigations."

"Hi, good lookin'." Crap. It was Dusty.

It seemed that no sooner had I solved one relationship problem than another reared its ugly head. "What do you want?"

"We need to talk. You blew out of here pretty fast last night."

"I was tired." Was it my imagination, or were Jimmy's ears growing longer? One certainly appeared to be stretching itself in my direction.

"Lena, I just want to explain…"

"There's nothing to explain."

A long silence at the other end. I could hear him breathing, a horse squealing in the background—at least I hoped it was a horse. Then, "You don't have to be so touchy."

"Who's touchy? Listen, I've got work to do here, calls to make. I can't be tying up the line with these personal conversations."

"Fine then." He slammed the phone down.

I hoped that horse I'd heard in the background kicked him.

The day crawled like a centipede with a broken leg. I needed to interview Clarice's brother, but for now, there was billing to be done and notes to be typed. At the best of times, I'm not wild about computer work, but getting these monthly statements out was pure torture and I could only make myself do it because of the large amounts of money the bills generated.

Mid-way through the morning I had a thought.

"Jimmy, didn't you say that your uncle owned a body shop?"

Jimmy looked up from his keyboard and nodded. "Yeah. He does major collision work, but he can handle dings and dents, too. Painting, detailing, stuff like that. The re-upholstery stuff he farms out to his brother."

"How much do you think he'd charge me to paint the Jeep?"

Now he turned all the way around, a pleased expression on his face. "Well, it being a Jeep and all, there's not really a lot of surface there, so I wouldn't imagine it'd cost too much. What color you thinking of?"

That was the question. The pink was awful, certainly, but what else was there? Red? White? Black? Puce? What looked good on a Jeep besides the standard Army-issue green? Then I had an idea. "Look, why don't I just drive it out to your uncle's, let him take a look at it, and let him decide. Any color will be fine, as long as it's not pink and doesn't clash with the steerhorns."

He raised an eyebrow. "That's a little trusting, don't you think?"

"I can use the practice."

Jimmy called his uncle and made an appointment for me to take the Jeep in that afternoon. "He said he's got a loaner he can give you, but it's not anything fancy."

"Neither's the Jeep."

On the way out to Jimmy's uncle's, I stopped for lunch at Native Hands, the Pima restaurant-cum-gift shop that now sat almost directly under the new freeway overpass. After enjoying a mesquite-smoked barbecue sandwich and a small cup of lamb stew, I went into the gift shop portion and purchased a pair of turquoise and silver cuff links. Not that I had anybody to give them to, anymore. But it was always best to be prepared.

The flat land of the Pima rez was better suited for growing crops than was the San Carlos, which is why early Indian wanderers had settled just outside the area that came to be known as Phoenix. Although today the Salt River Valley was frequently too dry and hot for comfort, it had at one time been quite lush. Up until relatively recently, the Salt was an active, flowing river, so the Hohokam had designed a two-hundred-mile network of canals with which to irrigate their crops during the long, hot summer months. It made all the difference to *their* descendants, the Pimas.

For staples, the early settlers grew corn, beans, gourds, grain amaranth, and squash. Antelope, land tortoises and other animals provided an occasional feast. For clothing, the Hohokam and Pima both cultivated and wove cotton. Everything they needed, they gleaned from the land. They lived in such close harmony with nature that more than two thousand years later, the area the Hohokam originally settled bore few scars.

But when the White Man moved to the Salt River Valley in the early 1800's, he rerouted some of the old Hohokam canals to water his own gardens. Not content with this minor water rights theft, in the early part of the twentieth century the Anglos built the Roosevelt and the Laguna dams, which deflected the river's entire flow onto Anglo land. The Pima's crops withered and died. Within a generation the tribe was reduced to poverty.

But now they had begun to fight back.

Like their more warlike cousins, the Apache, the Pimas were building casinos as quickly as they could get them up. For those Pimas who still preferred a rural way of life, mechanical irrigation systems now replaced the old canals, although at a much higher cost. And a few Pimas, like Jimmy's uncle, had gone into business for themselves.

PIMA PAINT AND COLLISION—MICHAEL SISIWAN, PROPRI-ETOR sat just outside the Scottsdale border, on the western edge of a large Pima cotton field. This being August, most of the cotton had already been harvested, leaving only a few white tufts blowing around the field, driven by a hot wind. Across the road, where a tractor was preparing the ground for the next planting, a dust devil whirled along a gully. I wondered again how anyone could work in 100-plus temperatures, especially when the monsoon season had spiked the humidity.

As I drove up, Mr. Sisiwan and his crew came out to meet me. "I've heard plenty about this Jeep," Jimmy's uncle said, patting the steer horns, his vowel sounds stretched out in the melodious Piman accent.

Other than his considerable height and breadth, he looked little like his brother's son. Where Jimmy's face was cantaloupe round, his uncle's harkened back to some ancient ancestor. Recent theories say the Pimas may be descended from South Sea islanders, not Asiatics. It was angular, liberally creased with weather lines and worry. Well, owning a business will do that to you. And then there was the lack of facial tattoos. Mr. Sisiwan's face, as well as the faces of his entire staff, remained unmarked. Jimmy was the only Pima I'd ever known who had resurrected the custom.

"Jimmy tell you what I want?"

Mr. Sisiwan looked worried. "Well, yes, but I'm not sure I understood him correctly. He said you, ah, wanted to be *surprised?*"

"That's right. This is your chance to get creative. I'm sick of the pink, but I still don't want a Jeep that looks like every other Yuppie-mobile in town."

The crew, all of them Pimas, looked around at each other. Here was living proof, their body language seemed to say, that Anglos should stay out of the summer sun.

"*Any* color?"

I nodded. "I don't care if you paint stripes on it. Just make sure it looks different."

Mr. Sisiwan, still hesitant, took me inside the office and filled out a service ticket, writing "Customer says be creative" inside the color selection box. "You'd better sign off here," he said.

I signed with a flourish, also initialing "Customer says be creative." "Great. When can I pick it up?"

He checked a work list. "How does day after tomorrow sound?"

"That sounds fine. Ah, Jimmy told me you'd have a loaner for me?"

After being warned by Jimmy, I didn't expect much, so I was pleased at being led to the almost-new Toyota pickup truck in the back lot. "If you don't like this, we've got a Taurus around here somewhere."

I shuddered. The last time I'd seen a Taurus up close, its occupant had shot me. "No, thanks. The truck'll do just fine."

He handed me the keys, and with a final wave, I drove off.

I didn't want to go back to the office in my present mood—my relationship with Jimmy was already strained enough—so I decided to use the key Serena gave me and take a look inside Clarice's house.

I knew the neighborhood. Clarice's house was nestled among the few remaining horse properties in downtown Scottsdale. Sparkling white paddocks fronted the narrow streets, and as I drove along, dish-faced Arabs and long-nosed Thoroughbreds snorted at me from velvety muzzles. The houses themselves were huge—long, low ranch-styled homes that had been built approximately thirty years ago, before the California exodus began gobbling up the land.

Clarice's house turned out to be one of the biggest, at least six thousand square feet, and as I steered the truck into the driveway, I couldn't help but wonder what she and Jay had done with all that space.

Serena had been right to worry about rain damage. The dining room with its sagging beam was a mess. Its priceless rosewood paneling was streaked and buckled away from the walls. Judging from the notes I found scribbled on a yellow pad on the dining room table, somebody—probably Clarice's brother—was already making an estimate of the needed repairs. He'd better not wait long. Already the smell of rot and mildew was overpowering. When the ceiling began to creak, I hurriedly backed out of the dining room and went into the gigantic living room.

And there I stopped, stunned, not knowing whether to weep or laugh. Instead of utilizing the ever-popular Southwestern Saltillo tile, Clarice had floored the thing with white Berber carpeting flecked in grays and blues. The blue had been picked up on the walls. Every single one of them. Given that the furniture—from the sectional sofa and occasional chairs, to the clumsy marble etagere near the sliding glass doors—was white, I felt for one dizzying moment as if I were trapped inside a giant Wedgewood bowl.

As I investigated more carefully, I found that nothing in the room was as it first appeared to be.

Silk and plastic plants lined a white-painted shelf that ran the length of the living room. More silk plants rested in a long, glass-topped "planter" that served as a coffee table. A white enamel and gilt birdcage played home to a stuffed parrot, and the water in a lavishly landscaped eighty-gallon aquarium bubbled around a school of bobbing artificial fish.

It got worse.

Apparently Jay hadn't retrieved his paintings yet, because the blue walls were cluttered with dozens of portraits of questionable Indian maidens, mostly nude with glowing tits; expensive show horses apparently set free to roam the desert; and cowboys who bore a suspicious resemblance to either John Wayne or Gabby Hayes.

Nothing in the house was real. Regardless of its true cost, everything looked cheap, artificial.

Like its owner? a little voice whispered.

I forced myself to stop thinking about Clarice's god-awful décor and began to search the premises.

Two hours later I had found nothing, other than a closet still filled with Jay's clothing and even more of his lousy paintings tucked away in a studio at the back of the house. Why hadn't he cleared it all out? Could he possibly have been hoping that somehow, someday Clarice might take him back?

Anything was possible, I thought, as I shouldered my carryall. But if Clarice *had* let Jay come home, would she still have been murdered?

Back at the office, I made the phone call I'd been putting off all morning. "Mrs. Hyath? This is Lena Jones. I talked to you and your husband a few days ago?"

"I remember you. What do you want?" She sounded relatively sober.

"Do you think it might be possible to meet for…" I started to say "lunch," but then remembered who I was talking to. "…to meet for a drink sometime in the next couple of days?"

I could almost hear her frown. "What for?"

There was no point in lying, so I told the truth. "There's a lot more I think you could tell me about Clarice, and I'd really like to talk to you away from your husband."

A phlegm-filled laugh. "Why should I do that?"

The obvious answer—out of maternal love—never crossed my lips. Instead, I said, "I'm not working for Jay Kobe anymore, so look at it this way. While professional ethics prevent me from actively working against a former client, if my investigation reveals evidence that he did kill Clarice after all, he can't inherit. Got that? He can't inherit. That means Clarice's money will revert back to the next of kin. Namely, you."

"And my husband," she muttered. Then I heard her brighten. "But fifty percent of a couple of million is better than zero percent, isn't it?"

I agreed with her, disliking the woman more and more.

"Tell you what, Miss Jones. I'm all booked up for the rest of the week and through the weekend…"

With what, I wondered. A case of gin?

"…but next Monday looks pretty good for me. Would you like to meet at the Hacienda Palms? Say around lunch time?"

Ouch. The Hacienda Palms was one of the most expensive resorts in the Valley. I hated to think what lunch and drinks would cost. Still, I owed it to Clarice.

"Next Monday. Noon. See you there."

"And Miss Jones? Please make sure you're dressed appropriately. We're judged by the company we keep."

Fuming, I hung up the phone.

I made two more calls, both less aggravating than the last one.

Yes, Evan Hyath would be happy to see me, the sooner the better. Tomorrow, even, if I wished. Since the police weren't getting anywhere with his sister's murder, maybe I could. He gave me directions to the company trailer on the Tudor Hills construction site, a mixed-use development going up just west of the Boulders. The location surprised me, because it was just down the road from Serena's house, making me wonder how Serena felt about sharing her neck of the woods with comparable riff-raff. Then again, since these homes would go from four hundred thousand dollars upwards, they weren't for the true riff-raff, just riff-raff compared to the Hyaths. But then I remembered the long ridge that separated the Boulders neighborhood from the rest of the Valley, and realized she wouldn't mind. She'd be making a small fortune off the project, but *her* million-dollar view would still be unobstructed. It was just too bad for her neighbors across the ridge, who had been promised "undisturbed, scenic desert vistas" when purchasing their homes.

The next call was easier still. It had occurred to me on my drive back from Pima Paint and Collision that I needed to take another look at the murder scene. The last time I'd been there, I'd been crawling around on all fours, which wasn't the recommended way to investigate a crime scene. Perhaps if I didn't have to worry about a murderer jumping out at me from behind one of her clunky pieces of sculpture, I might be able to spot something the police had missed. Not that the Violent Crimes Unit missed much, but you never know.

Kryzinski grumbled, but in the end, he agreed to send one of his officers over with the key to the Western Heart Gallery.

"You're not going to find anything in there," he said, echoing my fears. "As soon as we finished, Serena Hyath hired one of those crime scene cleaning companies and they scoured the place from top to bottom. There's not a piece of brain tissue or blood spatter left."

Frankly, I was relieved. Determining the direction of blood spatter, an all-too-frequent duty while still with the VCU, had never been one of my favorite jobs. But I had learned that there was a lot that a careful investigator could surmise just from a room itself.

Temporarily finished with my chores, I settled back in my chair and watched Jimmy type.

I didn't get to watch him long. Within a few minutes, a blue-and-white pulled up to the curb and disgorged Vic Falcone. He came into the office wiping his brow, his uniform damp around the armpits.

"Shit, Lena, it's hotter than the Devil's left testicle out there. Hi, Jimmy." He gave me a Groucho Marx eyebrow waggle, then headed straight for the refrigerator. After rooting around for a while, he finally emerged with a Coke. Full strength, sugar and all. That Falcone, what a wild man.

Falcone slumped down in a chair, chugged some Coke, then took some keys out of his pocket and jingled them at me. "These are the victim's, found them on her desk. They're supposed to be returned to her family, but we ain't got around to it 'cause of the rush."

"What rush?"

"Ain't you been reading the paper? Christ on a crutch, Lena, the whole city's gone nuts. We had us a couple of home invasion robberies up on McCormick Ranch, a suspicious carpet store fire near Papago Plaza, that damned bar over on Stetson had another big fight—the usual, you know, cowboys versus tourists with the tourists getting their asses whipped—a whole shit load of burglaries, *and* that damned kid-biting coyote is still running through town. Must be the heat, making everybody crazy, even the wildlife. Is it my imagination or is it hotter than last summer?"

"It's not one bit hotter this year than last."

Falcone shrugged. "I was thinking it might be that greenhouse effect. Or maybe the hole in the ozone layer."

It was obvious that Falcone wanted to stay in my air-conditioned office and chat all day, but there was work to be done. I stood up. "Let's go see what we can see."

He gave me a mournful look. "Hell, Lena. I'm supposed to stand outside and guard the place while you're messing around in there. It must be 120 degrees outside!"

"One-fifteen. Why don't you just stay here and have another Coke? You can see the Western Heart Gallery right through this window."

"You got all them big letters on the windows blocking my view!" Seeing my expression, he backtracked. "You're right, you're right. I'll move my chair over to the window, look through the center of the 'O', have some more Coke."

When I left, he was trying to hustle Jimmy into a hand of poker.

The Western Heart was almost as musty as Clarice's house had been, but a faint odor of antiseptic overlaid the odor of mildew. Clarice had been dead for almost three weeks now, and since the exit of the corpse cleaners—as the cops call the cleaning services specializing in crime scenes—no one had been in there. The corpse cleaners had done a good job, I noticed. No blood remained to be seen, not even on Jay Kobe's crappy horse portrait. But no trace of Clarice remained, either, no stray wisps of perfume, no echoes of edgy laughter. The Western Heart Gallery was as impersonal as a morgue.

I bit my lip and reminded myself that I was a professional. Letting the place get to me wouldn't help Clarice. Pushing aside my depression, I stood on what I believed to be the exact spot where she died—the cleaning crew had even removed all trace of the police chalk mark—and looked around.

At first I was surprised to see that all the paintings remained on the walls, the sculpture on their pedestals, but then I remembered how many legal steps needed to be completed before any artifact could be removed from a crime scene. This protected the heirs and also the artists who'd consigned their work to the gallery. Otherwise, anybody could come in, identify himself as the artist, and grab a painting. Not that anybody would bother in the Western Heart. We weren't exactly talking Rembrandts here.

The room itself appeared more or less as I had last seen it, discounting Clarice's body and all that blood, of course. The dolphin fountain had been turned off, but it stood in the same spot, as did Clarice's antique desk, chair, and the overly ornate credenza which served as her invoice cabinet. The gallery's walls were as crowded with bad art as ever. But something...

Something was missing.

Another look at Clarice's desk showed me that its formerly cluttered surface was now pristine. The corpse cleaners had removed the jumbled stacks of papers, a few knick-knacks, and all the rest of the desktop clutter we're prone to collect. And hadn't there been a small piece of sculpture or two decorating the desk's surface? I wondered what Clarice had been working on at the time of her death, because as any homicide investigator knows, paper trails solve more mysteries than smoking guns ever do. Fortunately, finding the papers turned out not to be a problem. The desk drawers were unlocked and inside them, I found unfiled consignment agreements, bills of sale, artists' bios, a Rolodex, a *milleflora* paperweight, and several loose pieces of paper with phone numbers written on them.

All well and good, but something was niggling at the back of my mind. That desk...

As I stepped back and took a good look at it, I realized the desk was a near twin to the one in Cliffie's gallery. And hadn't Cliffie once shown me that his desk contained a cleverly disguised secret drawer, at the time all the rage among the courts of France? Nothing ventured, nothing gained. I opened the bottom right drawer halfway out, then felt around on the drawer's surface until my forefinger felt a looseness in the center of a carved rosebud. Smiling with satisfaction, I pressed the flower hard.

The false bottom of the drawer slid back, revealing a Dayrunner lying calmly on the drawer's true bottom.

Gloating over my find, I tucked the Dayrunner in my carryall, then slid the false bottom back and closed the desk drawer. I'd turn over my find to Kryzinski.

Eventually.

I looked around some more, taking careful note of the back door through which Kryzinski believed the killer had escaped. I studied the door facing and the lock closely but could find no pry marks. This was interesting, because most gallery owners I knew kept their back doors locked during Art Walk.

Which meant Clarice must have let her killer in.

Or did he have a key?

This once again brought the investigation right back to Jay Kobe, a member of the family, or—and this was a new thought— a lover who had not yet stepped forward. Clarice had not only been a rich and beautiful woman, but she had considerable charm. There was no reason why she couldn't have already replaced Jay's rough affections with those of another man.

But who?

Still thinking about this, I opened the back door and looked out upon a parking lot empty except for the Dumpster Clarice shared with Cliffie. The smell of mesquite-broiled steak wafted from the restaurant across the alley, reminding me that it was almost dinnertime. I walked outside and took a quick look around, only to find nothing. If there had been any clues lying around outside, they were long gone. Sighing, I went back inside the gallery, locking the back door firmly.

For a moment I stood there inside the gloom, feeling the emptiness of the place.

"I won't let him get away with it, Clarice," I said out loud, listening to my voice echo around the room. "That's a promise."

As I crossed the street to my office, an old pickup truck came rattling around the corner and squealed to a stop right in front of Desert Investigations. Alarmed, I reached into my carryall for my gun, but I let my fingers relax when I recognized George Haozous in the driver's seat. A tall plastic-wrapped object sat propped in the truck bed.

"Brought your painting," Haozous said, emerging from the truck, a tool belt cinched around his waist. "Where do you want it?"

I noted once again what a handsome man he was, especially now that he wasn't covered with paint. His long hair glistened and his features were as flawless as a Greek statue's. His long, muscular legs were encased in tight-fitting Levis, and a black shirt mirrored his eyes. If George Haozous ever went to Hollywood, he'd make a fortune. Today there was no trace of his famous temper, and in fact, the man seemed positively genial. Probably because my check had cleared the bank.

"I bought the painting for my apartment upstairs," I told him. "But I've got to go in my office to return something first. You want to come in with me and get a drink? Coke? Tea? Ice water?"

He shook his head. The heat didn't seem to bother him. "I'll just start hauling it up the stairs. Maybe you can give me something to drink when we're finished, okay?"

I nodded, then went inside the office and slid the keys across the desk to Falcone, who was sitting in my chair, an odd expression on his face. Jimmy sat across from him, looking smug. A weathered deck of cards lay spread out between them.

Uh oh. "Seven card stud?" I asked, already knowing the answer.

"Yeah," Jimmy said. "Your friend here insisted on playing a couple of hands." For relaxation Jimmy played poker on his computer, and he was as good at that as he was everything else. Certainly too good for Falcone the Open-Faced, Falcone the Fumble-Fingered.

I threw Jimmy a dirty look. "You didn't."

Jimmy gave me a look of studied innocence. "It was just a friendly game. And he wanted it. Practically *begged.*"

Falcone cleared his throat. "Um, I'll drop off what I owe you on payday, okay, Jimmy?"

"No problem," Jimmy said. At least he didn't smirk.

Falcone put the cards back in his pocket. Eager to change the subject, he asked me, "Well, did you find anything over there?"

"Not a thing," I lied.

Chapter 14

I could look at Clarice's Dayrunner later, but now I had a painting to hang.

Jimmy was already packing to leave, so I left him to lock up and met George Haozous at the top of the stairs. The artist smiled, revealing the straightest, whitest teeth I had ever seen. "First a real life private detective and now an art collector. Well, well."

"Well, yourself." I took out my keys and opened the door. Notwithstanding the fact that I had a six-foot Apache at my back, I still took my gun out of my carryall and did the usual. When I returned from my search and destroy mission, Haozous was waiting for me in the living room.

"A little paranoid, are we?" His smile had dimmed.

"Even paranoids have enemies."

Haozous didn't look eager to explore this. Instead, he began untying the thick cords that kept the plastic wrapped around the painting. I held my breath. Would I like it as much today as I had the first time I saw it? But as the black plastic fell away and the colors rushed out, I released my breath in a satisfied sigh.

It was even more horribly beautiful than I had remembered.

Apache Sunset, ready to hang," the painter said, all business. "I attached wire to the stretchers before I left the studio. So. Where do you want it? Over the couch?"

"If I put it over the couch I won't be able to see it." I thought for a moment, then unplugged the television and hauled it over to the small table by the door. It would mean that I'd have to watch CNN at an angle, but who cared? "Let's put the painting on the wall behind where the TV used to be. That way I can sit on the couch and look at the painting, instead."

Haozous looked inordinately pleased. "Wish I had more collectors like you. Most people just buy paintings to give their sofas something to do."

He took some hooks out of his pocket and unattached the screwdriver hanging from his tool belt. "The painting's pretty heavy, so I usually use these wing nuts. You mind?"

I shook my head. I didn't care if he bolted the painting to the wall.

"Now stand where you want the painting to be. The middle of a painting should be hung at the eye level of a standing person."

For a change I did as I was told, taking note of the way Haozous's eyes raked the rest of me before he checked my eye height. But he was an artist and artists were into anatomy, right?

"You can move now."

I stepped away and he walked to the wall, brushing my arm as he passed. Unusual. Out of respect for personal boundaries, most Indians avoided unnecessary bodily contact. Or even unnecessary eye contact, for that matter.

But Haozous looked me straight in the eye. "This about right?" He pointed to a spot three-quarters of the way up the wall.

"Looks fine to me."

He nodded, then began screwing the wing nuts into the wall.

He was still working when the phone rang. For a second, I thought of letting the machine downstairs pick it up, but worried that it might be Kryzinski with some new tidbit to offer, I picked up the receiver. No such luck. It was Dusty.

"We've got to talk, Lena." He sounded half apologetic, half irritated.

I looked over at Haozous, now wrestling the painting onto the hanger. "Sorry, I can't talk now. I've got somebody here."

A few seconds of silence, then the irritation swallowed up whatever was left of the apologetic tone. "What do you mean, you've got somebody there? You *never* invite people over."

The painting was a little high on the right side, but before I could point it out, Haozous straightened it. "That's wonderful,

George!" I called to him, not bothering to cover the phone's mouthpiece.

"What's wonderful? Who's George?" Dusty sounded suspicious.

"I told you, I don't have time to talk now." Without giving him time to argue, I hung up the phone. Hey, the world is filled with men, right? So what do I need with a man who likes redheads better than blondes?

I don't love him, I don't love him, I don't love…

If I repeated that mantra enough maybe I'd even start believing it.

I came out of my funk to see Haozous watching me intently, his bronze arms folded across his broad chest. I tried to remember if I'd ever seen a handsomer man. Sean Connery in his 007 days? Brad Pitt? The young Elvis? Nope. None of them could hold a candle to George Haozous.

"How do you like it?" he asked.

"Like… like what?" Then I felt my face flame. "Oh, you mean the painting. I like it fine. It's magnificent."

And it was. The brilliant colors raged across the wall, totally transforming the beige-locked room. But for some strange reason, my eyes kept drifting away from the painting to its creator.

Haozous smiled. "Want anything else?"

"Wh…what?"

He lowered his arms and stepped away from the painting, approaching so closely that I could see my blond hair reflected in his dark eyes. "Lena, I asked if you wanted anything else." His voice was softer now, almost seductive. Or was that just my imagination?

For a minute, I felt like a jackrabbit hypnotized by a rattler. He looked so good, he smelled so good… Then I stepped back, putting a more discreet distance between us. I already had enough trouble with the men in my life and I certainly didn't need the added trouble of a married one. "No, George, I don't want anything else. Now, how about that drink I offered you earlier? It's a long drive back to the rez and it must be 115 degrees out there."

He smiled slowly. "I'm real comfortable with heat."

I waited until Haozous's truck was completely out of sight before I undressed and changed into my jogging outfit. I still hadn't regained my strength since being shot, so I was only able to make it halfway to the buttes before slowing to a walk. But at least the long walk cleared my mind.

As I finally limped across the McDowell median and into Papago Park, I was wondering if Haozous had ever made any moves on Clarice.

And if so, what she had done about it.

When I got back from my run—oh, hell. Let's be honest about it, from my *walk*, I found a note slipped under my door.

Don't you think it's time you quit pouting about that redhead? Dusty

I tossed the note into the garbage, all the while chanting, *I don't love him, I don't love him, I don't love him.*

Chapter 15

The next day, I left the office to Jimmy and left for Tudor Hills. Since the monsoon weather had calmed for a few days and was tormenting Mexico instead, Scottsdale Road was back in full working order. All debris from the storm had been removed, the flooding had drained, and the detour signs were down. As the Toyota ate up the miles, subdivisions slipped away and the road climbed higher into the desert. The crisp scent of sage surrounded me.

Just before the Boulders neighborhood where Serena Hyath lived, I followed the TUDOR HILLS—MODELS OPEN NOW! signs and took a hard left, crossing over the granite ridge. What I found on the other side was appalling.

On a once gentle hillside, a few finished Tudor-styled homes— exposed black beams and phony wattling on the second story perched over gray monastery rock on the first story—overlooked bulldozers busily carving flat terraces out of the vanishing slopes. Below them, deep trenches now criss-crossed the desert, awaiting the miles of sewer pipe that lay alongside the ditches stacked like stranded sea serpents. What appeared to be several hundred mesquite trees, creosote bushes, and saguaro cacti sat in giant wooden tubs awaiting banishment to other areas, leaving the denuded area looking like a giant, unpaved parking lot. The Hopi tribe had a word for such desecration: *Koyannisqatsi,* the world is out of balance.

I tried unsuccessfully to battle the rage that boiled up inside me. The sage-swept paradise of my childhood had vanished forever.

But there was nothing I could do about that now. The damage had already been done.

The Hyath Construction Co. trailer was located near four homes in various stages of completion. I parked the Toyota pickup between a fairly new but beat-up Dodge Dakota and a sleek gold Infiniti I-30. I was standing there admiring the Infiniti's taupe leather upholstery when the trailer door opened and one of the biggest men I'd ever seen stepped out. He was so tall he had to duck, and at the same time, so wide that he had to turn sideways to get through the narrow doorway. His massive frame filled out his work clothes in an almost alarming manner, but his ebony face projected an affability that belied his menacing bulk.

"I'll phone a friend of mine up in Flagstaff," he called over his shoulder into the trailer. "He should be able to send somebody down in the next couple of days. We got to get this show on the road."

The person in the trailer muttered something I couldn't quite hear, then the big man closed the trailer door and started down the steps. Spying me, he stopped halfway down.

"I wouldn't get too close to that Infiniti if I were you. There might still be broken glass scattered around."

I looked down at the car. "Broken glass? Everything looks fine to me."

He shook his head. "Somebody busted out the driver's side window the other day and stole the car phone. Third time in six months. We had the Glass Doctor out and he replaced the window, but Evan's still having a fit." He paused, then asked, "You here to see him?"

I nodded. There was something about him that looked familiar, but I couldn't quite place him. "Do I know you?"

He grinned, revealing flawless teeth. "Maybe. How many football games you see in college?"

Now I remembered. Malik Toshumbe, former fullback for the ASU Sun Devils. I'd watched him mow down an entire line of U of A Wildcats more than once.

"You went on to the Cowboys." I said, taking his extended hand. Although my own hand seemed little larger than his pinky, I found his handshake surprisingly gentle.

He pumped my hand a few times, then released it. "Tore my knee up the third season. But, hey, I had a good run. That's all you can ask."

He'd been one of my heroes, a role model of sorts, because Malik, who'd been two years ahead of me at ASU, was another foster home kid who'd beaten the odds. At the time, I'd been a lot more emotionally fragile than I was now, so whenever my memories threatened to overwhelm me, I had simply pictured Malik. I knew he had experienced so much worse. Once he'd even been pulled from a foster home because they'd "forgotten" to feed him for a week.

"You had quite a few good runs, as I remember," I said.

He looked pleased. "I guess I did."

Hero and fan stood there grinning at each other for a few more seconds, then Malik raised his hand and waggled it at me. "Well, I'd love to stay here recalling old glories, but I got to get shakin'. We're about three days behind schedule, and if we don't make up the time, it's my butt on the line. Flagstones. I ask you. Who in their right mind wants flagstone floors down here in the desert, what with all our grit and grime? What's the matter with good old Saltillo tile? When you use indigenous products you don't get in this kind of trouble. But no, Evan's just got to have flagstone driveways in front of his phony-ass Tudors!"

His already dark face darkened even more and he swept a beefy arm around, taking in the remnants of the Sonoran Desert, the uprooted mesquite, the toppled saguaros. "This look like Elizabethan England to you?"

Duly prompted, I shook my head. It didn't even look like Arizona anymore.

Malik was on a roll. "When folks have more money than taste the ecosystem gets raped. And flagstones? What's the point? Saltillo tile-layers are a dime a dozen around here, but lose just one flagstone guy and you're in a world of hurt. These construction types..." He paused for a moment, apparently remembering he was now a construction type himself, however high he'd clambered up the totem pole. "Well, a lot of them aren't the most dependable guys around. Hardest part of my job, keeping track of them."

Just then the trailer door opened and a dark man bearing a strong resemblance to Serena Hyath-Allesandro looked out. He was almost as tall as Malik, although much less broad. His eyes were red, which I attributed to either allergies or grief.

"I don't want somebody in the next couple of days, Malik," the man snarled. "I need another flagstone guy *tomorrow!*"

Malik nodded. "I'll do what I can but I'm not promising anything." Then he climbed into the battered Dakota and drove off.

"Shit," Clarice's brother said, watching the truck kick up a long line of dust. "Shit, shit, shit, shit." Then he looked down at me, irritation plain on his face. "Do yourself a favor. Don't ever go into business for yourself."

"Too late," I said, climbing the stairs. "Lena Jones, Desert Investigations."

"Oh, yeah. I recognize you from that time you were on TV. You'd proved some guy on Death Row was innocent, and I don't think the prosecutor was any too pleased with you, a cop who actually went around proving people innocent, not guilty."

Uncomfortable, I acknowledged my fifteen minutes of fame. The whole incident had been overblown, but that was the media for you. "The prosecutor got over it, especially when we found the real perp."

He nodded. "It was the mother, wasn't it? Christ, what a world!" He started to say something else, then changed his mind. "Let's get out of this god-awful heat. I've been wanting to talk to you for some time. I'll do anything I can to help put that bastard back behind bars."

"Which bastard is that?"

He gave me an odd look. "Jay, of course. Who else do you think I mean? Here. Let's get inside out of this damned heat. Christ, I hate the desert!"

I bid Elizabethan England goodbye and followed him inside the construction trailer.

The trailer was exquisite. My surprise must have shown on my face, because Evan said, "Since my last divorce I just about live in this thing, so I figure I might as well make it as homey as possible."

Last divorce? The Hyaths certainly had their problems with personal relationships.

Homey wasn't quite the word for what Evan Hyath had done to the trailer, which now resembled the foyer of an expensive men's club. Although the floor was carpeted in the same industrial-strength tweed I'd seen in a dozen other mobile offices, a brightly colored Navajo rug did its best to disguise the blandness. An expensive-looking burgundy leather sofa and matching chair sat at right angles to each other against walnut-paneled walls.

The pre-digital cell phone charging on a polished rosewood end table provided the only incongruous note.

Evan caught me staring at it and threw me a rueful smile. "Goddamn thieves, they…"

Not wanting to hear the car phone thief story again, I interrupted, "Yeah, Malik told me."

In front of the sofa, another rosewood table served as a display area for several pieces of Western sculpture, including a copy of Remington's *Pony Express.* I only gave it a cursory glance because I'd seen knock-offs of it in every cheap souvenir store in Scottsdale—even Clarice's gallery.

"Just a copy," Evan said, stating the obvious. "Of course, it'd be crazy to keep a real Remington in here—but copy or not, all the lines are there. The man knew horses, didn't he?"

"And human anatomy." Then I remembered the horrible pieces in Western Heart Gallery and for a moment, I actually missed them. There were worse sins in the world than bad art. Murder, for instance.

The corner of Evan's mouth turned up in a sad smile. "I loved my sister, Miss Jones, but she called in sick the day God passed out good taste. I tried to get her to take an art appreciation class down at the Phoenix Art Museum, but you know Clarice. You couldn't tell her anything."

That was true. Once I'd realized she was in an abusive marriage, I'd told her to get counseling. She'd laughed in my face.

Evan settled himself onto the sofa and gestured me towards the chair. "Now, what can I do for you?" Then he immediately stood up again. "Sorry. Where are my manners? You want Coke?

7-Up? Tea? Fucking overpriced designer water? Or how about an Anchor Steam? That's what I'm going to have."

I asked for tea, then settled back into the deep chair, enjoying the feel of cool leather on my backside. Evan's clumsy but genuine courtesy reminded me of Serena's, making me smile. As troubled as the woman had proven to be, I'd found myself admiring her attempt to bring some tenderness into a violent world. And now her brother appeared to be following in Serena's footsteps. His appointment of the very black Malik Toshumbe as construction foreman hinted that he didn't share Clarice's racism. Families are funny.

Evan interrupted my thoughts by returning with a tall glass of ice tea and a frosty bottle of Anchor Steam. Collapsing onto the sofa, he took a long swig of beer, then said, "Okay. Now that neither of us is going to dry up and blow away, tell me what I can do for you."

At closer quarters, Evan bore a startling resemblance to his father. His face shared his father's lean angles, and his hair was beginning to gray in the same distinguished manner. His blue eyes, however, held considerably more warmth than had the elder Hyath's.

I chugged some tea, then set it down on the table next to the faux Remington. "Look, Mr. Hyath…"

"Evan, Evan. I'm not into formality."

"Look, Evan, you might as well accept the fact that the police consider Jay Kobe, bastard though he may be, not a particularly viable suspect right now. I'm sure Captain Kryzinski has already given you the bad news on that."

Evan clenched his jaw. "Yeah, Captain Kryzinski gave me some shit about Jay's having an alibi, but for God's sake, Lena, you're not buying into that crap, are you? I mean, the police have to follow certain procedures, we all know that, but you're a private investigator. You must have other methods."

"Like what? Cattle prods and baseball bats?"

He set the bottle of Anchor Steam down so abruptly that beer sloshed out of the opening. "This is some fucking country, isn't it? When men like Jay Kobe can run around beating and killing women while the rest of us have to play nice."

Which made me wonder again about his own divorce. Or, as he had mentioned, divorce plural. "Look, Evan, I'm continuing to check out Jay's alibi, but I want to make sure we've got every other angle covered. As you know, I was Clarice's friend so I've got my own motivation here. So let's lay off Jay for a minute. Instead, why don't you tell me where you were the night she was killed."

For a moment I thought he might pick up the faux Remington and throw it at me, but the anger on his face faded quickly. He gave a heavy sigh which seemed to make his shoulders collapse inward. "You're just doing your job, I know. But..." Another weary sigh. "All right. I was having dinner with Malik that night, down at the Pacific Seafood Company, I think. We were having some labor troubles and I wanted to get away from the site while we discussed them."

I wrote the information down in the notebook I'd pulled out of my carryall. "Malik will verify that?"

Evan shrugged. "Probably. I don't know if he wrote it down or anything, but I probably paid for the meal by credit card, and there'll be a date and time on the receipt, I think. You want me to dig it out?"

I shook my head. Maybe later, if it turned out to be necessary, but I doubted it would. Evan sounded like he was telling the truth. After taking Malik's cell phone number from him, I said, "Now tell me anything you can about your sister. I already know that Jay wasn't the only person she had trouble with."

The mulish look on his face told me Evan had already made up his mind Jay had killed Clarice, but my years in homicide had taught me how to deal with the most recalcitrant of witnesses. I took a deep breath, leaned across the coffee table, grasped his hand in mine, and looked deep into his eyes. "Evan, I know how much you loved your sister. Please help me help her now that she can no longer help herself."

To my horror, the mulish look faded and tears welled up in his eyes. I snatched my hand back and watched helplessly as he buried his face in his hands and tried to muffle his sobs. Since I am not one of those women who is all that comfortable with "sensitive" men, there was little I could do other than to fish a few tissues out of my carryall and thrust them into his wet hands. "Blow."

Evan blew his nose until I thought it would fall off, then groped around blindly for more tissues. I was all out, so he began mopping his dripping nose with his sleeve. Disgusted as much with myself as with him, I jumped up, ran down the narrow hall to the bathroom, grabbed a roll of toilet paper, and trailed it back to the couch.

"There." Hating myself, I handed him a wad of toilet paper. Feeling like I should do more but not knowing exactly what, I moved over to the sofa and put my arm around him. I felt like I was holding a child, and maybe I was. No one in the Hyath family, Clarice included, had so far impressed me with their emotional maturity.

After a few minutes, Evan looked up, red-eyed and red-faced. "I'm so sorry," he managed, his voice jagged as cut glass. "But you don't…you don't know what it's been like. I had to make all the funeral arrangements. I've never done that before, and I just didn't know what to do. The funeral… It was a mess. Hardly anyone showed up."

So I had noticed. "Didn't Serena help you make the arrangements?"

He shook his head and gave his eyes a final swipe with the toilet paper. "Serena has always had problems, as I'm sure you noticed, and Clarice's death made her even worse. I actually thought I was going to have to check her into some rehab center somewhere before it was all over. That husband of hers is worse than useless. Calls himself an investor, but if you ask me, it's just a cover for something else, god knows what."

This was interesting. I made a mental note to have Jimmy run a check on Serena's husband. "What about your parents? Didn't they help?"

Anger flooded back into his face, chasing away the remaining ravages of grief. "Them! Can you see my mother doing anything for anyone? Or my father?"

I shook my head. I couldn't see either of the senior Hyaths bothering to see that any of their children were buried properly. But this, at least, explained one thing; why Clarice's funeral had seemed so slipshod. Judging from her brother's condition, Clarice was probably lucky she'd actually made it underground.

Evan looked down at the Navajo rug, as if ashamed to meet my eyes. "Hell, I'm no paragon of mental health, myself. Three wives already and I'm not even forty yet." He sighed. "It's different when I'm here at work, I can forget about... well, you know. I can concentrate on getting these homes in for people and not think about..."

I nodded. "I understand."

His eyes welled up again. "Clarice was so sweet."

Clarice had never seemed particularly sweet to me, but then again, I wasn't her brother. I made a sympathetic noise and let him continue.

"When we were kids, Clarice and Serena and I kind of took care of each other. We had to. We didn't have anybody else, just the hired help, and they never stayed long because of Mom. Dad was usually gone, but when he was home it was even worse. And Mom...Well, you've met the Gin Queen."

I nodded again.

"Maybe the three of us leaned on each other too much. I mean, look at us. Not one of us can seem to find a healthy relationship. Clarice wound up with Jay, Serena got that crook from Madrid, and me? Christ. I got Liz, Amber, and Tiffany. Money-grubbing bimbos, every last one of them."

In deference to his grief, I refrained from pointing out that he'd chosen the money-grubbing bimbos himself. Why not teachers? Social workers? Ex-nuns?

Evan's next words stole my thoughts. "But I've only got myself to blame, right? Nobody pointed a gun at my head and told me to marry them. The warning signs were all there. I just chose to ignore them, like Clarice chose not to pay any attention to Jay's temper when they were dating. Or Serena not listening to anybody about her drug problem."

I took another long drink of tea. Was it my imagination, or had the trailer become hotter? Maybe I was simply responding to the emotional temperature of the room. I'd never been comfortable with naked expressions of emotion, a shortcoming that had made my life in the Violent Crimes Unit tougher than necessary. All that suffering. All that grief.

"Relationships are tough for us all," I said, falling back on the truth in a desperate attempt to change the subject. "But there's nothing either of us can do about that right now so why don't we just concentrate on helping Clarice? Tell me who else might have a motive to kill her. Then I'll put the cattle prods to Jay."

My attempt at humor worked, and Evan managed a wobbly smile. "I'm still convinced it was Jay, but I know she was having trouble with one of her artists. Some Apache guy."

"I've already talked to him."

He picked up his Anchor Steam and lifted it to his lips. "Other than that, I'm afraid I don't..." Suddenly his eyes narrowed and he slammed the bottle down. The glass resounded on the rosewood table like a gunshot. "Jesus, why didn't I think of her earlier?"

"Her?"

"That damned Albundo woman. She's been gunning for Clarice for years."

"Albundo?" The name rang a bell, but I couldn't quite place it.

"Dulya Albundo. You must remember the Museum of Western Art project. When we got those old homes condemned, Dulya's mother refused to leave. Magadalena Espinoza, her name was, ninety if she was a day. Senile. Dulya hauled her out of there, not that she had much choice, really, what with the court order and all. But the old lady somehow managed to sneak back into that old house of hers one night and got killed when the bulldozers took it down next morning. Dulya blamed Clarice. Said she'd get even with her if it was the last thing she ever did. I thought the lawsuit she brought against Hyath Construction was what she meant."

I felt like slapping myself. How could I have forgotten the tragedy and the part Clarice had played in it?

It had been four years ago, but the scandal over the building of the Museum of Western Art still hadn't died down. The lawsuit Dulya Albundo filed was still winding its way through the courts. Every attempt at reaching a settlement had been spurned, because Albundo was determined to have her day in court and—as she had once told the newspapers—"prove to the world what a despicable woman Clarice Hyath is." It had all started when the

Scottsdale city fathers bought Clarice's idea that the city needed a museum devoted to the "art of the American cowboy." Working from a list of the Valley's wealthiest families, Clarice had almost single-handedly raised the fifteen million-plus required to purchase a good-sized parcel of land and design and construct the huge building.

But the land purchase went terribly, terribly wrong.

Clarice had zeroed in on Scottsdale's last remaining Hispanic enclave as the museum's target site. She knew that the homes there, hand-built by Mexican laborers a century earlier, would be less expensive to buy than any Anglo neighborhood within Scottsdale city limits. The fact that the thirty-plus homes were genuine adobes, passed from father to son, from mother to daughter, meant nothing to her. In the end, it didn't mean anything to the city fathers, who let themselves be persuaded that *real* adobes weren't constructed of caliche mud, straw. Besides, they resented the fact that some of the families kept sheep and chickens on their property, a right that had been grandfathered in when the zoning laws changed. Bulldozing the entire area in order to get rid of some chickens and erecting a shiny new museum for the tourists sounded like an answer to the zoning commission's prayers.

Hence the quick and dirty nighttime condemnation hearing, attended by no one from the Hispanic community. By the time the families figured out what was happening, the homes their families had lived in for generations had been condemned. A quickly assembled protest group with a lawyer who'd just passed the Bar exam joined the fray too late and their attempt to obtain a restraining order failed. Justice had a price tag in Scottsdale and as usual, the Hispanics came up a day late and several million dollars short. Checks for "fair value" for their properties were hand-delivered to all the residents and the matter was considered closed. Soon sheriff's deputies were stacking the families' belongings into U-Haul trucks and arresting any individual who refused to leave. A couple of the neighborhood's men put up a fight. Both were serving time in Perryville Prison.

Six months to the day after Clarice got her bright idea, bulldozers mowed down every adobe within a four-block radius.

And one ninety-year-old woman.

"Have you heard anything lately from Dulya Albundo?" I asked Evan.

Evan shook his head. "I never thought…"

"We can't jump to conclusions here but I obviously want to talk to her. Do you have an address? Your lawyer should know how to reach her."

He jumped up, walked quickly over to the desk, and picked up the phone. Within seconds he was talking to his attorney. After a few minutes, he scribbled down an address, hung up, and brought it back to me. Tears had filled his eyes again and he didn't look at me as he handed the address across. "Here's where she's living now. It… it looks like she's down in South Phoenix."

From Scottsdale to South Phoenix? Where the deer and the gangbangers played? What a come-down.

I stood up, eager to escape from Evan Hyath and his grief. "I'll check it out."

When I left, he was sitting on the couch, his head once more in his hands.

As soon as I walked back into the office, Jimmy announced that he had beaten the investment banker's encryption system. "But whoever set it up was good. You want to know what it turned out to be?"

I shook my head, convinced I wouldn't understand it even after he'd explained it to me. For once I was wrong.

"It was Navajo, with all the words spelled backwards!" Jimmy threw back his head and laughed. "Remember the Navajo Code Talkers in World War Two? The Japanese never broke that code, but all it was, really, was just a bunch of Navajo guys yapping all the classified information in their own language. After I recognized the sentence structure, I got Harvey Gray Hills over here and within ten minutes, we had it."

I laughed with him. "You've got to admit, though, that's one savvy investment banker. And he's obviously got a Navajo working for him."

"They're probably both World War Two buffs."

"But no match for The Flash."

To celebrate, I went over to the fridge and poured Jimmy a tall glass of prickly pear juice. Then I poured myself a tall glass of fucking overpriced designer water and toasted my partner.

"To The Flash!" I said.

Jimmy shook his head. "To the Navajo Code Talkers!"

Chapter 16

After replenishing my bodily fluids, I called Malik Toshumbe and verified that Evan Hyath had been having dinner with him the day Clarice had been killed.

"I'm never that hungry at five, but Evan wanted out of that trailer real bad so we went down to that fish restaurant on Scottsdale Road and scarfed down some oysters."

"You get the labor problems straightened out?"

Malik laughed. "Not much. Evan started drinking as soon as we arrived and by the time we left, he couldn't tell a labor contract from a summons. I even had to drive him back to the trailer."

The trailer? "Why not home?"

Malik made a disgusted sound. "That trailer *is* his home. His last wife got the house and the Rolls. You know, Evan's a great guy, but he's a goof. Show him a couple of big tits..." he trailed off into stuttering. "I, uh, I'm sorry. I mean he, uh..."

It was my turn to laugh. "No offense taken, Malik. I know exactly what you mean. He gets blinded by the light."

Malik laughed back and we finally hung up with me in receipt of an invitation to share an Arizona Diamondbacks game with him and his wife. They had season tickets, right down on the third base line.

Jimmy, who had been eavesdropping again, turned away from his computer with a jealous look. "Third base line? I've never been out of the nosebleed section."

I flashed my teeth at him. "Hurts, doesn't it?"

I fooled around the office for the next hour, making a few more phone calls. So far, we'd been unsuccessful at finding out the whereabouts of the department store chain CEO's ex-mistress, or the missing diamond necklace. I canvassed a few more pawnshops to see if anybody'd unloaded it, but came up empty-handed again. Still, I wasn't ready to give up. The woman had to be somewhere, possibly with friends, possibly with relatives.

Possibly in Vegas.

I told Jimmy to check out her credit card purchases since the CEO had finally admitted that he'd been silly enough to give her a platinum Visa, too. I then hopped back in my loaner and left for Dulya Albundo's house.

The trip took only twenty minutes, but it was like entering another country. South Phoenix was the Valley's version of the ghetto, the 'hood, the barrio—the place you moved when times were hard and not going to get any better. Granted, the area still maintained a few decent pockets guarded zealously by Neighborhood Watch groups, but for the most part, the area from Buckeye Road south to South Mountain, 32nd Street west to 19th Avenue was a no-man's land ruled by the Crips, Bloods, West Side Chicanos, and Wetback Power. Most Scottsdale residents pretended South Phoenix didn't exist, even though most of Scottsdale's maids and resort workers commuted from there.

Dulya Albundo lived on Buckeye Road, almost dead in the middle of the barrio. As I crept along Buckeye, checking out the street numbers on the rundown frame houses, I was very much aware of the group of youths lounging against a graffiti-covered wall near the corner, watching me with narrowed eyes. They were dressed almost entirely in brown, with baggy chino pants and long, wicked-looking chains which looped from their belts almost to their knees. West Side Chicanos. As luck would have it, Dulya Albundo's house was only three houses down from them, so I eased the pickup to the curb, hoping Michael Sisiwan's theft insurance was paid up.

The Albundo house was a single-story wood frame needing paint, but both the house and its small yard were spotless. Several well-used, unmatched chairs sat on the wide porch. Windchimes tinkled in the soft breeze, and from somewhere behind the house, a rooster crowed.

I locked the truck carefully, noticing one of the boys break away from the group and walk towards me. The chain at his side jingled, but it didn't sound like Santa Claus coming to town. Trying not to make too big a deal of it, I reached into my carryall and rooted around for my gun. Once my hand wrapped around the handle of the .38, I felt a lot more secure.

"Hey there, Blondie, you lost or somethin'?" the boy asked in an Hispanic accent, his busy eyes checking out my carryall. He couldn't have been more than fourteen and hardly came up past my chin, but I'd learned long ago that the little banty roosters were more apt to kick your ass than the big doofus noisy leghorns.

"Nope," I said, forcing myself to sound casual. "Just looking for Dulya Albundo."

His mahogany eyes were not welcoming. "What you want with her?"

"That's private." I didn't let my own eyes waver.

He considered my words, my manner, then took careful aim and spat. A green gob landed uncomfortably close to my Reeboks. "There ain't nothing private around here, Blondie."

This was nothing more than the standard Pecking Order Waltz, with the banty rooster trying to estimate my position on the dance card. Nevertheless, I couldn't let it get too far. "You spit on my Reeboks, *compadre*, and you'll be licking them clean."

A little fire jumped in those cold eyes. "You think you tough?"

"Tough enough." I kept my voice steady, even though I could see his friends were now approaching us, the same measuring look in their eyes. They didn't like Anglos down here. Anglos had never done them much good.

Then the little banty surprised me by laughing. He looked over his shoulder and rattled off a stream of Spanish to his friends. They laughed, too, and went back to their huddle at the wall, planning god knows what. My language skills being highly limited, the only words I had understood were "cute" and "Mama." But that was enough. The banty was Dulya Albundo's son.

"You come on, Blondie. I take you to Dulya Albundo. Give me five bucks, I even watch your truck. Keep it nice, just like them pretty Reeboks of yours." Then he surprised me even further by winking.

Without a word, I hauled a five dollar bill out of my carryall and handed it to him. Hey, good security's cheap at twice the price.

"Yeah, you a tough lady, Blondie," the banty said, stuffing Abraham Lincoln into his jeans. "But you got brains, too."

He opened the screen door and let me inside. The house was dark, and for a moment I couldn't see at all, but when my eyes finally adjusted to the gloom, I saw a woman praying quietly in front of a small tabletop shrine. Plastic flowers flanked a small candle that lit up the photograph of a boy who bore a strong resemblance to the banty at my side. A younger brother? Next to the boy's picture was that of an elderly woman. I recognized her from the *Scottsdale Journal's* coverage of her death—Magadalena Espinoza. On a shelf above the child and the old woman, a small statue of the Madonna looked down with sorrowful eyes.

Dulya Albundo rose when we entered the room. She was older than I had expected her to be after meeting her son, well into middle age, but then I remembered that her mother had been in her early nineties when she'd been crushed under a collapsed adobe wall. Unlike some Hispanic women for whom age lent a comfortable plumpness, the years did not set lightly on Dulya. The high cheekbones which revealed her Aztec ancestors only increased the dark shadows under her eyes, and her black polyester waitress's uniform merely accentuated the unhealthy sallowness of her skin. Her back was as bowed as her mother's. Even her gray-streaked hair looked tired.

Without a word, she moved away from the shrine and went to her purse. She opened it and began to count change, a nickel at a time, into her palm. "Manuel, why do you bring someone here when you know I need to leave for work?"

Still not looking at me, intent upon her counting, she said, "If you are from the school, you are too late. I must be at work." In contrast to her son's barrio-thickened speech, Dulya's words revealed hardly any accent at all. But then again, she had been born and raised in Scottsdale.

Manuel shrugged, winked at me once more, and went back out. Hopefully, to guard the truck.

The room's closed drapes reminded me of Serena Hyath and her drug-induced paranoia. But here the darkness was an obvious attempt to keep out the scorching sunlight. Like so many homes in South Phoenix, the Albundos' house had no air-conditioning. Given the triple-digit heat, the room was close to unbearable.

As my eyes became accustomed to the gloom, I was able to see an overstuffed but threadbare sofa. Matching chairs were shoved up against the wall, separated by a dark-stained end table on which perched a lamp in the shape of a matador. On the floor, thin, floral-patterned linoleum testified to years of use. The scrubbed white walls were hung with family photographs, a crucifix, a print of the Madonna, a framed cover of *Time* magazine depicting Cesar Chavez on the march. A woman with a familiar face marched behind him. A younger Dulya Albundo?

Seeing me staring at the picture, she said without inflection, "Yes, that was me when I still believed that with faith and courage, things could be changed."

"You no longer believe that?"

"What do you think?" Her face was as immovable as her statue of the Madonna.

I knew better than to disagree with her. In this life, money talks and bullshit walks. Dulya Albundo had access to neither. But the room's claustrophobic heat gave me an idea. "Mrs. Albundo, I understand that you're in a hurry, but I can drive you to work and we can talk, ah, about Manuel along the way. My truck's got great air-conditioning."

Still no smile. "I work in Scottsdale."

I smiled for her. "Isn't that a coincidence! I'm headed in that very direction."

She stood for a moment in thought, her face giving nothing away. Then she suddenly gathered up her purse and started for the door, obviously expecting me to follow. I did.

Standing in front of the screen, she finally began to unbend. "My Manuel, I know he has caused you problems but he needs his summer school classes. They are necessary if he is to go to college. This year, well, you know that it was a bad year for him."

I said nothing. All I wanted was to get her in the truck and we'd sort the truth out later.

Believing that I held the fate of her son in my hands, she forced a smile but it failed to erase the solemnity from her face. "Manuel is a good boy, but after his brother was shot in the drive-by last Christmas, it changed him. He gave up, I think. You and I, we must stop that. We must give him back his heart."

Heart. There was that word again.

I held the screen door open with my left arm, and with her at my right side, we walked into the glaring sunlight towards the truck. Halfway there, I heard her gasp. Startled, I turned to find her staring at me, a shocked expression on her face.

"What is it?"

She shook her head. "It is nothing. It is just that... I do not like that boy Manuel is with."

I looked slightly to my left and saw Manuel talking to an older boy who appeared to be pretty far along in the gangbanger process. A long red scar, the mirror image of my own, marred an otherwise handsome face. His arms were so thickly tattooed that the natural skin color hardly showed.

Mrs. Albundo spat a stream of Spanish at Manuel, who made a great point of ignoring her. The tattooed boy looked down from his superior height and sneered. He was trouble, all right.

"Dios, Dios," Mrs. Albundo muttered. "What should I do?"

Even if it had been my place, I had no advice for her. Given where the Albundos now lived, gang affiliation was an almost necessary survival mechanism for teenage boys. The problem was, the survival tended to be short term.

Trying my best to look like a high school counselor, I made a sympathetic noise. We climbed into the truck and I turned the air-conditioning up full blast, and for the first time, her face began to relax.

"Roberto and Manuel, they used to have jobs delivering groceries to the old people from Alvarez's Market. They were saving up their money for some wheels. That's what they called them, wheels. They did not want me to take three buses to Scottsdale. But I used the money to help bury Roberto."

We sat in silence while she basked in the unusual luxury of air-conditioning. We'd made it all the way to Central and McDowell in downtown Phoenix before she began to get suspicious.

"Why are you not asking me questions about Manuel?" she said, a frown creasing her face. "Why are you sitting there so quiet?"

I took a deep breath. "Mrs. Albundo, I'm not from the school."

She pursed her lips in disapproval. "But why would you lie to me?"

"Did I tell you I was from the school?"

She digested this and for the next few blocks, the only sounds I heard were the usual traffic noises and the comforting hiss of the truck's air-conditioning. Eventually, though, she sighed. When I looked over at her, her expression displayed a peculiar combination of anxiety and acceptance.

"Well, then, Miss-Not-A-School-Counselor, what do you want from me? If you are selling insurance or magazine subscriptions you are out of luck."

I flashed her an apologetic smile. "I'm sorry, Mrs. Albundo, but my name's Lena Jones, and I'm a private detective. I need to talk to you about Clarice Hyath."

An intake of breath, then, "That *puta!*"

I winced. Even though my investigation had uncovered many unsavory facts about Clarice, I hated hearing my dead friend called a whore. I didn't rebuke Mrs. Albundo, though. A dead mother, a murdered son, and a family banished to the streets of South Phoenix were enough to make even a saint coarse-tongued.

"I hear you threatened to kill her," I said instead.

Mrs. Albundo crossed her arms across her chest in what appeared to be satisfaction. "Somebody did and I say good for them."

She was either an honest woman or a foolish one. I wondered which. "Do you have an alibi for the evening Clarice was murdered?"

"I work three days and five nights a week, Miss Private Detective. What do you think?"

The truck rolled east towards Scottsdale, caught up in the afternoon rush hour. We were going nowhere fast, but even at our snail's pace, we were traveling faster than the fume-spewing buses. For a while we said nothing, but just before we cut through the Buttes at the Scottsdale city limits, Mrs. Albundo surprised me.

"I am going to be very early for work," she said, her expression suddenly Sphinx-like. "Let us stop and get coffee. If you will buy."

This sounded promising, so I hooked a left and went up to Thomas Road, which had a string of espresso bars, some of which even sold regular coffee. Pretty soon Mrs. Albundo and I were hunkered down in Einstein's over two caffe lattes, a dash of vanilla in hers.

"Mmmm," she said, licking the froth off her upper lip. "They are always ordering this on *Friends*. Do you know what would also be good? A sesame bagel with a veggie cream cheese schmear. Toasted."

I went back through the line and got her bagel and schmear. Toasted.

She ate daintily and with great satisfaction, every now and then giving me that peculiar, stoic look again. Finally, when she was finished, she asked me, "That scar on your forehead, it is like Juan's, that gangbanger friend of Manuel's. He was shot holding up a Circle K. He would be in prison but he is only fifteen, too young. Six months in the Adobe Correctional Facility and he is back on our street telling all the boys in the neighborhood how macho such a life is." Then she gave me a sly smile. "Were you also shot holding up a Circle K?"

I smiled back. "I was shot, all right, but not holding up the Circle K. It happened when I was only four years old, and I can't remember anything about it."

Her expression changed to one of sorrow. "Four years old? I am sorry. That is a wicked act, to shoot a child."

Remembering her youngest son, I shrugged. At least I was still alive. "The social workers told me some Hispanic woman carried me into the emergency ward at St. Joseph's and just left me there."

She frowned. "But your mother and father? What do they tell you about this? Surely they seek justice for you, just as I seek justice for my Roberto."

Since there was no point in distressing her further, I gave her the short, expurgated version of my childhood. But the brief digression worked to lower the ice between us, and while the Scottsdale yuppies slurped their half-decaf cappuccino around us, she finally began answering my questions about Clarice.

"Do you know what it is like to be ninety years old and live all your life in one house?" she said. "My mother, she was born in that house. My grandfather built it for my grandmother before they were married, he built it with his own hands. His sweat and his blood were mixed into that adobe. My father, he added two rooms, working in the same traditional way my grandfather did. Sweat, straw, adobe mud. You must understand that for my mother to leave that house, it was like leaving the body of her father, the body of her husband. Our neighbors, with them it was all the same. Our homes were... They were..."

Here words failed her. Amidst the hiss of a nearby cappuccino machine, she took a few deep breaths and tried again. "Our homes were not *things*. They were a part of us, our blood and our bones. And our neighbors, they were good people, decent. They all had calluses on their hands from work. You saw where we live now, how far I must travel to come to my jobs. I must take three different buses, each way, so it take me almost two hours to come to work and then to return. And when I get home, what do I have? You have seen my house, where it is. Do you think I have a nice life? Do you think my son has a nice life, Miss Detective?"

Although I felt sympathy for her, I didn't like being blamed for an act I had not personally committed. "Surely you don't have to live in South Phoenix, Mrs. Albundo. Why not some place closer?"

Her eyes narrowed. "Do you know how much money they gave my mother for her house? After they had her house condemned, they gave her $32,000, Miss Detective. Have you tried to buy a house in Scottsdale or even Phoenix for $32,000? This will make a *down payment*, not a purchase. My husband, he died right after Roberto was born, and my mother and my sons and me, none of us had enough money—or credit—to make house payments or pay rent. We had to buy for cash."

Her eyes took on a faraway cast. "Do you know what one of those lawyers called our neighborhood? They called it urban blight. Our houses were trash, they said, and that our *trash* should be torn down to make way for their idea of beauty. I ask you, Miss Detective, why are Hispanic things, the creations of earth and dreams, always called trash? And why are Anglo things, no matter how strange and ugly—like that museum—always called beautiful? Does beauty only exist in blue eyes and steel?"

I had no answer for her, having often wondered that very thing myself. Setting aside its unsavory origins, most people found the new museum grotesque, but the architectural magazines termed it "glorious," "impressive," and "magnificent." In one newspaper article, E. Hampton Lockspur, the museum's architect, was described as "the possessor of a far-reaching vision."

Lockspur was, of course, Anglo. From Boston.

I doubted if it would make Mrs. Albundo feel any better to know that I hated the new museum, too, so I just waited until she continued. It didn't take long.

"We were not asked to vote on the museum. The city council did that themselves. And then the lawyers, the rich Anglo lawyers, they were able to get our property condemned. In the court papers they filled, they said all our homes were..." Here she paused, quoting the exact wording. "'...not fit for human habitation.' This was a lie. Our homes were beautiful, made from the earth, built from history. But truth has no place in the courtrooms, so after it was all decided by those blue-eyed men with the English names, I told my mother, 'This is a thing that has been done, there is no hope. This Clarice Hyath and her lawyers, they will have their way. The rich always do. We must take that money and we must move.'"

She looked down at her caffe latte. "I thought she understood what I was saying. After we moved to South Phoenix, I thought she would give no more trouble. But she was an old woman and she was frightened of the new place. I got up that first morning and found her gone. By the time I thought to look for her in our old house, she was already dead. Buried under the wall her father had built."

Now it was my turn to stare into my cup. I didn't see anything there, just guilt. At the table behind her, a red-faced man in an expensive suit was telling a joke to his friends, something about a Frenchman, a Scotsman, and a Texan on board an airplane. The plane was losing altitude, so the pilot told them they needed to lighten the load or they'd all die. They ditched the luggage, but that was not enough. The pilot said three people would have to sacrifice themselves for the good of the others. A selfless Frenchman jumped out the plane's door, crying, "Vive la France!" Then a Scotsman jumped out, crying, "For bonny Scotland!" Next, a Texan pushed a Mexican out the door and cried, "Remember the Alamo!"

Mrs. Albundo gave no indication that she had heard the joke but I knew she couldn't have missed it. She was sitting closer to the man than I was.

"So you must understand how happy I was when I read that Clarice Hyath had been killed," she said. "These rich people with the Anglo names, they should pay for the things they did to us."

This sounded awfully like a confession. Trying to keep my voice steady, I asked, "Was Clarice murdered because of what she did to your family?"

Mrs. Albundo's smile chilled me. "The good God, he has his ways."

When I dropped Mrs. Albundo off at the restaurant where she worked, she was still smiling.

Chapter 17

The next morning I went down to the office, determined to study Clarice's address book and the Dayrunner I'd lifted from the gallery, from beginning to end.

But the headline on the *Scottsdale Journal* changed my plans.

"JAY KOBE ARRESTED!" the headline screamed in eighty-point Gothic. The sub-head explained, "KOBE TIED TO BODY IN DESERT."

Body, I wondered? What body?

But as I read, it came back to me.

> SCOTTSDALE—On Thursday, the medical examiner's office announced that a body found in the desert last week was that of Gus Baylor, of Bakersfield, California. The autopsy showed that Baylor had been shot at close range with a .45.
>
> The Scottsdale Police Department investigation revealed that Baylor, who was on parole after serving six years for a 1992 murder conviction, met Jay Kobe in the Bakersfield jail, where they briefly shared a cell.
>
> Last week, Kobe—who had earlier been arrested for the murder of Clarice Hyath Kobe, his socialite wife—was released from jail for lack of evidence. With this new finding, however, police theorize that Kobe contracted with Baylor to kill his wife, then murdered Baylor to keep him quiet.

The police arrested Kobe at Sky Harbor Airport, where he and his fiancée, Alison Garwood, were preparing to board a flight to Las Vegas where they were to be married. "We're certain of a conviction now," stated Capt. Edgar Kryzinski, of Scottsdale Homicide. "Kobe got off before because he had an alibi for the time of death, but now that we have the link between him and the actual killer, his alibi means nothing. We'll get him, and for two murders, this time. Not just one. I promise you that Mr. Kobe is on his way to Death Row."

I noticed the politic way the *Journal* had cleaned up Kryzinski's language, making him sound like an Oxford scholar. Too bad. I'd have liked to see him revealed to one and all as the low-life, sneaky weasel he really was.

Fuming, I picked up the phone and dialed Kryzinski's direct line. When he answered, I started right in. "You shit. You could have told me!"

"If you still worked for me, kid, you'd already know everything I know." I could almost hear the bastard smile.

Somehow I kept from slamming down the phone. "Is there any other information you'd like to share with me—before I read it in the paper, that is?"

He actually chuckled. "Well, you remember that our old client Jay was beatin' up on females when he was young and foolish and livin' over in Bakersfield? We checked around a little more and found out that when he was booked—and this is where the paper screwed up—the Bakersfield cops put him *next* to the cell where they was holding Baylor. Reporters never get this stuff right. So, kid, you want to know what Baylor was in for?"

"The paper said murder," I mumbled, choking back my anger. "Or did the reporters screw up there, too?"

"Nah, they got that one right. Seems Mr. Baylor beat his wife to death for having the nerve to start divorce proceedings. *And* Baylor had been married before, beat that one up, too. But the first wife, that gal had enough sense to start her divorce from a woman's shelter. Soon's it came through, she hit the road and ain't been seen since."

I could see where Kryzinski was going. Two aggrieved batterers sharing stories of female duplicity. It held together, all right. But I still didn't like it. I was allergic to coincidence and this was one helluva big coincidence.

"So you're telling me the two kept in touch all these years? C'mon, Kryzinski. Does that sound right to you? Jay's one of those *classy* batterers, not your common, blue collar batterer. The two seldom hang together."

He chuckled again. "Oh, well, they ain't been exchangin' scented letters or anything like that. What happened was, they ran into each other up at one of those fancy developments Kobe's wife owned some kind of interest in."

I sat up straighter. "Developments? What do you mean?"

"You know Tudor Hills? That English-looking piece of shit up near Carefree?"

I nodded, then realized he couldn't see it. "Yeah, I know it." But I wished I didn't.

"Anyway, ol' Baylor was working up there, laying flagstone for those fuckin' driveways. Here's how it all came down, we think. Remember the day the First Lady was in town, touring all the fancy-schmancy developments with the governor? Hell, the local politicos couldn't kiss her ass fast enough. So Kobe and the entire Hyath clan, they was all up there at Tudor Hills, trailing around after her, contributing their part to the community ass-kissing. The way we figure it, Kobe and Baylor musta recognized each other then. Two hearts beating as one, and all that shit. It was only two weeks later that Clarice split on him and filed for divorce."

"Are you telling me that Gus Baylor was actually working for a Hyath-owned company?"

"Life's just filled with strange and wondrous surprises, ain't it?"

I thought hard. "Tell me," I began, trying to sound casual. "Did anybody else know about Baylor?"

"Whattaya mean, know about him? That he'd served time for murder? Give me a break. Nobody knew but Kobe. Although there was one incident…" He paused for a minute, then said, "It made the papers. I'm surprised you don't know about it, you bein' such a great reader and all."

"What incident, Kryzinski?"

"It was quite the little scandal for the Hyaths, I hear."

"*What* incident?" I was ready to strangle the man.

"You know, that thing that happened when the First Lady and her entourage was all up there with everybody and his prize jackass. Old man Hyath was there, that boozehound wife of his, the skinny sister, the doofus brother, Clarice, and Kobe the Magnificent—not to mention all their snooty friends. After all, it's not every day the wife of the U.S. President bestows a blessing on your nasty little houses."

"*What* incident?" Maybe I would have to kill him after all.

"You mean the fight?"

I took several deep breaths. "What fight?"

"Seems Baylor, who was hanging around the site goggling at all the politicos instead of working, said something ugly about the First Lady. Compared her ass to a barrel cactus. Or was it a cholla? Anyway, before that, he'd been insulting one of the secretaries, too, even said something off-color about Clarice. But it's when he made the remark about the First Lady's ass that one of the other construction workers jumped him. Probably a Republican. Well, anyway, the fight got pretty nasty, right in front of the First Lady and all, and it took that big football star the Hyaths' got working for them to break it up."

"You mean Malik Toshumbe?"

"The very Malik Toshumbe I once won a bundle on at the Rose Bowl. Shame about that knee, wasn't it?"

I flashed back to my visit to Tudor Hills, when Toshumbe had been bitching about losing a flagstone layer. It was neat, all right. Maybe a little too neat?

"Look, Kryzinski, hasn't it occurred to you that if all the Hyaths saw the fight…"

"Saw *and* heard. They say it was quite the deal. And if what they say about the First Lady's gambling jones is true, she was probably makin' book on it."

I ignored him. "If the Hyaths saw the fight, then they all knew Baylor was a violent man who didn't like women."

He got my meaning and was quick to respond. "Doesn't track, Lena. Maybe they all saw the fight, but how'd they know they was watching a potential hit man in action? You're way off base there, kid, been reading too many of them detective thrillers. You need to be gettin' back to real police work and stop putzing around with those dinky computers."

"It's Jimmy who putzes around with the computer. And it's not dinky. It has millions of megahertz or whatever."

"Whatever."

"Anything else you'd like to tell me before I read it in the papers?"

"You mean like the traces of latex and talcum powder they found on Baylor's hands? I'll tell you everything when you come back to work for me, kid."

My patience ran out. "That'll be a cold day in Yuma, you bastard." I slammed down the phone.

Jimmy looked up at me from his computer. "Did I just hear you casting aspersions on the parentage of the captain of the Violent Crimes Unit?"

"Damned right you did."

The tone of my voice warned him off, so with a baleful silence, he returned to his computer.

After working my way through the address book Stephen Hyath had given me, I was more disturbed than ever. The address book dated from the days long before Clarice's marriage to Jay and should have contained the names of old friends, but the phone calls I'd made proved just the opposite. Not one of the people I'd talked to had seen or heard from her in years.

"Clarice wasn't one for keeping close ties," one woman told me. "She'd be all over you for a few months, then drop you and move onto the next conquest. Not the deepest person I've ever known."

The Dayrunner proved more helpful. I was studying it when the phone rang and Hal McKinnon's voice floated out of the receiver. "I'm sure you've heard about our client, Miss Jones."

Our client? I'd been paid off, and my association with Jay Kobe was history. "I read the papers."

"How'd you like to come back on board? Jay would certainly be appreciative of your help. You and I both know that somebody's trying to railroad him."

I snorted. "Couldn't happen to a nicer guy."

My eyes kept scanning the Dayrunner, then stuck on a name. The day of the murder, Clarice had pencilled in, *Gus. 5:30 p.m.* A different Gus? Or had she actually made an appointment with her murderer, the man she had seen involved in a very ugly fight at Tudor Hills? I felt the hair stand up all over my body.

McKinnon was oblivious to my shock. "Come now, Miss Jones. Remember your promise to Albert Grabel, and that Jay is his wife's nephew."

"I don't care if he's the nephew of the fucking Pope," I said, slamming the phone down.

When the phone rang again immediately, I ignored it. I was too interested in the Dayrunner. I returned to studying the appointments Clarice had penciled in during the last two weeks of her life.

Lawrence Sallis. Her divorce attorney. Three different appointments there.

Emily Ruzan. The attorney representing her in the civil case against her father.

Cliffie. Why pencil in an appointment for your next-door neighbor? Wouldn't you just walk over and see him? But the appointment was for six o'clock, so maybe they were headed out some place for dinner.

Mom, lunch. Drinks with the girls?

Dad. Stephen Hyath appeared four times, which I thought was odd, considering the fact that she was suing him. But maybe they were on the verge of reaching an out-of-court settlement. The last appointment was two days before her death.

Serena and Evan. Noon. Hacienda Palms Inn, Patio Court Restaurant. Clarice met with her brother and sister a week before her death.

I checked back through the book and found that the three met for lunch on the average of two times a month. This didn't surprise me, since both Evan and Serena had told me they were close. You couldn't fake the kind of grief both her siblings displayed when I interviewed them.

George H. George Haozous? If so, the artist was pencilled in every Tuesday evening after gallery hours, all the way back to February. There had been a break in May, but then his name began to appear again in early June. But after the last of June, his name vanished from the book.

There were a host of other names, too, many with phone numbers beside them. I spent until two o'clock checking them out and discovered most of them to be artists or artists' agents. A few of the numbers pencilled in for lunches belonged to society women who professed themselves shocked—*shocked!*—over Clarice's death, then couldn't get me off the phone quick enough. None of them expressed any real grief, however.

As soon as I finished my calls and replaced the phone in the receiver, it rang. I picked it up, only to find Dusty on the line.

"Woman, we have to talk."

"Don't call me woman."

"Okay. Guy, we have to talk."

"No we don't." I hung up the phone.

I don't love him, I don't love him, I don't love him.

Jimmy looked over at me, frowning. "Are you going to fight with everyone today?"

"Don't start with me."

I picked the phone up carefully, listened for a second to see if anyone was still on the line, but heard nothing but the reassuring dial tone. I dialed Pima Paint and Collision. After a few rings, Michael Sisiwan answered, out of breath. He told me the Jeep was ready.

Suddenly the day looked a whole lot better.

Ten minutes later I was at Michael Sisiwan's garage, feeling a mixture of excitement and trepidation. What color had they chosen? Yellow? Maroon? Army green? The whole thing was like Christmas, but I reminded myself not to get too optimistic. After all, I'd experienced more than a few downer Christmases in my lifetime.

Mr. Sisiwan and his crew looked as apprehensive as it's possible for Pimas to look. Some looked towards the Superstition

Mountains, some towards the ground, some towards the concrete sound barrier that kept the freeway noise out of the quite streets of Scottsdale. No one met my eyes, and I didn't think it was because of the usual tribal politeness. They were worried.

I forced a bright smile. "I'm anxious to see it. What color did you decide on?"

Mr. Sisiwan elevated my own anxiety when he said, "You remember that you told us to be creative?"

I made my smile wider. "I sure did."

There was silence for a while as we watched a coyote chase a roadrunner across the field next to the body shop. Just like in the cartoons, the coyote lost again.

As the coyote trotted off, disappointed, Mr. Sisiwan apparently decided there was no point in putting off the moment of truth any longer. "You wait here. I'll bring your Jeep around."

The coyote disappeared into a drainage ditch, and the other men went back to looking at the mountains, the freeway, the city limits. I did some looking around myself, picking out a particularly odd-shaped saguaro across the road. The cactus was holding up two arms, as if caught in a bank holdup. But lower down on the main trunk, another limb had begun to grow straight up in what could have passed for the groin region, if it had been human.

It reminded me of Dusty.

I heard the crunch of gravel, then the familiar motor of the Jeep behind me. The Pimas stared even harder at their various focal points as I turned around to see what color they had chosen for me.

"Oh!" was all I could say, when I saw the Jeep. "Oh!"

Mr. Sisiwan climbed down from the driver's seat. "You don't like it?"

"Oh!" The lump in my throat made it impossible to talk.

"If you don't like it, we'll repaint. No cost."

I blinked my eyes, hoping they would think it was just the desert's damned, ever-present dust. "It's... Oh, it's..."

"How about a nice white? Or black? Very neutral. We can do that, easy. I know that this... Well, what we did, it's not for everyone. Here, let me take it back to the shop."

Now the other Pimas focused on a hawk floating in an updraft. It hung there, as silent as the old Pima gods.

"Don't you touch that Jeep!" I yelled, finally breaking out of my trance and snatching the keys out of Michael Sisiwan's hands. "Don't you even *think* of re-painting it!"

One of the Pimas rolled his eyes towards me as I slid my hand along the Jeep's fender. "It's the most beautiful thing I've ever seen," I managed, before my voice failed me again.

Why was it that anger raised my decibels, but when it came to joy, I usually fell silent?

The Pimas had painted the body of the Jeep the color of sandstone buttes at sunset. But the deep, heady rose served merely as background for the pale Hohokam petroglyphs which now marched across the Jeep's hood, sides and fenders. On the driver's side of the Jeep stood Earth Doctor, the father-god who built the earth and everything in it. Walking away from him were his first creations—Elder Brother, Coyote, Snake, Eagle. Splashed across the hood was the labyrinth where Earth Doctor sought refuge when Elder Brother humiliated him by usurping his power.

Along the passenger side door were the rising waves which destroyed First World because of the people's wickedness, but riding atop the waves was Coyote in his reed boat. Clinging to the sky by their sharp talons Night Singing Bird and Sky Hawk.

On one fender danced Kokopelli, the flute player. On another, Spider Woman wove her magic.

The old gods were not banished to the Underworld—they were still alive and living in the Arizona sky, its mountains, in the Pimas' hearts.

And on my Jeep.

Weeping didn't go over big with the Pima so I struggled for control. "You have honored me," I managed.

The soaring hawk above lost its fascination for the Pimas and they walked slowly over to the Jeep, a rarely revealed pride in their eyes.

"You know them, then, the old gods?" one asked, a man of about sixty. "We're all Christians now, and even most of our own tribe has forgotten them."

Thanks to Jimmy, I knew them. I began calling out the gods' names and telling their stories. "After the flood destroyed First World, Elder Brother angered Earth Doctor by making a new race of people," I recited, Jimmy's lesson fresh in my mind. "But these Second World people, they were as selfish as most of the First World people were wicked, and they did not appreciate the life Elder Brother had given them. So they rose up and they killed their creator. They reduced Elder Brother to nothing but bones.

"But it's hard to kill a god. After several seasons had passed, the bones of Elder Brother rolled towards one another and Elder Brother sprang up, resurrected. Oh, he was angry!" I pointed to the jagged lightning they had painted above Elder Brother's head.

"Seeking vengeance, he traveled east to the road of the sun and he walked that road all the way across the sky to the west where it went into the Underworld. There he found Earth Doctor and the few good First World people the gods had allowed to escape the flood. With them, Earth Doctor created an army."

Here I paused and smiled. "The army traveled to Second World and gave Elder Brother the vengeance he desired."

Now the Pimas were all smiling at me. Genuine smiles, not business ones. Except for one, a young man with a shaved head, wearing gang colors.

He frowned. "I didn't know that."

Mr. Sisiwan gave him a long, hard look. "You would if you listened to your elders."

Now the frown turned on Mr. Sisiwan. The young Pima glared at him for a moment, then walked back towards the shop. Apparently my glib and perhaps insensitive recital of Pima legend had landed me squarely in the middle of a family dispute.

My discomfort must have shown plainly on my face, for Mr. Sisiwan said, "Paul is Jimmy's brother. Are you as familiar with Christian legend as you are with Pima?"

I nodded, remembering the Baptist family I used to camp with. They'd drilled me in scripture for two years, and then gave up in disgust when they discovered all that Bible reading I'd been doing was concentrated on one book, the X-rated *Song of Solomon*.

"Then you remember the story of the Prodigal Son, who was welcomed home with open arms."

I nodded again. Where was Mr. Sisiwan leading?

Now Mr. Sisiwan looked grim. "A lot of the times people forget that not everyone was glad to see the Prodigal Son return. His brother, who had been living at home and behaving himself, resented the big fuss the family made over the Prodigal." He paused, began to say something, and then apparently changed his mind. "It is good that you like your Jeep. We enjoyed painting it for you. Now. Let us go settle up the bill."

The other Pimas went back to their various work assignments and I followed Mr. Sisiwan out of the glare and into the shop. When the bill turned out to be surprisingly low, I began to argue, but he would have none of it. The paint job was a paint job. The Jeep didn't have much surface area, so they'd saved on materials. And the petroglyphs? An opportunity to bring the old gods alive again and maybe educate the Anglos at the same time. Why charge for that?

As I drove my freshly painted beauty away, I remembered something the writer Dorothy Parker had once replied, when a friend of hers, who had been having trouble with her family, turned to Parker and complained, "Oh, Dorothy, life is hell!" Parker, whose parents were both dead, grinned and said, "Not for orphans."

Parker knew something I was just finding out, that belonging to *any* family set you up for disappointment, anger and heartbreak. So why did the whole world insist on singing the praises of family? As a counter-argument, why not take a look at Clarice, Evan and Serena. Their parents had a marriage intact enough to please the Pope, but what good had that done the siblings? Had the lack of divorce truly kept the family together? Hadn't the family's very intactness helped set up a system of dysfunction that wound up crippling them all? Serena was certainly a mess, and Evan wouldn't be winning any medals come Mental Health Week. And poor Clarice? She had been so desperate for love that she'd run straight into the arms of a psychopath.

None of this was very comforting for a foster child searching for her real family. If I ever found my people and they turned out to be like any of the Hyaths, who knew what I'd do. Slink off into the sunset? Move somewhere and change my name?

When I arrived back at the office, I couldn't bear to hide the Jeep in the parking lot so I parked it in front. A few tourists still milled around, checking out the galleries. Their faces lit up when they spotted the Jeep, and a couple of them wandered over to look at her more closely. Even Cliffie emerged from Damon and Pythias to ogle her.

"Well I'll be damned!" he said, patting me on the shoulder. "You're finally rid of that Pepto-Bismol pink. High time, neighbor."

"Yeah, I was tired of being the neighborhood eyesore."

Now he winced. "I'm afraid Clarice's place was that." Then he turned and went back into his gallery.

Leaving me wondering.

Just how far would Cliffie go to raise the tone of the neighborhood?

Chapter 18

The next morning, the *Scottsdale Journal* read like a Jay Leno monologue.

A hot air balloon sailing over a Phoenix suburb was struck by what the chamber of commerce called "the world's tallest artificial geyser," and had to make an emergency landing in a lake. Fortunately, all the tourists on board could swim.

The Arizona Puppet Theater was robbed, the thieves making off with Mr. Creepy, a ridge-nosed rattlesnake; Ms. Crawly, a desert tortoise; and Mr. Wild, a bald eagle.

Another article informed me that a new study had discovered that Arizona was the sixth most dangerous state in the nation. To help combat those statistics, the Arizona legislature had voted to chemically or surgically castrate the rapists of children.

I groaned, and said to Jimmy, "If you value your mental health, don't read the paper this morning."

"Already have. Which one bothered you the most? The new crime statistics? Or the castrated rapists?"

I thought for a while. "Nah. I'm all tore up about Mr. Creepy. What have we come to in Arizona when not even a puppet is safe?"

Still, the morning turned out to be fruitful. Jimmy's check on Gerado Allesandro, Serena Hyath's husband, revealed that yes, he was a bit of a crook. A naturalized citizen, he'd once been convicted of telemarketing fraud, although his attorney had been able to get his sentence reduced to time served and a lengthy probation. He was now the focus of a government securities investigation.

Those Hyaths. They certainly knew how to pick 'em.

The morning got even better. Alicia "Bunny" Germaine, the department store CEO's missing girlfriend, had made recent charges on her platinum Visa, all local. Wonder of wonders, one charge turned out to be for the first and last month's rent deposit on a luxury apartment not too far from Desert Investigations. Chortling with satisfaction, I picked up my carryall and headed over there.

After a few quiet knocks at the apartment door, a young woman answered it. She was blond, very pretty in a Hollywood starlet sort of way, and she looked like she'd just crawled out of bed.

"Miss Germaine?"

The young woman nodded. "What can I do for you?" Her voice was husky, filled with erotic promise.

I flashed my ID, and instead of looking frightened, she smiled. "Brian's caught up with me already, huh? Well, come on in, Miss Jones. You don't have to keep standing out there in the heat like some encyclopedia salesman."

Feeling oddly off-balance, I walked into an exquisitely furnished apartment. Bunny had either hired a decorator or she had a much more highly developed sense of taste than the average department store CEO's mistress. The living room was decorated in cool off-whites, accented with dashes of turquoise and copper. Large bouquets of fresh flowers filled the air with subtle scent. And hi-de-ho, boys and girls, above the eight-foot-long cream brocade sofa hung a George Haozous almost as gloriously bloody as my own.

"Nice painting," I said.

Bunny raised her eyebrows. "You think?"

"I've got a Haozous, too. *Apache Sunset.*"

She smiled. "Mine's called *Revenge.* Tasteful, isn't it?"

"I especially love the nicely placed arrow through the cavalry captain's eye. Look, Ms. Germaine, we have to talk about a certain diamond necklace." Without being asked, I sat down on the sofa. It turned out to be filled with down and I sank about two feet. Just the kind of sofa I needed in my place. I made a mental note to look at her credit card receipts again; I wanted the name of her furniture store.

Still smiling, Ms. Germaine sat down next to me. "Call me Bunny."

"Well, Bunny, I'm sure you know why I'm here. Your boyfriend needs his diamond necklace back."

She didn't look in the least embarrassed or frightened. Instead, her smile broadened as a voice with an English accent interjected, "You mean *my* diamond necklace, don't you?"

I turned to see another woman emerging barefoot from the hallway. She was wrapping a pale violet robe around an obviously naked body. "My husband gave me that necklace for my fortieth birthday, and quite frankly, I think it was terribly tacky of him to loan it to Bunny. Even though she's certainly worth it."

Although she had to be in her fifties, the woman was still beautiful, with the perfect oval face of a china doll, and a willowy figure any twenty-year-old would envy. Her eyes, with their penetrating hazel irises, were permanently crinkled at the corners, betraying a lively sense of humor.

I was feeling more and more off-balance. *"Your* necklace?"

The woman sat down next to Bunny and after giving her a quick nibble on the earlobe, stretched diamond-studded fingers towards me. I didn't know whether I was supposed to kiss her hand or shake it. I settled for shaking it.

Her smile was blinding. "I'm Gwendolyn. *Mrs.* Meeks, dear. Don't look all shocked on my account."

As she told me her story, it turned out that several months back, Gwendolyn, a.k.a. Mrs. Brian Meeks, suspecting that her husband was cheating on her, had hired a detective. After receiving his report, she'd confronted Bunny herself.

It had been love at first sight for the both of them.

They'd used the Platinum Visa Mr. Meeks had given Bunny to set up their little Scottsdale love nest and were now planning a vacation in Paris. Both art lovers, they were dying to spend some time in the Louvre.

"How long did you think you'd get by with this?" I asked.

Gwendolyn shrugged her elegant shoulders. "I was hoping we'd get by with it for as long as Brian got by with cheating on

me, but now that you've uncovered our dirty little secret…"—
here she flashed that blinding smile again—"…I guess the jig, as
you so charmingly say in America, is up." She turned to Bunny.
"Time for Plan B."

Bunny leaned against her and giggled.

"What's Plan B?" I asked, intrigued.

"Plan B: When lies stop working, simply tell the truth,"
Gwendolyn answered. "What the hell. My children are grown
and have enough problems of their own to keep them from
obsessing about mine. So I think it's time for me to divorce Mr.
Department Store and go back to England. With Bunny, of
course."

They treated me to a perfectly brewed cuppa before I left.
Without the diamond necklace.

Once back at my Jeep, where several roller bladers had gathered
to study its gleaming petroglyphs, I checked my watch and
discovered that I had more than two hours left before my lunch
date with Eleanor Hyath.

After interviewing Dulya Albundo, I'd grown curious about
the Museum of Western Art, so I decided to swing by on my way
to the Hacienda Palms. It would be interesting to see if their
collection was worth the life of one old lady.

The museum was less than five minutes from Bunny's, and by
the time I'd turned into the parking lot, the Jeep's seats hadn't
even begun to cook. Then again, it was still early and only about
105 degrees out.

The exterior of the museum didn't bode well, I thought, as I
slid my Jeep into a too-tight parking spot. The building had been
purposely designed to resemble a stage set for a movie about the
Apocalypse, with portions of wire netting protruding from raw
concrete, and dimly lit green fiberglass panels designed to represent… Represent what?

Urban decay?

I winced and averted my eyes from the architect's "artistic
statement." I paid my fee at the front and rushed in, hoping
things were better inside.

To my surprise, they were.

Whoever had pulled this collection together, it hadn't been Clarice. One long, cool gallery after another showcased the best and the brightest of modern Western art.

In the first gallery hung a massive Paul Pletka oil which depicted a religious procession of Hispanics bearing a life-size crucifix. In brilliant deformity, each of the marchers' hands were painted twice their normal size, signifying unleashed power.

In the next room hung a bright collage by Juane Quick-to-See Smith, an amalgam of Plains Indian symbols overlaid on a gouache wash. Next to the Smith hung several Fritz Scholders, documenting that artist's evolution from abstraction to postmodernism. While providing a delight for the eye, the multi-layered glazes on the Scholders hinted at varying takes on perception.

My favorite painting, though, turned out to be the goofy Anne Coe, which showed a wry cowgirl staring at a Scottsdale pool while two steaks carbonized on a barbecue grill. Her horse stretched hungry lips towards a parboiled sun worshipper with hair the color of straw. As usual, Coe had captured the true heart of the tacky New West.

I was still laughing when an elderly docent, one of the great legions of Scottsdale volunteers, walked over to me. "Would you like me to explain the work to you?"

I wiped my eyes. "You know what they say, a picture is worth a thousand words."

The docent's eyes twinkled and he said, "Yes, that's what they say."

I had an idea. Pulling my card from my carryall, I asked to see the curator. "If he's in."

"She."

The docent took my card away and returned in less than five minutes, during which time I'd worked myself over to the haunting pastels of Lynn Taber-Borcherdt. Pastels or not, Borcherdt's work was reminiscent of William Turner, and I fell in love with a near-abstract rendering of a storm over the Santa Catalina Mountains. She'd used the same colors Turner had when he'd painted his breathtaking view of ships burning at sea.

Studying the painting, I was reminded of my Baptist foster parents, who'd once taken me camping in the Catalinas. The memories rose up before I could stop them.

Here was the problem.

Like so many foster home kids, I preferred to live in the present. Opening the door to happy memories, such as camping with the Baptists or learning color theory from Madeline, also opened the door to other memories not quite as pleasant: The foster father who'd raped me, the foster brother who'd set my kitten on fire. What lunatic would want to remember shit like that?

Being only a partial lunatic, I'd long ago decided it was preferable to forget all my joys as long as it meant I'd also forget all my pain.

But the siren song of painting worked like a back-alley mugger. Art knocked you over the head when your guard was down.

I'd shut my eyes against the Taber-Borcherdt when the docent returned. "Anne Amherst, our curator, has a few minutes free right now."

We left the main part of the building and entered a long, hushed corridor, where Anne Amherst's office took up a goodly portion of the northern side of the building. As I entered, I noticed that the large windows overlooked the remains of the orange tree orchard that had once separated the Hispanic neighborhood from their Anglo neighbors.

"Pretty," I said, turning towards the woman sitting behind the massive desk.

Anne Amherst was leafing through a Sotheby's auction catalogue. She was as brown and skinny as an old piece of rope and her pale blue eyes missed nothing. "But you don't approve."

I sat down in the chair the docent pulled out for me and wiggled my fingers at him as he returned to the galleries. "You've got a nice collection here but I'm afraid I miss the old neighborhood."

She winced. "Miss Jones, are you in the employ of Dulya Albundo? If so, I must warn you that I simply cannot discuss any museum business that might be part of her lawsuit. You'll have to speak to our attorneys."

I reassured her, explaining my connection to the Clarice Kobe case. "I'm just trying to find out more about Clarice. You see, at one time I thought I knew her well. Turns out I was mistaken."

But hadn't that been my fault as much as Clarice's? I'd always been most comfortable with relationships that demanded little of me, preferring acquaintances to real friendship. Whenever anyone attempted to get too close to me, I withdrew. In her way, I guess, Clarice had been the perfect friend. Like the Lady of the Manor, she delivered her little gifts to Desert Investigations and then returned to her own turf, leaving me untouched, unthreatened.

Poor Clarice.

Poor me.

Amherst shocked me out of my musings. "Clarice Kobe was a heartless bitch."

I sat up straight in my chair. *This* from a museum curator?

She expanded on her theme. "A heartless bitch who has done untold damage to the Arizona arts community. Do you have any *idea* what she made us look like? It'll take years to recover from the bad publicity that woman's actions have caused."

I leaned forward, smelling blood. "Are you talking about the eminent domain order she rammed through the courts?"

Amherst made a motion with her hand as if waving away a gnat. "Of course. And it was all so unnecessary! There was a perfectly good property up near the new freeway interchange but for some reason Clarice fixated on this one. She wouldn't listen to advice, just rode hell-bent for leather getting those poor people thrown out of their homes. What in heaven's name did the stupid woman think she was doing?"

I spread my hands helplessly. I didn't know what Clarice had thought she was doing, either. Except that maybe the profit margin on the in-town construction was higher. I floated that theory by Amherst.

She snorted. "When you're that rich, what's a million here or there? I think Clarice wanted to run those people out of their homes simply because she enjoyed the exercise of raw power. Some people do, you know. Plus, she was the most awful bigot and the residents around here *were* Hispanic, which by her lights meant they were somewhat less than human. But fat lot of good her little power-play did the bitch. What she really wanted, in the end, was the directorship of this museum. When poor Mrs. Espinoza died, that was the end of that."

"Clarice really believed she'd be made curator of the Museum of Western Art? With *her* taste?"

Amherst threw me a grim smile. "In a sick sort of way, Mrs. Espinoza did not die in vain. If she hadn't been crushed under that falling wall, today this museum would be filled with Jay Kobe's vulgar crap."

I spent the next half-hour looking through the rest of the museum's collection, and another half-hour trying to figure out exactly which room was on top of the remains of Dulya Albundo's ancestral home. Or maybe she had given her life for the parking lot. Evan and Serena notwithstanding, I was coming to the conclusion that I didn't like the Hyath family.

When I finally climbed back into my Jeep and took off to meet Eleanor Hyath, I'd built up a full cargo of dread.

Back in my days with the Scottsdale Violent Crimes Unit, this particular type of interview had always been the most difficult for me. It was hard for me to hide my contempt for certain suspects, and when it came to child molesters or abusive parents, I damned near frothed at the mouth during interrogations. Kryzinski was always calling me out of the interrogation room to calm me down— which made me even more agitated. After a few years, though, I finally learned how to put my own emotions on the back burner and ask the questions in a normal, conversational tone.

Which is how I became a resident of Ulcer City.

Now I'd need every bit of the distance Kryzinski taught me. I despised Eleanor Hyath, both for what she had been and what she had allowed herself to become.

But I knew better than to let it show.

The Hacienda Palms is located just off Paradise Valley Road, at the base of Camelback Mountain. As the valet drove my Jeep away after giving it an admiring look, I looked up and saw the Hyaths' home perched one thousand feet up the mountain. Didn't it look like Paradise?

The Hacienda Palms is one of Scottsdale's oldest resorts. The original Spanish Colonial Revival complex with its plastered brick walls and red tile roofs had been erected just after the turn of the century as a magnet to wealthy tuberculosis patients from back East. Here, legend has it, they lay on silk sheets in their private casitas and, with the aid of the sanatorium's resident priest, prayed for a cure. While the disease ravaged their lungs, they suffered amidst elegance. Sixteenth-century fountains imported from Italy played water music behind lush plantings of bougainvillea and hibiscus. A reflecting pool lined in Moorish tiles echoed the tall palms that gave the sanatorium its name.

When the discovery of penicillin made the old sanatorium redundant, the place changed hands. The priest was booted out and the complex found new life as a resort. And now the *serious* money began to roll in. Who else, other than millionaires, could afford a couple of thou a night?

In contrast to the huge resorts that lined Scottsdale Road, the Hacienda Palms' main building and its attendant casitas took up fewer than twenty acres and catered to only two hundred guests at a time. In their financial (if not ecological) wisdom the new owners had bulldozed the workers' shacks at the back of the resort and installed a nine-hole golf course. While the little putt-and-chip course couldn't compete with the big professional courses further north that hosted such world-class events as the Phoenix Open, the course's sheer beauty had the others beat.

The green backed up to the mountain itself, snaking around granite outcroppings, meandering alongside a man-made stream operated by huge pumps. Throughout the years, the course had remained popular with Old Money families, families who knew they couldn't hold a candle to the likes of Arnold Palmer or Tiger Woods and had more sense than to try.

I'd wondered about Eleanor's common sense in choosing an outdoor restaurant for lunch, but as the maitre d' led me from the guest reception area across the elegant Patio Café, I discovered that the entire area was cooled by an elaborate misting system. The temperature might be in the triple digits, but under the misters, it was cool as spring. I clattered along the Saltillo tiles, passing at various tables a local anchorman, the star of a popular TV sit-com, and a former First Lady.

Eleanor was waiting for me at a table just off the ninth hole, the emerald slopes behind her contrasting nicely with her blood-shot eyes. She sat surrounded by a blue haze of cigarette smoke, but at least she appeared sober. For now. She was already halfway through a margarita served in a glass the size of a goldfish bowl. Crystals of salt speckled her lips, and as I watched in disgusted fascination, a coated tongue snaked out and licked them away.

I forced a smile. "Mrs. Hyath, it was so good of you to agree to see me."

She didn't bother to smile back. "The lunch is on you, re-member. And the drinks."

"Of course."

As I took the menu from the waiter, I realized the lunch would gut Desert Investigations' petty cash fund for the next three months. I tried my best to contain my horror as I ordered a salad *(Curly Radicchio Crowned with Edible Flowers, Kissed by a Calorie Conscious Honey-Dijon Dressing)*—at $24.50, the cheapest thing on the menu. To drink, I contented myself with the lemon-garnished water. I'd pretend it was lemonade.

Mrs. Hyath didn't follow my cheap lead. For an appetizer, she ordered Oysters Rockefeller *(Flown in Fresh Daily!)*, then the same small salad I'd ordered, and for the main course, *Mesquite-Broiled Milk-Fed Reindeer Medallions from Norway, Nestled on Slices of Crispy Rusk Topped with a Sensuous Smattering of Paté de Fois Gras, then Smothered in Silver Palms' Award-Winning Bordelaise Sauce— A Delightful Culinary Escapade!*

Eleanor's culinary escapade would set me back more than one hundred and fifty dollars.

Smiling until I thought my ears would pop off, I handed the menu back to the waiter. I thought I detected a brief glint of amusement in his eyes, but he was too well-trained to show it for long. As he turned to leave, Mrs. Hyath called after him, "And I'll want to see the dessert selection afterwards."

My glued-on smile felt as if the glue was eating a hole through my skin. To calm myself, I began counting the broken capillaries on Eleanor's nose.

She misinterpreted my close study. "So what do you want from me now?" she asked. "And don't hand me any more bullshit condolences. I couldn't stand Clarice and she couldn't stand me, which you well know." Another drag on her cigarette, more sucking noises at the margarita. She'd be ready for a new one soon. God. How much did they cost here?

When I dropped the smile, my face thanked me for it. "Look, Mrs. Hyath, I just wanted to talk to you away from your husband, get your side of the story, who you think might have killed Clarice."

She snorted, and a few drops of moisture landed on my hand. I hoped they were from the misting system. "They arrested Jay again so you don't need anything from me."

"Let's just say I'm hedging my bets. What if Jay didn't do it?"

She sucked at her margarita some more, then wiped her hand across her mouth and answered, "Oh, he did it, all right."

Eleanor sounded so certain I didn't have time to disguise the look of surprise on my face. "You sound pretty sure."

Her raspy laugh brought stares from some of the other guests. "Of course, I'm sure. And you would be, too, if you could see your nose in front of your face. By the way, why don't you ever wear any makeup? Those blond eyelashes of yours make you look like some Georgia cracker. You could at least do something to cover that ghastly scar."

"It's against my religion," I answered, deciding not to tell her the real reason, that I was still hoping to be recognized by someone who knew me a lifetime ago.

Another snort. "And I thought I made it clear you were to dress well."

Poor Clarice. And for that matter, poor Serena and poor Evan. "This is the nicest dress I own, Mrs. Hyath. It's from Saks."

"It takes an unusual talent to go to a good store and find something so cheap-looking."

She smeared the remnants of her cigarette across a clamshell-shaped ashtray and lit another. Although her nails had been manicured the polish had begun to flake off, and underneath some of the clear areas, I could see dark ridges of dirt. Perhaps she believed that if she was critical enough of others, her own shortcomings would go unnoticed.

"Oh, dear, it looks like you've got egg yolk on your expensive dress," I said, pointing a clean, unvarnished finger at the offending area. "Right there under that, um, what *is* it? Merlot? Sloe gin?"

Her eyes lit up and the wattles under her chin danced merrily. "Well, well. You're not exactly a pushover, are you, Miss Jones."

"I never told you I was, Mrs. Hyath. Now, do you want to continue this juvenile dissing contest, or do you want to get down to business?"

The wattles wobbled. "How's this, then? Jay told me he killed her."

Just at that point, the waiter delivered her Oysters Rockefeller, and I composed myself as she slurped away. Her noisy enjoyment didn't surprise me. At $6 per oyster, the slimy little bastards should deliver multiple orgasms.

After the waiter took the shells away and returned with our salads, I finally managed, "So when did Jay tell you he'd murdered Clarice? When you went to visit him at the Madison Street Jail?"

She flushed. *Damn!* So I was right! She had visited the creep! I wondered briefly what kind of woman would visit her daughter's accused murderer, but the answer was obvious: A woman who enjoyed maliciousness in all its forms. This insight complicated the interview considerably, because I had no way of knowing if she was telling the truth or merely trying to make as much trouble as she could.

"As a matter of fact, I did visit Jay," she said. "I'm not without a heart, you understand, so I went down to see the poor boy, just in case there was anything he needed. That's when he confessed to me. Jay and I have always gotten along well, you see. Anyway, he told me he had slipped out of bed that night and gone down to the gallery to see if he could talk her out of the divorce. I hate divorce. It's so unnatural. But Clarice didn't want to listen to him and started calling him names.

"She wasn't the innocent little victim the world likes to think, you know. She was always a difficult girl, very self-centered. I had to take a firm hand with her when she was growing up, I tell you. Her father spoiled her rotten." The wattles began to dance again. "Anyway, Jay told me he just lost control of his temper and popped her one."

Popped her one. "Did you see Clarice's body? You don't lose an eye just from being *popped* one. And I must tell you that the confession you say Jay gave you doesn't jive in any way with the forensic evidence. Or did Jay also tell you he was wearing latex gloves at the time?"

She shrugged. "Whatever. I just thought you should know he did confess." Then she leaned back in her chair and sighed. Looking out over the golf course, she said, "Isn't that just the most magnificent sight? This is a real Garden of Eden, isn't it. But have you heard the rumors?"

I was puzzled. "What rumors?"

She smiled nastily. "About the golf course."

I shook my head. The conversation was drifting off into the ozone and it was time for me to take a stronger hand.

"Look, Mrs. Hyath, I don't care what the rumors are about the golf course, not even if they're going to start playing an abbreviated Masters Tournament here in the nude. I want to hear more about Jay and Clarice."

"Awfully short-sighted of you." A curl of radicchio hung from her lower lip. I couldn't take my eyes off it. "But I should be used to short-sighted people. None of my children ever had any foresight, not even Clarice, and she was the smartest one of the whole stupid lot."

Our waiter approached with a small plate of what appeared to be tiny veal steaks. Rudolph smelled great, making my still-empty stomach rumble. I reminded myself to stop off for a Big Mac on the way home. With fries.

"I don't agree about your children," I said, hoping to draw her further. "Other than in his personal life, Evan seems to be doing well, and Serena has made quite an impact in the Valley with all those charitable organizations she's part of."

"*Used* to be part of. That crowd she likes to run with doesn't fraternize with junkies."

Somehow I kept from spitting in her face. "Still, they've all managed to make a contribution to the community."

A sucking announced to the entire restaurant that Eleanor Hyath was through with her margarita. As the former First Lady and the sit-com star glared, the waiter whisked the empty glass away and replaced it almost immediately with a fresh one. Apparently they didn't mind how drunk you got here, just as long as you were quiet about it.

"What'd you say?" she said, licking more salt off her lips. I thought her words were beginning to slur, but maybe it was just that she tended to talk with her mouth full. I'd never seen anybody eat so fast.

"That all your children have made some kind of contribution to the community." But you haven't, I finished silently. You just take up space.

"You don't know what you're talking about."

"Oh?"

Eleanor leaned over her margarita and snapped, "They're failures, each one of them! As for success, that idiot son of mine gave almost everything he ever owned to his ex-wives, and Serena herself wound up paying alimony to her ex-husband. Now she's in another bad marriage and didn't even have the sense to ask for a pre-nupt. What a stupid, stupid girl! She's headed for divorce court again and that greasy Mex she's married to is going to fleece her like the last one did."

"He's Spanish."

"Just another Beaner with pretensions."

Our waiter, who was Hispanic, looked like he wanted to hit her, but his training stood him in good stead. "Madam wishes to see the dessert menu?" he asked, removing Rudolph's remains.

"Isn't that what I told you? Christ, is everyone around here deaf?"

The former First Lady threw down her napkin and started for our table, fire in her eyes. Just before she reached us, the young man she was with put a restraining hand on her arm and returned her to her seat. I breathed a sigh of relief. Bar fights were a pain, no matter how classy the bar. Or the combatants.

Our waiter exhibited more control. "Very good, Madam," he said, his face now totally devoid of expression. "I'll bring the dessert menu immediately."

"You'd better."

I took a deep breath and let it out slowly. One. Two. Three. "Ah, you were saying that Serena didn't have a pre-nupt, and that her marriage is on the rocks?"

Cigarette time again. She lit up and blew smoke into my face. "By the time that Beaner's through with her, she won't have a pot to piss in."

I didn't bother waving the smoke away. It would give her too much satisfaction to know that she'd managed to annoy me.

"I thought Serena received a steady income from the construction company."

"As of now," Eleanor cackled. "But she won't when Pedro or whatever his name is gets through with her!" Then she shook her head in a great show of sorrow. "I just don't know why none of my children ever learned anything from my example."

I wasn't certain I heard her right. "Your example? What do you mean?"

The waiter delivered a tall dessert menu and Eleanor took it with a crooning noise. She disappeared behind it for a while, then finally re-emerged with a genuine smile on her face. "Prickly Pear Crepes with Brandy Sauce! My, my. I haven't had them in years. Who would ever have known that this outdated old sand trap still served them." Then she handed the menu back to the waiter. "You know what to do," she told him.

He looked confused. "Does Madam mean she wishes the crepes?"

She would have looked more fondly at a bug. "What do you think I mean, José?"

The waiter, whose name tag announced his name as Gilberto, gave her a deep bow—to cover the fury on his face, I think—then rushed away. I wanted to rush away, too, sticking the evil old bitch with the bill, but she still hadn't answered my last question.

"What did you mean, Mrs. Hyath, when you said your children should have followed your example? What example are you talking about?"

Another genuine smile. "Why, my pre-nupt with their father, of course. It was one of the first pre-nupts my attorney ever put together. For a woman, that is."

This was news. "You mean, you and your husband have a pre-nupt?"

"Like I said, everyone around here must be deaf. Of *course* I have a pre-nupt. Why do you think I'm still living with him?"

In response to my urging, Eleanor revealed the realities of love among the Upper Classes. When she and Stephen Hyath had first married, he'd already been a rising developer and she was little more than an impressionable teenager from an old Arizona copper mining family. The deal for her fair hand, much like any business deal, had been this: Hyath would provide an interest-free loan to Eleanor's father for some obscure business venture he'd embarked upon, and in return, the father would re-write his will to give Eleanor a larger inheritance that had been originally planned.

As Eleanor related this, I thought I saw a brief flash of pain in her eyes. But it disappeared so quickly that it might have been just my imagination.

But Eleanor, although young, had already learned a thing or two from her money-grubbing father. Before agreeing to the marriage contract, she demanded a pre-nupt that would make her an equal partner in Hyath Enterprises, which included, of course, Hyath Development. And in a coup de grace that took my breath away, the attorney, a Phoenician who'd been around the track a few times himself, had added a startling codicil: Who-ever filed for divorce first would forfeit three-quarters of the corporation's profits for a ten-year period following the date of the final decree.

Talk about until death do you part.

"It's a man's world and a woman has to protect herself," Eleanor said. "If it hadn't been for that eleventh-hour codicil, Stephen would have traded me in for some dumb blond long before now. Maybe even one like you."

The expression on her face was bleak beyond words. As Gilberto, whose face appeared set in concrete, delivered the prickly pear crepes, I couldn't help but wonder if Eleanor's financial security had been worth all the pain.

When she called for another margarita, I had my answer.

I arrived back at Desert Investigations a little after two o'clock, still shaken from the size of the luncheon bill. And just what had I learned? Very damned little. That confession Jay supposedly gave Eleanor sounded like a figment of her malicious imagination. And as for the rest of her ramblings, she hadn't told me anything I didn't already know.

Except for the sordid details of the Hyaths' pre-nupt. No wonder the Hyath siblings hadn't had their own drawn up. With their parents' marriage as an example, they were probably trying to achieve the exact opposite, no matter how risky the attempt.

The lunch had given me a raging headache, so I told Jimmy I was quitting early. He nodded sympathetically, and I dragged myself up the stairs, swallowed a couple of Excedrin, and jumped into a cold shower. I stayed in there long enough to turn into an icicle, then wrapped myself in a white terry bath sheet and fell across the bed.

After lying there for a while staring at the ceiling, I suddenly felt my eyes begin to burn. Then a tear slid down my cheeks.

I was crying.

But I didn't know why.

Chapter 19

When I woke up, the shadows in the room had lengthened. I checked the clock and discovered it was almost six o'clock. I'd been asleep for four hours.

At least my headache was gone.

I got dressed and readied my fanny pack for my evening run. The hip was fine and the shoulder hardly twinged at all. It was time to stop babying myself.

So I ran. And ran. And ran. I ran so swiftly that even my friend the blond-faced coyote looked amazed. She followed me for a short while up the slanting side of the Buttes, veering away into the underbrush only after she spotted another runner.

A yellow cloud of pollution hung over the Phoenix end of the Valley, making the Buttes glow with a sick fire. Nonetheless, I sang the Pima Corn Song as if the desert was as pristine as a century earlier, when Pima songs were in the ascendancy, not the twilight.

Then I limped home.

A shadowy figure was waiting for me on the stairs. As I drew my .38 from my fanny pack, a familiar voice floated to me on the magnolia-scented air.

"Shoot me, Lena, and I'll haunt you for the rest of your miserable life."

It was Dusty.

I don't love him, I don't love him…

Ah, who the hell did I think I was kidding? I holstered the gun and walked towards him.

He stood up, his face soft. "I love you, you silly bitch. I'd do almost anything for you."

Almost? Where was all this unconditional love I kept reading about?

But I opened my arms anyway.

Chapter 20

"On the whole, I prefer CNN," Dusty said, frowning at *Apache Sunset*. "The wars are a lot more cheerful."

"Philistine."

We'd made love through the evening and half the night. Now it was morning and we were still damp from the shower, sitting wrapped in bath sheets on the sofa, where Dusty was—unasked— playing art critic. "That artist must be nuts."

"He might be," I agreed. "That's the guy Clarice kicked out of her gallery."

"Gee, I wonder why."

"He's pretty good, actually."

Dusty got up and walked over to the painting, the bath sheet slipping down around his hips. I smiled. He had the best buns I'd ever seen.

He leaned down and peered at the signature. *"George,* huh?"

"Yeah. George."

"The guy who was here when I called."

"The very same."

Dusty didn't ask me if I'd slept with George, just as I didn't ask him if he'd slept with the redhead. As we had many times before, we just continued in the present, not bothering to discuss what had gone wrong and how we could prevent it in the future. Who knew if we had a future, anyway?

"I've got to get back to the ranch," he said, his voice trailing after him as he headed for the clothes he'd left in a pile by the bed. "I've already missed morning feed time, but I left word with a couple of the other guys to help out in case I didn't make it back. The horses won't starve."

I followed him into the bedroom. It was understood that I would never try to talk him into staying once he'd announced he had to leave. "I was kind of starved."

He turned, his Jockey shorts dangling from his hand. "Yeah, I noticed that. But you're not now, are you?"

How could I tell him that when it came to sex, too much was never enough? When you can't allow yourself to love, you still have to reach out, to stroke, to caress, to kiss. "I'm fine now," I lied.

He smiled. "You look fine. Real fine."

I smiled back. "You do, too, Cowboy. Y'all come again, y'hear?"

For a brief moment, the sound of his laughter chased my loneliness away.

My morning copy of the *Scottsdale Journal* informed me that Animal Control officers had finally located the biting coyote's den and had staked it out. In accordance with the locals' wishes, they were armed only with tranquilizer guns. They promised to merely stun the coyote, haul it off for rabies quarantine, then release it into the wild a long, long way from Scottsdale.

Not a perfect solution, I thought, but probably the best solution for everyone concerned. If left to its own devices, that coyote would probably wind up getting flattened by a Mercedes someday.

I spent the morning on the phone, putting out fires and rustling up new business. The most rewarding phone call came when I told Brian Meeks that I'd found his runaway girlfriend shacked up with his wife. His hypocritical outrage was something to hear, but I finally calmed him when I said that as far as the divorce courts were concerned, adultery was adultery, no matter with which sex or species.

Of course, that held true for *him,* too.

He was still thinking about the implications of that when I hung up.

Around lunchtime, when my stomach began to growl, I remembered being at the Hacienda Palms with Eleanor Hyath. Something she said was still bothering me, but every time I tried to remember it, it eluded me. Disgusted with my Swiss cheese memory, I wandered over to a deli and picked up a hot pastrami for Jimmy and a corned beef for myself. As I walked back through the noontime heat, the memory still eluded me, like an itch at the back of my brain that I couldn't scratch.

The rest of the day was slow, except for the now-routine phone call from Jay Kobe's attorney, crowing that he had bailed his client out again.

"Isn't this getting just a little bit boring?" I asked Hal McKinnon. "The cops arrest him, you bail him out? The cops arrest him, you bail him…"

"You wouldn't think it was boring if it was you sitting in Sheriff Joe's jail eating green bologna," he snapped. "Now are you going to help us again or not? My client did *not* do this murder."

"If he didn't, it's only because he's the luckiest man alive and someone else murdered Clarice before he got around to beating her to death."

McKinnon begged some more, then finally began to threaten. "Albert Grabel is going to be very unhappy with you."

He obviously didn't know that Grabel had called me that very morning and told me that my duties to Jay Kobe had been well and truly performed, and that he wouldn't hold it against me if I refused to do any more work on the case.

"If I'd known everything about Jay I know now, I'd never have asked you to do this, Lena," he'd said, his voice heavy with regret. "I'm sorry about the whole thing."

I was off the hook.

So when McKinnon finished his threats, I smiled into the receiver. "Tell Jay he can stick it, Mr. McKinnon. And you can, too."

I hung up, vowing never again to do any work for wife beaters. No matter who they were related to.

The rest of the day proceeded calmly, and by the time the little hand hit five and the big hand hit twelve, I was ready to close up shop. I told Jimmy to go home.

"Sounds good to me," he said. "I think I'll drive over to Uncle Sisiwan's, learn a few more Ant Songs, talk to him about painting my truck."

"Your truck?" I looked out the window at Jimmy's almost-new Chevy pickup truck. It was a gleaming burgundy, with a metallic gold racing stripe streaking along the side. "I think your truck looks pretty good."

"Not half as good as your Jeep."

The pall of pollution that had hung over the Valley for the past few days remained and as I jogged across McDowell and into Papago Park that evening, I noticed that no other runners or mountain bicyclists could be seen. Apparently only mad coyotes and private detectives were crazy enough to jog under such conditions. It was a sad irony that the Valley's pure, dry air, which had attracted tuberculosis sufferers for decades, was speeding down the same smog-clogged road as Los Angeles. As I squinted up at the yellow-tainted sky, the feeling that I had forgotten something important returned. What the hell had Eleanor Hyath told me that was so important?

The thick air made it hard to breathe, and by the time I reached the Papago Amphitheater at the foot of the buttes, I felt like I'd run twice the distance. The exhaust from the rush hour traffic seemed even thicker up here, and I chastised myself for not being farsighted enough to stay on flat ground. Hoping the old Pima gods would forgive me, I decided to skip the steep climb to my usual perch above the amphitheater and instead dropped down on a rock cement seat. The pollution exaggerated the heat effect, and my skin felt dangerously clammy—a warning sign. Any savvy desert dweller knows that clammy skin can be a precursor to heat stroke. I needed plenty of liquids and I needed them right now.

Which turned out to be a good thing, because reaching around for the water bottle attached to my fanny pack's belt probably saved my life. I heard the shot from above me and the bullet's whine almost at the same time, then the concrete just beyond where my head had been a half-second earlier exploded.

Quite literally hitting the dirt, I scooted along on my belly to a broken-off piece of seating and hunkered down behind it. Dust entered my nostrils, making me want to sneeze, but I didn't dare make a sound. I froze, unmoving, heat stroke a concern of the distant past. At moments like these, when you are paralyzed by terror, time itself seems to stand still. Overhead, a yellow and orange Southwest Airlines jet appeared to hang suspended above the Salt River as it made its way towards Sky Harbor. The traffic noise from below merged into one humming wave of sound, as if some prehistoric monster was making its noisy way through the sandstone buttes.

Time began moving again when a lizard, panicked by the gunfire, or maybe by the big white person lying atop its home, scuttled out from behind the concrete and tore ass towards the underbrush. Released from my terrified paralysis, I hauled my .38 out of the fanny pack. The shooter was hidden somewhere in the rocks above the amphitheater, looking down on me. I couldn't be in a more precarious position. Raising my head over the sanctuary of the concrete might get me killed, but I couldn't just cower until he finally scored a bull's eye. There was an added danger, too. The commuters below us were oblivious to the drama taking place above. If he kept firing, the shooter might kill an innocent driver. Or two. Or three. How many families were in those cars? How many children?

I couldn't allow him to keep shooting.

Squirming around, I wedged as much of my body as possible behind the concrete and peered carefully over the top.

He didn't disappoint me.

Another gunshot, another rock exploding. This one even closer.

But I'd seen what I wanted to see, the burst of fire from a gun muzzle. The shooter was tucked away into a dark recess near the gap in the buttes that led to the Eliot Ramada on the south side. I snapped off a quick defensive shot, more to make the shooter realize I was armed than to do any real damage, but my shot missed him by only a few inches. An iron oxide boulder at the edge of the recess exploded. He yelped, but his voice was too distorted by the traffic noise below for me to identify it.

My return fire accomplished its purpose. The shooter realized he was facing an armed adversary instead of a helpless victim, and that changed the entire equation. I heard feet scraping along rock, then the sounds died away as the shooter dove through the gap in the buttes. His footsteps echoed as he scrambled down the other side.

I picked myself up, gun held high, and ran up the amphitheater steps towards the gap.

"Halt! Halt or I'll shoot!" I ordered.

But I was too late.

By the time I reached the gap, I heard the roar of a motor from the ramada parking lot. I looked down just in time to see a silver Taurus round the corner on two tires and head towards Phoenix.

Chapter 21

Once home, I called Kryzinski and told him what had happened. He cursed for a while but finally shut up when I promised to go down to the station first thing the next morning and file a report. Then I stripped my grit-embedded clothing off and stepped into the shower. While I hadn't felt anything while scooting around in the amphitheater, my breasts, stomach, and knees proved to be scored by tiny cuts. I looked like someone had dragged me through a cactus patch backwards. But hey, at least there were no new bullet holes. After toweling myself off, I dabbed some antiseptic ointment on the worst of them and counted myself lucky.

When I finally wandered back out to the living room, I noticed that the message light on the phone was blinking. Dusty, I bet. Smiling, I hit the "play" button.

But it wasn't Dusty.

Dulya Albundo's voice floated out to me. "Miss Jones, I need to talk to you again. I'm working at Julio's tonight, and should get off at ten. I'll meet you in the parking lot."

I frowned.

At ten in the parking lot. Did the woman think I was an idiot? Then again…

At 9:30 p.m. I walked into Julio's, sat down at the bar, and ordered a glass of iced tea. It being late on a week night, the restaurant was nearly deserted. In the dining area, I could see Mrs. Albundo

making small talk with the last dinner customers as they slid out of a booth. I saw the man hand her a twenty. No wonder she made the two-hour commute.

When the bartender informed me they were closing, I walked into the dining room and tapped Mrs. Albundo on the shoulder. The polite smile on her face faded when she saw me.

"Miss Jones, I thought I said I would meet you in the parking lot."

"I'm allergic to dark places."

She didn't know what to make of that, but it didn't seem to bother her as much as I thought it might. "We cannot talk here. We must go somewhere else."

"How about some more caffe latte?"

That seemed to please her so as soon as she was finished in the kitchen doing whatever it is that waitresses do, I escorted her out to the Jeep I'd left parked directly under a tungsten light. I kept a close watch on the shadows, but I saw nothing other than a stray cat rummaging through the Dumpster. On the soft night's breeze I could smell magnolia and garlic.

"Where is your truck?" Mrs. Albundo said, when she saw the Jeep. "The truck with the wonderful air-conditioning."

Was she just trying to cadge a free ride back to South Phoenix? Funny, she hadn't seemed the type. "Oh, that was just a loaner. This is mine. I was having it painted when we talked before."

"What are those designs on it?"

As we traveled south on Miller Road, I gave her a short course on Pima mythology. It didn't seem to me that she really was all that interested, but I noticed that she did her best to keep me talking. I'd seen this sort of thing before. It usually stemmed from a guilty conscience.

The espresso bar was still open, so we found a seat near the back. She ordered another bagel with veggie schmear with her caffe latte. I did, too. She kept me talking until our orders arrived and I decided to end her clumsy manipulation.

"Now, Mrs. Albundo, I want to know why you wanted to see me tonight, and don't tell me it's because you wanted to learn all about Earth Doctor."

She stared into her steaming cup. "I should have told you before."

I said nothing. Sometimes it's best just to wait. Was I going to get a confession?

The caffe latte appeared to fascinate her. She watched the steam curl upwards as if it were protoplasm about to coalesce into earthly form. Who did she expect to see? The ghost of her mother? A visitation from the Madonna? I was almost ready to prod her again when she finally spoke.

"I think my cousin was the person who carried you to the hospital that night."

A woman sitting at a table by the window laughed and the man with her leaned over and whispered something in her ear, making her laugh even harder. The counter man watched them both, his expression bland. He was wearing an ASU T-shirt and a lame attempt at Coolio's hair style—four thick braids sprouting from his head all directions. I preferred corn rows, I decided. Corn rows with beads. Even Afros were nice as long as they weren't too extreme. I wondered if Afros would ever come back. I hoped so. Some of these rapper-influenced hair styles verged on the hilarious. I missed grace. I missed beauty.

"Miss Jones, did you hear my words?"

"Huh?"

She was staring at me now with an expression bordering on pity. "I said, did you hear my words?"

"Ummm, yes. Yes, I did. I heard your words."

Now it was the man's turn to laugh, the woman's turn to whisper in his ear. The counter man rolled his eyes. Another couple entered. They took seats at the table next to us. I liked the woman's dress, a pretty shade of blue. Periwinkle, I think it was called. Blue with just a hint of lavender. Total artifice, and no artist would be caught dead using it, but flattering nonetheless. I wondered where she bought it. Neiman Marcus? Saks?

"Miss Jones, please look at me. You are scaring me."

I closed my eyes for a moment and exhaled a deep, trembling sigh. What a bitch of a day. Then I summoned up the tattered fragments of my courage and looked straight at her. "Why didn't you tell me earlier?"

"Because my cousin was an illegal. I did not want to get her or me into any trouble with INS."

As active as the Immigration and Naturalization Service had sometimes been, after a few recent ugly incidents they'd become much less knee-jerk about picking up innocent Hispanics off of Valley streets. I reminded Mrs. Albundo of that.

"Maybe so, but you must understand that I do not trust the government, not any of it."

I finally understood the peculiar expression she'd worn on her face during our previous interview. She'd been hiding this secret for years, afraid the INS would swoop down and do even more hideous things to her family than had already been done.

Seeing the fear in her eyes gave me courage. "Tell me."

She shook her head. "There is not much I can tell you. It was so many years ago. My cousin Agnezia, she and another cousin of mine, Annuncio crossed over down by Nogales, where we were waiting for her. They wanted to work and there were jobs here for them, the dirty jobs that you Anglos do not like to do."

"Mrs. Albundo, I don't give a flying fart how your cousin got here, so skip the soapboxing and get to the point."

Anger hung in her face for a moment until a wave of guilt drowned it. "I am sorry. I have been angry for so long."

"Haven't we all."

She sighed. "Agnezia, she worked as a cleaning woman for some rich people who lived up on one of the mountains. One night she came home late covered with blood and very, very frightened. She would tell me nothing, just there had been a shooting and she took a little girl to the hospital with the statue of St. Joseph and the Baby Jesus in front. She did not know if the child was still alive when she got there and she was afraid she would be blamed and sent to prison. She would tell me no more of what had happened and made me promise never to tell of this to anyone."

Then she spread her hands. "What more can I tell you? Agnezia was only seventeen, a young girl away from her country and scared of your Federales. She was afraid they would make her go back to Mexico."

It held together. Ever since I learned that the woman who'd left me in the Emergency Ward was Hispanic, I'd suspected that she was an illegal. Otherwise why not stay and give the police a statement?

Unless, of course, she'd had a hand in the shooting herself. But for some reason, I'd never believed that.

"I want to talk to Agnezia. Right now."

Mrs. Albundo smiled, the first genuine smile I had ever seen on her face. It made her look a decade younger. "You have a long drive ahead of you, Miss Jones. Agnezia went back to Mexico ten years ago."

Chapter 22

Some rich people who lived up on one of the mountains.

After I returned from driving Mrs. Albundo home to South Phoenix, I put some Honeyboy Edwards and some Johnny Shines on the turntable and collapsed on my cheap beige sofa. For the next hour, I stared at George Haozous's painting—at the little Apache girl with the bullet wound in her forehead.

Some rich people who lived up on one of the mountains.

Jimmy's computer search of the entire database for Arizona the day I had been taken to the Emergency Ward had come up with no killings, not even any shootings. No children had been reported missing, which only meant one thing.

That whatever had happened, somebody wanted it kept secret. Why?

What deed, what act could be so horrible that the permanent loss of a four-year-old child would seem trivial in comparison? I closed my eyes, shutting out the vision of the Apache girl.

Had no one ever loved me?

Cowboys go to bed early, and my phone call woke Dusty up. "It's after midnight, Lena," he moaned. "I need to be up by five in the morning."

"I just got back from South Phoenix."

Silence. Then, "What the hell were you doing down there in the middle of the night? Are you all right?"

I decided not to tell him about the shooting in Papago Park. "I'm fine. I just had to take someone home. Listen, can you skip work tomorrow? I need to go to Rocky Point and I'd like a little company."

"Rocky Point?" he said, he too using the English name for the Sea of Cortez resort village. The joke was that at any given time, there were more Arizonans down there than locals. "It's a pretty place, Honey, but isn't this kind of short notice for a vacation?"

I told him.

When I was through, he said, "I'll be right over. We can leave as soon as it's light."

He was at my apartment within the hour and I wrapped myself around him. "I'm scared," I managed to say, my nose smashed against his chest.

"I know, Baby, I know." I felt his lips on my hair, his arms holding me tight. Then he picked me up and carried me into the bedroom.

I was shaking too hard to make love, but he held me all night long.

Chapter 23

Rocky Point, Mexico is a fishing village only two hundred and fifty miles southwest of Phoenix. It is to Arizona what Ft. Lauderdale is to East Coast college students, and every spring break, the town of thirty-six thousand people is inundated with students camping, drinking, screwing, and puking their guts out on the pristine white beach north of town. The students tended to be a little tamer to the south, along the black beach of Malecon Fondadores, where they quietly passed out along the lava rocks. The locals are disgusted by this Ugly American behavior, of course, but for the main part, they endure it with grim politeness.

Because other than fishing for Rocky Point shrimp, some of the tastiest around, tourism is the town's main source of income. Accordingly, most of the residents were bilingual and most business establishments were more than happy to accept American dollars. You didn't need a visa to get there or trips to the money-changers. Just cash or a credit card, and not really much of those. You could stay in Rocky Point's finest beachfront hotel and get your own private balcony for about what you'd pay for a Motel 6.

The only thing I had against Rocky Point was the fact that I had to leave my .38 at home. Too many Arizonans had spent months in the Mexico jails because they'd forgotten the hunting rifle they always carried in their car trunk. For the past few years, Mexico had been in a state of political and social unrest, and more guns were being smuggled to the insurgents there from

Nogales, Tucson and Phoenix than from anywhere else in the U.S.

When the Federales caught you with a gun at the heavily armed border crossing, they didn't take it for granted you were a forgetful tourist; they saw you as a gun-runner.

The drive down took us less than four hours. The Jeep sped through the cholla-dotted desert southwest of Phoenix, slowed down only for the border crossing at Lukeville, then picked up speed again as it blasted past the sandy flats of Sonora, where tin-roofed shanties leaned against a merciless wind. The poverty we saw was so extreme that we were overjoyed when we finally arrived at the relatively flush resort town.

Dusty had called ahead and booked us into the Hotel Vina Del Mar, which sat high on a cliff edge overlooking the beach. As we checked in, we could hear the squawks of the caged parrots that lived in the hotel's cabana, and behind them, the incessant thunder of surf. I stepped out onto our balcony to be greeted by a spurt of laughter from the gringo tourists sitting on submerged barstools at the poolside bar. They were drunk on margaritas and telling stupid light bulb jokes. Miles of sapphire blue ocean available just yards away, yet more swimmers were frolicking in the chlorinated pool than in the ocean. Maybe because chlorinated water seldom played host to mean fish with big teeth.

"When do you want to go down to Agnezia's Cantina?" Dusty asked.

I stepped farther out onto the patio and looked up. The noon-time sun hung high over Rocky Point, bleeding the color from the tile roofs and gaily painted storefronts. "Mrs. Albundo said to wait until about two, let the lunchtime crowd go away. Then Agnezia would have time to talk to us."

According to Mrs. Albundo, Agnezia had saved the money she earned cleaning rich people's houses in Scottsdale and after returning to Mexico, purchased one of the brush-roofed *loncherias* that lined the Malecon, the old port. Now that she was secure in her own country, I doubted she would hold back anything that happened the night I was shot.

"As long as you truly want to know," Mrs. Albundo had said. "But did you ever wonder, Miss Jones, what kind of people would shoot a four-year-old child?"

More than once, I'd answered.

Dusty slipped into his bathing suit and headed for the pool. "You did nothing but toss and moan all night," he said. "Why don't you try and get some sleep?"

But I couldn't sleep, not even after a long, hot shower. While Dusty frisked in the pool with the other gringos, I lay wide-eyed on the bed, watching a cable news show from Los Angeles. That morning an eighteen-year-old television star had been found decapitated in her apartment; her drug dealer was under arrest. Further north, Charlie Manson was again petitioning for parole; his chances weren't considered good.

A basketball star, sentenced to fifteen years in prison for killing his wife, had given a shocking television interview where he'd admitted killing her because he "loved her so much."

I fingered the bullet scar on my forehead. No wonder love made me so nervous.

The newscaster was still describing recent killings when Dusty came back into the room, smelling like tequila and chlorine. "You've got a strange look on your face."

"I was thinking that love sucks."

"Jesus."

I glanced at my watch. It was 1:30. I rolled off the bed and combed my hair.

"You ready?" Dusty asked, his eyes still reflecting the hurt my thoughtless remark had inflicted on him.

"Not really." But I followed him out the door.

We left the Jeep at the hotel and walked along Malecon Fondadores, enjoying the cool breeze off the Sea of Cortez. A sports fishing boat chugged back into the marina where the commercial fishers had already moored. The ocean appeared calm with only the occasional whitecap marring its glass-like surface. As I searched the cobalt sky, a pelican swooped down towards us, veering away at the last possible moment.

A dark-skinned child of about ten, playing among the black lava rocks, laughed. "He thinks you are a great big fish." Like most of the children of Rocky Point, I figured he was on duty, paid to tout the excellence of one cantina over another. He didn't disappoint me. "If you are like him and eager for fish, you must stop by Agnezia's Cantina. My grandmother, she has the freshest fish in all Rocky Point."

I stiffened.

Dusty put a comforting hand on my shoulder and brandished a dollar bill. "Perhaps you could show us the way to Agnezia's."

The child's eyes gleamed. *"Si,* yes!" He danced towards us, took the dollar politely from Dusty's outstretched hand, and skipped ahead down the sidewalk. "Manolo will show you. It is not far, just beyond the statue of *El Piscadore."*

We passed vendors selling brightly colored *sarapes,* huge *piñatas* shaped like porpoises and llamas, hammered copper bowls. Without asking, Dusty ducked into a shop and emerged a minute later with two enormous sombreros. He put on one me, the other on him.

"With the sun bouncing off that water the way it is, we're headed for lobster time."

"Thank you, Daddy."

The look he gave me wasn't pretty. "Lena, do you always have to be such a bitch?"

"Just most of the time."

Agnezia's Cantina was perched so close to the ocean that if you got drunk and fell off the balcony, you'd go out with the tide. Like most of the waterfront establishments, it was little more than a bar and kitchen attached to a wide slab of concrete and shielded from the blistering sun by a thatch-covered cabana. Wafting from the kitchen, and almost smothering the pervasive odor of tequila, was the delicious smell of frying fish, garlic, and cilantro. It reminded me that I hadn't been able to eat breakfast. Or lunch. Maybe after I found out what I needed to know, I'd be able to choke something down.

Or maybe not.

The cantina was deserted except for a few lingering tourists hunkered over bottles of Carta Blanca and Corona. Manolo ushered us to a table and told us to wait there while he fetched his grandmother.

As soon as we sat down, Dusty took my hand and squeezed it. I snatched my hand away. I didn't want anyone touching me.

A shadow fell across the table and I looked up. The sun was behind her and I couldn't see her face.

Apparently she could see mine.

"Tina?" she whispered. "Tina?"

Before I could stop her, Agnezia fell to her knees in front of me and took my face in her hands. She kissed my scar and smoothed my hair, much like a mother comforts a weeping child. But I wasn't weeping. I was fine, just fine. Nothing could hurt me. I was invulnerable.

"Oh, my little one, I have prayed for you for so long." Not content with these hesitant caresses, Agnezia then threw her arms around me, pressed my head to her huge bosom and began to cry. Fat tears dropped onto my hair but I could not move.

I had been embraced by this woman before.

Tina. The name floated back to me on the winds of memory. *Tina.* The name I had tried to tell to the social workers but which had come out of my four-year-old mouth as "Lena."

But I was Tina.

Above the ever-present surf, I began to hear other voices. Numerous hands patted my back, my hair. "It is our Tina! *Dios gracias! Dios gracias!*"

When I finally managed to struggle away from Agnezia's grasp, I found we were surrounded by a crowd of teary-faced men and women of all ages bearing a strong resemblance to either Agnezia or the child Manolo. As I stared at their faces, a hard kernel of fact fought its way through all the emotion.

They were so dark and I was so pale.

I swallowed hard, fighting to keep my voice steady. "I don't understand."

Agnezia leaned forward on her knees again and caressed my face. Her hands were careful, soft. What a wonderful mother.

But not mine.

"You are Tina, the little girl I have asked the good God to protect all these years."

"Our mother has told us all about you, about the little girl she saved," said a woman of about my age. "She has made us pray for you every day since we were all children. She has told us to keep you safe in our hearts."

Why? None of these people were related to me. Why should they give a shit?

"Please, tell me who I am," I begged.

Agnezia got off her knees, not bothering to brush the grit away. She slid onto a chair beside me while several family members trouped back to the kitchen. Now that I could see her clearly, I recognized the strong resemblance to Mrs. Albundo, but where the South Phoenix woman's face was thin with worry, Agnezia's face was round and merry, even while she wept. Like many cooks, she was plump, and as I had already experienced, she had a large, soft bosom ideal for comforting sobbing children.

But now her own tender eyes were sorrowful. "I am sorry, Tina, but I do not know who you are. After that woman shot you I picked you up and ran away. I ran as fast as I could to the hospital with the statue of St. Joseph carrying the Christ child, praying to him that he would not let the good God take you."

A cold snake wrapped itself around my spine. "After *what* woman shot me?"

Brown hands began to load the table with bottles of Corona, Cokes, glasses of iced tea, baskets heaped with tortilla chips, bowls of pungent salsa. I reached for the tea. It was excellent, flavored with mint and some other mysterious spice, but I could hardly swallow. The snake had slithered to my throat, and it was squeezing, squeezing.

"The woman with the yellow hair shot you," Agnezia said. "Then she screamed, 'Tina!' It was a horrible sound, a sound I still can hear. Then she shoved you out the door with her foot— I saw this with my own eyes!—and you fell on the ground. I picked you up and I ran and ran."

The woman with the yellow hair. I grabbed Agnezia's wrist. "Where was this? Did it happen at the house where you worked?" But I didn't see how that could be possible. Mrs. Albundo told me Agnezia had worked for some 'rich people' up on one of the mountains. There were no mountains within running distance of St. Joseph's Hospital.

"No, no. Not where I worked. This happened near my apartment on the west side of Phoenix, on the street named Thomas, only a few blocks from the hospital. It was dark and I had just gotten off the bus, coming home from my job on the mountain. I was walking along the street when I saw this other bus, a strange bus, very plain. It was not a city bus like the one I had been riding."

I held very still, waiting. The snake didn't move. It was waiting, too.

"The bus passed me. It was going slow along the street and it was all lit up inside. The people inside were making a lot of noise. Some were singing. But someone was also screaming, a woman. A child was screaming, too, crying, 'No, Mommy! No!' Then the back door to the bus, the one people are supposed to leave from, it flew open and I could see the yellow-haired woman holding you with one hand. In the other hand she had a big gun. She was pointing it at you. Above all the singing voices, I could hear her screaming, 'I'll kill her! I'll kill her! Get away from me and let me do it!'

"Then some man, I could not see him well but he was darker than her, he reached down to grab the gun. But it was too late. The yellow-haired woman, she fired the gun. You stopped screaming and fell into the street. You fell right at my feet, where the good God had planned for you to fall."

The snake squeezed tighter. "You say the man tried to take the gun?"

She nodded. "He had his hands around the gun. He must not have wanted her to shoot you."

"You are certain that the woman who shot me had yellow hair? Hair like mine?"

The low buzz from the family surrounding us quieted. Agnezia picked up a Corona and took several hesitant sips. She didn't drink like a drinker. She set her beer down slowly, wiped her mouth, and gave me another sorrowful look.

"I am sorry, Tina. The light from the bus was very bright on her and I will always remember her face. She looked much as you do today, very beautiful. Except she had no scar."

No, of course she didn't. Just as my face was free of blemish until my mother shot me.

I couldn't stand to hear any more. I stood up, brushing away patting hands, arms that offered clumsy embraces. "I'm going for a walk."

Dusty jumped up and reached for me. I brushed his hands away, too. "Leave me alone."

I left them all staring at me, staring at the odd, scarred, yellow-haired woman who had wanted to know so much and who now wanted to know so little. With my back straight, my eyes wide against the glaring sun, I walked back along the tumbled-rock beach towards the hotel, away from the noisy cantinas, the music, the laughter. The only things I wanted to hear were surf and gulls. I wanted to think nothing, to feel nothing, to be nothing.

I don't know how long I walked but when I finally stopped, I could no longer see Agnezia's Cantina and the Hotel Vina Del Mar was little more than an angular shape on the cliff. Volcanic boulders cast long shadows on the beach. At some point, the gulls had ceased their raucous cries. The roar of the surf had descended to a murmur. Suddenly exhausted, I sat down on a volcanic rock and stared out to sea.

Part of me, I realized, had always known. The nightmare I'd had right after Clarice's murder had not been about her, it had been about my mother. The gun was my mother's gun. The voice was my mother's voice. The promise to kill, my mother's promise. Somewhere in my unconscious mind, the memory of that night lurked to ambush me again and again in my dreams. No wonder, then, that all my life I had been plagued with insomnia, that I always went to bed terrified of sleep, surrendering to it only when sheer exhaustion lowered my defenses and the book I'd taken to keep me awake slipped from my hands. Wherever she might really be right now, my mother remained a constant fixture in that twilight life, waiting for me with a gun.

What had my mother found so unlovable about me that she had tried to take my life? I was four years old, a child. What were my sins? What acts could a child of that age perform to earn so much hatred, so much rage? I remembered the beatings I had endured from some of my foster homes, the rapes, the thousands of humiliations, the betrayals. What had all those people, in total agreement with my mother, seen in me that I couldn't see?

What was wrong with me, had always been wrong with me?

The knowledge the afternoon had thrust at me hammered home a hard lesson. Almost everyone I had ever known, even Malik Toshumbe, had taken their right to live for granted. But that wasn't true of me. I'd always felt like a cheat, as if by simply breathing in the earth's air, I was stealing precious resources away from the rest of humanity. I felt like a nothing, a creature with no right to live. Something precious, something that all other human beings owned in abundance, had been left out of the biological stew as it formed in my mother's womb.

And that's why I'd always felt that I had to *earn* my right to life, the real reason I became a cop. To protect all the others, the lucky stiffs who had a right to be here. I wasn't really human. I was just a tool to be used in defense of the others, little more than a human gun.

Now that I knew that, really understood it, I didn't want to go on. It was just too hard.

Crimson and violet streaked the sky as the sun slipped towards the ocean. Two pelicans waddled up the beach towards me, their mouths open, hissing dark threats. Twilight would fall soon, bringing the evening's chill. It occurred to me that if I was going to kill myself, I might as well do it now while the water was still warm.

But I sat there a little longer, imagining how it would be to start swimming towards that fiery sun, to swim and swim until my arms grew too tired to swim any more. Then I thought about how it would feel to slip beneath the surface, to sink towards the ocean floor, to lie dreamless among the seaweed.

I thought about it until I realized that although I did not really want to live, I wasn't yet ready to do anything about it.

After that realization, there was nothing else to do but turn around, go back to the cantina.

To hear the rest.

The others had gone, but Agnezia and Dusty still sat at the table I had abandoned earlier. Agnezia's face was taut with strain, but Dusty's looked no different than usual. He was used to my ways.

"Tina, I am so sorry." Tentatively, she put her hand on mine, expecting me to brush it away again.

But I didn't. Grasping her hand firmly, I told the biggest lie I'd ever told in my worthless life. "Thank you for saving me."

She began to weep again. "The good God, he put me there for you."

If the good God was so protective of me, I wondered bitterly, why did the bastard let me get shot in the first place? And then shot two more times? How about that drug dealer who knifed me back in '92, and who left me with a six-inch scar on my left breast? Or the batterer who had almost choked me to death before he could be subdued? These God-worshippers were always so blind to the truth. I wanted to stand up and scream that there was no God, but if there was, He was a serial killer with a sadistic sense of humor.

But I didn't. Agnezia had saved my life and deserved respect. "Yes, God sent you to be my guardian angel," I lied again.

I heard a choking noise and looked around to see Dusty sitting there with a half-smile on his face. He'd heard my diatribes about religion, knew what I thought about the fools who packed the pews every Sunday. He shook his head slightly at me, warning me not to lay it on too thick.

Agnezia was oblivious to my dishonesty. "You must come with me to my house where my family has prepared a great meal in your honor. You must tell us all about your life, about what you have done, where you have been. We all want to know. You have grown into a beautiful, strong woman, my Tina, and we want to know what glories you have accomplished."

Glories?

I'd disappoint them, just as I had disappointed everyone else. My mother had just been the first of a very long list. But I smiled and agreed. I was hungry.

And acting halfway normal was always easier during a meal.

Agnezia had married as soon as she returned to Mexico. She had seven children, ten grandchildren, and a handsome husband named Umberto who was the chef at her cantina. She had done well for herself. Her house was neither large nor luxurious according to American standards, but it placed her squarely in Mexico's middle class. The rooms were freshly whitewashed, with bright sombreros and serapes covering the walls. Above the tiled fireplace in the living room hung a picture of a laughing Jesus, one of the first I had ever seen of him with dark eyes and hair—which if he really existed, he probably had.

Gaily painted wooden chairs completed a conversational grouping made up of gold-crushed velvet, and on the floor, hand-woven rugs used all the colors of the rainbow. Oddly, the overall effect was not gaudy, just cheerful. Madeline, my artist foster mother, would probably have told me that was probably because all the colors used were colors that existed together in nature. Blue for the sea, gold for the sun, red for the bougainvillea that cascaded over the town, green for the palms lining the seafront. The colors might be bright, but when used in the same proportions found in nature, they worked.

Near the door leading into the kitchen was an altar surrounded by fresh flowers, the Madonna guarding this one as she had Mrs. Albundo's. The pictures included every person sitting at the dining room table, and even a few people I didn't recognize. But one picture stood out, a picture cut from a Phoenix newspaper of a blond-haired child with a bandage over her eye. Underneath was the caption, "Do you know this little girl?"

Mine was the only picture with a silver frame.

"My family, it is still growing," Agnezia said, as she finished introducing all her family members. "Angelina, my youngest, she is pregnant again. We think it will be twins."

Angelina, who was sitting next to a startlingly handsome young man, blushed and ducked her head. He nudged her in the side with his elbow and said something in Spanish I didn't understand. It made her giggle and cover her mouth.

"Angelina, Stephan, I have told you not to be dirty at the table," Umberto, Agnezia's husband, admonished even though his eyes were laughing. He and the grandchildren were loading the long dining table with serving platters heaped with shrimp, oysters, chicken- and beef-stuffed enchiladas, chili rellenos, rice, beans, and piles and piles of hot tortillas.

I started to reach for a tortilla, then stopped when I saw everyone's hands assume the prayer position. Agnezia began saying Grace, and out of consideration for her Anglo guests, she said it in English. She thanked God for the table's bounty, the success of her cantina, and called down blessings upon family, friends and neighbors. Then, in that sing-song voice common to those who have committed a long list to memory, began petitioning her deity to help the troubled members of the family. She prayed for someone name Olivera who lived in Nogales and suffered from some sort of secret trouble. She prayed for Carlos, jailed in Los Angeles. At the very end, Agnezia prayed, "And may the good God keep our Tina safe and protect her always, wherever she is."

There was a gasp around the table, then giggles. Blushing, Agnezia looked over at me. "I guess He has already answered the prayer."

Umberto smiled at his wife and asked, "Now that we know Tina is safe, do we drop her from the list?"

Agnezia shook her head. "No, *mi corazon*. I think our Tina still needs our prayers."

By the look she gave me, I felt that Agnezia had somehow heard my thoughts as I'd sat on the rock, staring out to sea. But I'd be damned if I ever admitted to them. "I'm fine," I said, looking her straight in the eyes. "Just fine."

In all my life, I'd never seen a woman's eyes grow so loving yet at the same time, so sad.

I decided to consider Agnezia my mother, and let the real one remain in the past.

I never wanted to look in *that* woman's eyes.

Chapter 24

"So do I call you Tina now?" Kryzinski asked.

I was sitting in his office filling out the police report about the Papago Park shooter, even though Kryzinski and I both knew that the chances of finding him were slim to zip. Or at least slim until we I.D.'d Clarice's murderer.

It was Saturday. Dusty and I had stayed another day in Rocky Point, getting to know Agnezia's family, walking on the silver beach, making love on clean, white sheets. But now Dusty had returned to the ranch, and I was trying my best to continue my life as if I didn't know what I knew, as if what I'd discovered hadn't half killed me.

"Lena will do fine, thanks." Why should I feel loyalty to a name given to me by an attempted murderer?

Kryzinski shifted in his seat. I couldn't tell if he was as uncomfortable with the expression on my face as Jimmy had been, or if it was just his silly suit. Today he was wearing a shiny blue Western suit with cream-colored piping, and ostrich-skin boots.

He looked at me warily, as if unsure whether I'd cry, scream, collapse, or heave his computer through the window. "Ah, have you read the paper yet this morning?"

I shook my head. I'd been too busy convincing Jimmy that I was fine, thank you, just fine.

"Then you need to hear about Alison Garwood," he said.

"What about her?" I was still struggling with the incident report. Even during my own days on the force, I had hated filling out police reports. Too many lines of tiny print, too many pages, too much attention to detail. A misquote now, a faulty recollection committed to paper, and perps walked.

"Kobe put her in the hospital."

I jerked my head up. "What?"

Kryzinski nodded. "You remember she was pregnant? Well, not anymore. He beat her so bad this time that she miscarried. She's also got her jaw wired together and a couple of cracked ribs. Her left eye socket? The creepoid shattered it. She's gonna have to go a few rounds with the plastic surgeon this time."

The pencil snapped in my hand and I let it fall to the floor. It wasn't that I was surprised. I wasn't. Once a man begins to batter, he's started down a road from which there is no turning back. The violence escalates until slaps turn into punches, bites become knife attacks, thrown ashtrays become bullets. Yet such was the denial on the part of the victims that they pretended they couldn't see the increasing savagery of the attacks. Chances were good that Alison was right now lying in her hospital bed, wondering whether to call a cab to take her back home or to have Jay come and get her.

Then something Kryzinski said jogged a memory.

"Did you say she had a shattered eye socket?" I remembered Clarice's face, the shattered eye socket, and it occurred to me— could Jay have set up Gus Baylor? Was he smarter than any of us had given him credit for? Was Clarice's murder simply one more case of domestic violence after all?

"Yeah, a shattered eye socket. The left one." Kryzinski's eyes met mine. He was thinking what I was thinking.

I leaned over, picked up the broken pencil, and held out my hand for a new one. Within ten minutes I'd finished filling out the incident report and Kryzinski told me he'd find some sucker, probably the young patrolman I'd met a few days earlier, to type it up for him. Then I'd need to sign it.

"Yeah, yeah. Call me and let me know when you want me to come back down. Um, what hospital is Alison in?"

He looked at me hard. "Scottsdale Memorial. You sure *you're* okay?"

I threw him a bright, lying smile and left.

Alison looked even worse than I expected. Her face was swollen the size of a Phoenix Suns basketball and just about the same color. Purple and orange bruises obscured the skin to the point where she could have been any race, any sex. Her very humanity had been stripped, leaving her reduced to nothing more than a throbbing vessel of pain.

We had a lot in common, Alison and I.

I sat down on the chair beside her, knowing better than to ask her how she felt. "I know you can't talk, Alison, so I'm going to tell you what I need to tell you and then I'll leave. If you go back home, he's going to kill you, just as he might have already killed someone else. Men like Jay don't change. He may cry, he may beg you not to leave him, but once you give in and stay, he'll have learned that no matter how hard he beats you, you'll always forgive him. Save your life, Alison. Leave him now."

A tear slipped out of the purple slit that remained of her right eye. The left was invisible, hidden under layers of bandages. She tried to say something, but with her wired jaw the words emerged as gibberish.

Her grief took me out of my own so for a while, I sat there with her in silence. Eventually, I patted her hand and placed a card on her nightstand. "This is for My Sister's Place. It's a woman's shelter, and all you need to do is call them, and they'll take you to a safe place where Jay can't find you."

Her face was so damaged that I couldn't tell if she was receptive to what I was saying or not. I hoped for both our sakes that she was. If Jay wound up killing her, as he seemed ready to do, I didn't know how I'd handle it. Since leaving the police force, I'd lost my professional detachment. I wanted to get Jay Kobe in a small, dark room and do to him what he'd done to Alison...

And maybe Clarice.

Saturday or not, the office was open when I got back. Over my protests, Jimmy had decided to skip his weekend plans. He was on the computer again, checking out the history of every single bus that had ever been registered in New Mexico. Unlike me, he was humming with contentment.

He stopped humming when I walked through the door and he saw my face.

"Are you okay?"

Why did the whole world keep asking me that? "I'm fine, dammit, fine!"

He looked like he was about to say something, then changed his mind and turned back to his computer. I sat down at my desk and pretended to be busy. After a while, Jimmy spun his chair around and asked, "How's that woman? Alison Garwood?"

"I think she might go back to him."

Jimmy surprised me by looking angry, something he almost never did. "I had a cousin like that, up in Utah. Every time her husband beat her, she'd pretend it was the only time it had ever happened. Tunnel vision. She'd never look at the big picture, she'd just focus on the most recent beating, like—he wouldn't have done it if she hadn't served the steak medium instead of medium rare."

"It was always her fault, right?"

"Yeah. Never his."

"Did she ever leave him?"

Jimmy was quiet for a moment, then nodded. "In a way. One night he finally beat her to death and her spirit left for good."

There was nothing I could say to that.

I'd done all I could to help Alison and now Jimmy was doing all he could to help me. Both of us were failures.

Jimmy returned to his computer and I to the one skill I'd learned in a rather pointless life, piling theory upon theory, fact upon fact, cutting the murderer out of a whole herd of likely suspects. Clarice's Dayrunner in hand, I began making phone calls. The first was to Emily Ruzan, the attorney who was representing her in her civil case against her father. Ruzan wasn't thrilled about speaking to me on the phone, but since her client was dead, she made an exception.

"Clarice dropped the action," she finally admitted. "Two days before her death."

The snake I'd thought I left in Mexico was back and slithering up my spine. "Did she say why?"

"No."

"Was there some sort of out-of-court settlement?"

"Not that I'm aware of. And I am, ah, *was,* her attorney. She did, though, set up an appointment to see me on, ah…"

I heard the sound of papers rustling.

"Here it is. She was due in here on Friday. But, um, she didn't make it."

"Friday?"

"Yeah, she was dead by then."

The snake did the mambo. "Do you have any idea what she wanted to talk to you about?"

"I'm afraid not. I just assumed it had something to do with her father and the civil action she'd brought against him."

"And dropped."

"That's right. And dropped."

Ruzan couldn't help me further so I rang off. I sat at my desk for a moment, thinking. Ruzan was a civil attorney, but she handled no divorce work. Besides, Clarice had a divorce lawyer, and she'd seen him the week before she was killed.

I called Lawrence Sallis but he only reiterated what I already knew. The divorce was proceeding apace and there had been no hitches. Clarice wasn't even going to have to pay alimony, because the moment she had poked her battered face into Sallis's office, he'd had hustled her off to a photographer to document the damage Jay had inflicted on her. He'd also personally escorted her to Scottsdale PD where she'd filed a domestic abuse complaint.

"Financially we had Jay by the balls," Sallis said. "But just between you and me and the lamppost, a lot of these battered women turn out to be a lot more careful about their money than they are of their bodies."

I couldn't argue with that. I had one final question. "Do you know what set Jay off that last time, the one that made Clarice leave him?"

Sallis made a disgusted sound. "Just the usual."

"And what was 'the usual'?"

"Money. Jay wanted her to sign off on that contract, she didn't, so he beat the shit out of her. Wrong move, I guess."

"What contract?"

"Oh, you know, the development agreement for that golf course she and her family own, the one everyone's so upset about. The Hacienda Palms. Now, I'd love to talk to you some more, but I've got a very high profile and very unhappy client cooling her heels out in the lobby. But call me anytime, especially if you ever need my services."

I hung up and stared at the phone.

Have you heard the rumors about the golf course? Eleanor Hyath had said, and stupid me, I'd put her words down to mere conversation. If I'd thought about it, I'd have known that Eleanor wasn't the type to make "conversation." And damn the malicious bitch to hell, she'd made me pop for an outrageous lunch at a resort she actually *owned*.

I left the other phone calls for later and took off for Scottsdale City Hall where Mildred, a clerk I'd known since my days at the Violent Crimes Unit, had agreed to sneak me into the closed records office. She wouldn't even accept my offer of a bribe, the fact that I had once kept her grandson out of jail being good enough for her. My search didn't take long. The papers had been filed late Friday afternoon and the public hearing was set for next week.

Pre-application for Zoning Change, it brayed at the top of the form. After flipping through dozens of pages of legalese, I finally found what I thought I'd find. The Van Vechten Trust was listed as the owner of the Hacienda Palms Resort, with Eleanor Van Vechten Hyath, Evan Hyath, Serena Hyath-Allesandro, and Clarice Hyath Kobe as equal principals. At the bottom, where the notarized signatures were affixed, one was missing.

Clarice's.

"Awfully short-sighted of you," Eleanor had said when I told her I wasn't interested in talking about golf courses.

For once Eleanor had been right, because the forms in front of me revealed that the Hyaths were about to turn the legendary Hacienda Palms Golf Course into upscale condominiums.

As soon as I had calmed down, I waved the forms to Mildred. She might have been pushing seventy, but she was going down with all flags flying, wearing enough makeup to stock an entire Merle Norman counter.

"How's this kind of thing handled, Mildred? And how long's it been in the works?"

Crow's feet traveled all the way from her thin mouth to her crepe-bordered eyes. "The proposed Hacienda Palms zoning change? Oh, lord, Lena, word has it that thing's been hanging fire for a couple of years, but they managed to file the papers yesterday. I think they wanted things to settle a bit over the weekend before the newspapers got wind of it and took up residence in their assholes. The thing is, sure, the Hacienda Palms is private property and all that, but when something's as much of an institution as that place has been, the city's always gonna get involved.

"What's going to happen is, they've gotta bring their plans before both the public and the Zoning Commission. And they'll have to present an environmental impact study that proves there won't be any kind of negative impact on wildlife or desert areas. Not that it looks like there will be, because that resort's in the center of town now and there's no wildlife left to speak of. Just the coyotes and javelinas that trot in from the rez. But this kind of thing's always a long, drawn-out process and a lot of fingers are going to be dipping into that pie before it's out of the oven."

I looked back down at the forms. "You mean they can just do that, then? Rip out the Hacienda Palms Golf Course to build condos?"

She made a small moue of displeasure. "Lena, I've seen the city turn down only three re-zoning applications since I've been here, and I've been here since they were still herding cows down the middle of Scottsdale Road. Unless the City Council puts the brakes on the zoning change, the Hyaths can build any damned thing they want to. Hell, we're talking private enterprise here, and that still counts for something in this state. Now let's get out of here before we get caught. I think that Captain Kryzinski is a fine man even if he is from Brooklyn but I don't want to know him any better than I have to. Jail's jail, if you get my meaning."

She ushered me out of the building and locked up behind me. I drove back to the office deep in thought, not even responding to Jimmy's friendly wave.

I sat down at the desk and began dialing. Serena didn't answer the phone, so I tried Evan. The mumbles which came across the wire alerted me to the fact that he was having lunch, but I didn't let that faze me.

"Hey, Evan, I've just found out about the application for the Hacienda Palms zoning change and I'm wondering if I can ask you some questions."

I heard a groan, the rustling of paper, a few crunches. Was he just stalling?

"Whayawannaknow?"

"How long has the family been planning to replace that golf course with a housing development?"

"Eroulaivers."

"Huh?"

A few loud gulps, then his voice became clearer. "I said for about the last five years, when Mother got this bug up her ass about it. What started it all, I don't know, but I think it had something to do with this big fight Mother and Father had. When, uh, Clarice, um, started…saying things. You know. Anyway, the place was owned by my maternal grandfather who'd bought it from this old TB doctor, and for years it's been frozen in a family trust. The way the trust is set up, you see, we're all equal partners, and everyone has to agree on a plan before we can do anything. Now that you've met us, you probably know how *that* works out! And the Hacienda Palms was no exception. First Serena didn't want to do it. When she finally changed her mind, Clarice didn't want to do it. Then Clarice changed her mind and *I* didn't want to do it. I think over the years, we all changed our minds at least once. No. That's wrong. Mother never changed her mind. She always wanted to develop. Hates golf, loves money."

That part of his story didn't make sense. Anybody who's lived in the Valley for more than a year knows that golf is one of the main money-makers in town, accounting for millions of dollars of revenue. Any resort boasting a golf course could be considered permanently flush. Nope, it just didn't fly, and I told him so.

"C'mon, Evan, ripping out that cash cow makes no sense. Sure, you'll get the one time hit of the land sale, but after that, what have you got? Zero, zip, zilch, nothing."

Evan made an odd sound. Then I realized he was choking. I heard some slurps, a couple of more hacks, then he came back on the line.

"Miss Jones, you've been reading too many brochures from the Scottsdale Visitors' Bureau," he said, his voice only slightly hoarse. "Sure, if the Hacienda Palms Golf Course was a full eighteen-hole course, it'd be making us a fortune. But it's not. It's just *nine* holes, and at this point, watering the damned thing and keeping that artificial stream running is costing us more money than it's bringing in. People who really love the game aren't interested in any little ol' shot-and-putt piece of shit, and they're more than willing to pay those exorbitant fees up on the pro courses. Those are the big money-makers in this town."

While I would never have called the Hacienda Palms Golf Course a piece of shit, Evan's story held together. "Doesn't the Hacienda Palms have the room to expand it into eighteen holes?"

"Hell, no. We're butted right up against the mountain and we've got established housing developments on the other three sides."

"So from time to time you discussed the prospect of going for the money."

"Yep. Over the years, that damned golf course was responsible for more family fights than Mother's drinking. Or Dad's, well, you know."

One final question loomed large. "But you finally all agreed."

"Finally."

I wondered if he would lie to me. "Who was the last holdout, Evan?"

A couple of more munches, then a gulp. "Clarice, I think. I seem to remember her being pretty upset when the board of the Museum of Western Art wouldn't give her the curator's job. As I'm sure you know, they were horrified by that old woman's death and besides that, they'd always been pretty unimpressed with Clarice's artistic taste. When she realized it was hopeless, Clarice decided to make conserving the golf course her... her *artistic legacy,* as she termed it. Something like that, anyway. The family thought she was nuts. They were all, myself included, hot to get the money the redevelopment would bring, but Clarice wouldn't budge. God, did we all have one helluva fight! I'm surprised the neighbors didn't call the police. But they don't do that much on the mountain, do they?"

More munches, then finally, "Whaialaou?" A gulp. "Sorry. What's this all about?"

I told him I wasn't sure, apologized for disturbing his lunch, and hung up.

How much money were we talking about here? Hundreds of thousands? Millions? Enough to kill for? The Hyaths were richer than God, but that didn't mean anything. For some people, too much was never enough.

I'd think more about that later, but for now, I had a few more phone calls to make. I reached for the phone again and dialed up to the San Carlos Apache Reservation, where Mrs. Haozous volunteered the information that her husband was down in Phoenix for the next few days, dancing the Art Dealer Tango.

"I told him he's got to quit sulking and start doing some business," she said. "You were his first sale in months."

She told me he was staying with an old friend on the Pima Reservation and gave me the man's name, phone number, and directions on how to get to his house.

When I called the number she gave me, somebody named Lloyd Gray picked up. His voice was familiar. I identified myself and he said, "I remember you. You're the detective who brought that Jeep in to Michael Sisiwan's to be painted. How's it driving these days?"

"It's driving proud," I told him. "Um, is George Haozous there? I need to speak to him if he is."

"I'll get him."

He set the phone down and walked away. In the background I heard him yelling, "George! George! You got a phone call!" Footsteps tapped back to the phone. "He was out back petting my horse. He'll be here in a second. Say, how's that Jimmy doing? He's my nephew, you know. On his mother's side."

I handed the phone across to Jimmy, who said a few words in Piman, then handed it back. His smile had turned into a frown. "That Apache's on the line now."

I took the phone back. "George, it's Lena Jones. I need to talk to you."

He didn't say anything but I heard him breathing.

"George? George are you there?"

"Is there a problem with the painting?" he finally asked. "It giving you nightmares or something?"

"No, no. The painting's great, cheers up the room. Not that I bought it as an object of décor, you understand." This was not the time to offend him, however mad I was feeling at the whole world.

"Yeah, yeah. If it's not the painting, then, what do you want? I'm real busy over here."

Sure, pestering horses and stuff. "It's probably not important, but I need to talk to you about something concerning Clarice. Are you free to talk now? Or would you like to set up an appointment for me to come over there? I know my way around the rez pretty well."

Another long silence, more noisy breathing. Was it my imagination, or was Haozous's breath coming faster, as if he were nervous about something?

"Look, Lena, I don't want to talk about this over the phone and I don't want to talk about it anywhere near Lloyd's house. I'll drive to your apartment."

Now it was my turn to get nervous. Ever since my trip to Rocky Point, I'd felt emotionally needy and Dusty was the only person I knew who could comfort me when I was feeling blue. I didn't feel like risking our relationship again quite so soon. Which definitely included not inviting a sexy—and married—Apache up to my apartment.

"Want to meet for a drink at the Rusty Spur?"

The man had enough silences left in him to make a 1910 movie. But he finally said, "I don't drink anymore. How about coffee at Denny's? Ah, on second thought, not Denny's. Too public."

Now I was really curious. What did Haozous have to tell me that couldn't be shouted out to one and all at Denny's? I mentioned the espresso bar Mrs. Albundo liked, and we agreed to meet there at four o'clock.

After I hung up, I checked my watch and looked across the street. The OPEN sign on Damon and Pythias showed that Cliffie was back from lunch, so I told Jimmy I'd be gone for a few moments and walked over there.

Cliffie didn't look all that happy to see me. He was straightening some paintings when I walked in and gave me a feeble wave. Then he turned back around and continued messing with the paintings.

I really liked the painting he was working on, a Jacques Louis David in full neo-classical flight. It portrayed a Greek warrior, naked except for his helmet, restraining a rearing stallion. The horse was fluid, his colors appearing to float off the canvas, but the warrior was static, posed. The contrast was amazingly sexy.

"David or a copy?" I asked Cliffie, more to get his attention than anything else.

He turned, eyebrows raised. Was it my imagination or did he look downright hostile? "There are no copies in this gallery, Lena. And if you don't mind, I'm pretty busy here."

I gave the gallery the once-over. The floor had been polished to a soft glow and a gardenia-based perfume filled the air. Fresh yellow roses filled the window. Other than the David, the paintings all hung square.

"Busy doing what, Cliffie? Busy avoiding me?"

"I don't know what you're talking about."

I walked up behind him and stood close enough for him to feel my body heat. As I had hoped, it bothered him.

"Really, Lena, if you're going to do that, you might have the decency to use a better perfume. That *Eau de Dial* is somewhat less than subtle." But he didn't move away. He was probably afraid to.

"Cliffie, what was the subject of your meeting with Clarice two nights before her murder?"

A quick intake of breath, and the David was crooked again. "Now see what you made me do!"

"Better talk to me, Cliffie. It's either me or Captain Kryzinski."

He finally turned around, a resigned expression on his face. But he gave it one last try. "We just went out to dinner. That's what friends do."

Now I had him. Clarice was too civilized to eat at six. Her style ran to eight and sometimes even nine o'clock. "Which restaurant? I can check."

"Why can't you just leave it alone?" His baby's face was tight, drained of color. Even the gloss had vanished from his well-groomed white hair. Something was eating at this man, and eating hard. "Jay killed her. That's all you need to know. Why do you continue to pester everyone?"

I was on the verge of losing another friend, but what else was new. "What are you hiding?"

He darted a look at the door, but no customer walked through it to save him. "Lena, do we have to do this?"

"Yes, Cliffie, we do have to do this. Tell me what you and Clarice talked about that night."

His deep sigh told me that I had him. "All right, but let's go sit down. My back is killing me. I moved that damned desk all by myself this morning and it looks like I'm going to pay for it with a trip to the chiropractor."

I noticed then that he was walking hunched over like an old man. I glanced at the heavy Louis Quatorze desk. It appeared to be in the same position as I'd seen it last time.

He saw my look. "Last week I moved it to the alcove there..." Here he pointed to a niche near the window. "...but I wound up not liking it so this morning I moved it back."

It could even have been true.

"Sit down, sit down." He motioned me to a chair, then bustled around getting us drinks, apparently trying to stave off the inevitable by playing the proper host.

I didn't touch the Diet Coke he set in front of me. "Quit stalling, Cliffie. What did you and Clarice discuss?"

He gave me a look so naked with rage that for a moment I was frightened. I dropped my hand to my side, then remembered that I'd left my gun back at the office. Who would have thought I'd need it for my interview with good ol' Cliffie?

The rage vanished as quickly as if someone had wiped it out with a giant eraser. "It was a business meeting, if you have to know."

"About?"

The rage battled its way forward again but with steely self-control, Cliffie kept it hidden behind those plump, friendly cheeks. "She wanted to, um, talk to me about leasing my space."

Which must mean that Cliffie was thinking about moving out. Like most of the other galleries in this part of town, Damon and Pythias held a very tenant-friendly lease. The only reason to give that up would be because you'd found better quarters elsewhere. But there was no elsewhere. The city was locked down tight. The rents on Gallery Row up on Stetson Drive were higher because the Art Walk crowds were a little heavier there than down here. Cliffie would be crazy to move.

Unless he had to.

Suddenly his drawn face and bent back took on an alarming note. Frightened for him, I blurted out my concerns. "Are you sick?"

He offered a bitter smile. "That's what people always think, isn't it, when one of us isn't having a very good day? AIDS, the big homosexual bugaboo. Thanks for your concern, dear, but I'm fit as a fiddle and testing negative. Except for my back, which I really did hurt while moving this damned desk, may King Louis rot in hell for the grief he has caused me."

I felt better but that didn't mean I was going to let up on him. "Glad to know you're fit as a fiddle, Cliffie. Now tell me why you want to move out of here."

He looked down at the desk, as if contemplating the culpability of Louis Quatorze's craftsmen. "I never said I wanted to move out of here."

At that point, a customer entered the gallery and Cliffie jumped up, spry as a teenager. Relief will do that for you. But Cliffie's reprieve was short-lived. The customer's expression (he obviously hadn't understood the significance of the gallery's name) segued from befuddlement to disgust in the space of seconds. Cliffie winked at me when the customer left, slamming the door behind him.

"What is our educational system coming to these days when people don't know who Damon and Pythias were?" he moaned theatrically.

"C'mon, Cliffie. Half of them don't even know who Socrates was. Now sit back down and tell me what was going on between you and Clarice. You said she wanted your space but you said you weren't moving."

He sat back down. "Nothing's going on—now. Ding dong, the witch is dead."

Now it was my turn to feel befuddled, but I played along anyway. "Which old witch?"

"The wicked witch."

Suddenly it all came together. Cliffie's worried expression over the past few weeks, Clarice's look of smug satisfaction. "Clarice was trying to get you thrown out of the building, wasn't she?"

"Hole in one, kid."

"But *why?*"

Cliffie sighed. "She wanted to expand. I don't think you realize what not getting appointed to the board of that miserable museum did to her. It was a slap in the face, and she knew it. So she decided she'd show them all and operate the biggest cowboy art gallery in town. She'd already picked up the lease on that vacant spot next to me and the gallery west of hers, and now she needed my space to make a clean sweep of the block."

"But she couldn't do that, could she? You've got a lease!"

His smile turned grim. "Oh, sure, I've got a lease. But there's a couple of lines of legalese in there that make my lease dependent on the good will of my neighbors. Just like the sainted Rodney King said, we're all supposed to just get along down here, 'cause fussin' and fightin's bad for Scottsdale's image."

"Still…you weren't giving anybody any problems. It seems like Clarice was the real rat in the nest. Surely the landlord would see that."

He snorted a bitter laugh. "Oh, really? You seem to forget what kind of gallery I'm operating here. It's a *gay* gallery, dear heart. And while Scottsdale doesn't exactly hold pogroms for its gay residents, when it comes to business, Scottsdale basically enforces a 'don't ask, don't tell' policy. All it would take to get me booted out of here is for someone to start raising a stink, and that's what Clarice said she was going to do if I didn't back out of my lease and let her pick it up."

Then, surprisingly, he reached over and patted my hand. "I know you liked her, Lena, but you never really knew her. Sure, on the surface Clarice was all bright smiles and intelligent conversation, but inside she was as hard as that ugly granite fountain of hers. Whatever she wanted, she went after—no matter who it belonged to and no matter how much it would hurt them to lose it. The only times she ever thought about other people was in figuring out how she could use them. She cultivated an acquaintance with you—don't be shocked, my dear—because she thought knowing a private detective might someday come in handy. She'd noticed, you see, that you don't always charge for the work that you do. And…"

He paused, probably not sure if I wanted to hear any more.

I didn't, but I told him to continue anyway.

"Well, she was pretty hot for that cowboy of yours."

I felt my own face drain of color as I remembered Clarice always telling me to bring Dusty to her gallery openings and her obvious disappointment when he didn't show.

Seeing my expression, Cliffie said, "My dear, Clarice was a supremely selfish woman, and everybody knew it. Except you. Why is that, do you think?"

No problem answering that one. When you've lived like I have, under the rocks with the rest of the bugs, you don't want to look at anyone too carefully.

But I didn't tell him that. Instead, I said, "So now she's dead and you're off the hook."

Cliffie beamed. "Ding dong."

The espresso bar was filled with tourists and by the time George Haozous joined me at a table towards the back, I'd heard accents from Germany, Japan, France, and Brooklyn. Due to the heat of the day—a hundred and eighteen degrees—I'd ordered an iced café mocha. With two scoops of ice cream.

"Jesus, this heat," Haozous complained as he slipped into the booth across from me. "I can't wait to get back to San Carlos."

"I thought you didn't mind the heat."

"Yeah, usually I don't, but damn, this is ridiculous."

His mahogany face was beaded with sweat and dark circles had formed under the armpits of his snowy cotton shirt. I gave him time to order a root beer float, then shoved a photocopy of Clarice's Dayrunner under his nose. "If you and Clarice were on such bad terms, why were you seeing her every Tuesday night?"

He looked at the book and made a disgusted sound. "I can't believe she did that, pencilled me in. Jesus." Then he looked up at me. "C'mon, Miss Jones. You weren't born yesterday. Why do you think?"

I thought about his bronze skin, his buff body, his sexy moves in my apartment. "You were having an affair with her, weren't you?"

His laugh was ugly. "Affair. Yeah, I guess you could call it that. I figured as long as I was shagging her she'd keep my paintings in the gallery. It worked for a while, too. Then sometime near the end of June she got sick of me or maybe she found somebody else. Whatever the reason, she booted me and my paintings right out of her suck-ass gallery, slam bam thank you ma'am."

He attacked his root beer float greedily while I sat there stunned. When I could finally speak, I said, "You mean you prostituted yourself just to keep your paintings in there?"

"Damn right I did and you don't need to sound so righteous. I'm not the only artist who ever used his ass…" He grinned. "… or *her* ass to further a career."

I felt as naïve as a Sunday school teacher in a bordello. "Does your wife know?"

"Get real. Natuende would cut it off by the root if she ever found out."

A vision of the sweet-faced woman in the trailer rose up before me. Some judge of people I was turning out to be.

When he saw the expression on my face, he threw back his head and roared. The tourists looked around to see who was making that jolly noise. Their eyes bugged when they saw it was an Apache.

Gee whiz, Martha, these redskins laugh just like us! Now ain't that something?

After Haozous headed out the door, I sat there staring at the remains of my café mocha shake. Emily Ruzan, Evan, Cliffie, Haozous—everything they'd told me hinted at a terrible truth.

But I had to be sure.

Abandoning my café mocha, I went back out to the Jeep and headed towards the mountain. No, I had no appointment, but if the Hyaths refused to see me, I'd simply stand at the front door of that mausoleum and shout out what I suspected for all their high-toned neighbors to hear. And somehow, I didn't think that would be necessary.

Randall was waxing the Rolls again as I drove up.

"They won't…"

"Tell them I know why Clarice dropped the civil action and if they don't talk to me, I'll tell the whole fucking world."

His face lit up like a kid's on Christmas Eve. "You got some dirt on them, huh?"

"Believe me, Randall, you don't want to know."

"I might surprise you." But he told me to wait there while he announced my presence.

My threat worked. Within minutes, I was seated in the dead-animal living room with both of the Hyaths, trying my best to keep from clawing their eyes out. Eleanor wasn't entirely sober but neither was she entirely drunk. She wore a chartreuse-and-navy silk warm-up suit that had never been seen near a workout room. Its front was spotted with the usual food and wine stains. Her greasy hair hung in strings to her shoulders and a sour odor wafted from her body. The woman repulsed me but I knew that in her condition, she'd be easy to bait.

Stephen Hyath was his usual withdrawn self, but I figured that wouldn't last long. I remembered that the only photograph of Clarice that remained in the house was in his den. In his own sick way, he'd cared more for her than her mother ever had.

"Clarice was coming back to you, wasn't she?" I said to him.

He tried to restrain the pride from leaping to his face, but failed. "I was the only man in her life who was good to her."

Eleanor looked at him as if she wanted to kill him, and who knew, maybe she did. "Sluts. The both of you."

"Moi?" I put a hand to my heart in pretended hurt.

"No, you scarred-face bitch. Him! Him and her! Dogs in heat, that's all they were!" She belched a wet, noisy belch that hinted at all sorts of ugly liquid combinations.

Stephen, though, was as cool as ever. "You don't know what true love is," he said to his wife. "You never knew."

"Love!" She made it sound like a dirty word.

It was really none of my business, but I couldn't keep from asking the still-handsome man, "Why did you marry Eleanor?"

"I needed the money." His face was granite.

Eleanor's own face was immobile, too, and I realized she wasn't hearing anything she hadn't heard a hundred times before. Then I remembered our luncheon, and the brief pain that had flashed across her face when she'd talked about her marriage. Hyath probably hadn't even bothered keeping his lack of love a secret. The first time he'd revealed his contempt for his bride, it had probably hurt her. The second time, the bride had begun keeping score and proceeded to act accordingly—which meant in her case, to hate her husband's children. That they were also her own children meant nothing because her hatred had already infected every cell of her being, making her unable to love.

Eleanor Hyath was a modern-day Medea.

And what had the mythical Medea done? *To get even with the lover who had jilted her, she murdered her own children.*

Anybody who reads the papers knows that mothers killed their children all the time. We read about the slaughters, shake our heads and murmur, "How shocking!" then turn to Dear Abby. Each week, battered babies turned up in Dumpsters, suspected SIDS deaths turned out to be homicides, mothers torched their children, poisoned them, hacked at them with machetes, and hanged them from shower curtain rods. Arizona even had a woman on Death Row who had paid two men to shoot her four-year-old son in the head so that she could collect $5,000 in insurance money.

Maybe another child-killer was about to end up there.

Her soul rotted by a life-long jealousy, Clarice's mother had certainly wanted to kill her daughter, just as my mother had wanted to kill me. The question was: Did Eleanor possess the same follow-through?

I couldn't ask her outright. She was too wily for that. I asked another question instead, even though I thought I already knew the answer. "Was Clarice planning to move back in here? Or was she…?" The expression on Eleanor's face told me I'd already drawn blood.

Her eyes glittered. "I told her I'd kill her if she tried to move back in."

Stephen put a restraining hand towards her, as if afraid his wife would spring off the sofa and fly at my face. "That was never a consideration. Clarice and I were…" He paused, thought about the way he should phrase it, then began again. "Clarice and I were going to build a house of our own, a place in another country, where we could live our lives without censure."

Without censure.

I thought I'd been able to keep the disgust from my face, but Stephen's next words showed me I'd failed.

"You don't have to look like that, Miss Jones. Clarice was free, white, and twenty-one."

Eleanor had to make her contribution. "And perverted as hell."

I stared at her. During our luncheon, she'd told me that she was bound to her husband by a pre-nupt. When I brought that up, she smiled. It wasn't a pleasant smile.

"Why should I divorce him? Just because he was moving in with his little whore? I wouldn't give them the satisfaction—*or* the money."

I had all I could take. I stood up and walked to the door without looking back.

I didn't know if it was the triple-digit heat or the incredible conversation I'd just been a part of, but halfway back to the office, I had to pull off the road and sit there for a minute. My hands were shaking and the noise of the traffic around me sounded like an *arpeggio* in a discordant modern symphony. I reached over to the passenger's seat and picked up the bottle of water I always kept there. After taking a few swigs, I felt better. But I still needed a bath, if only to wash the memory of the Hyaths off me.

At what point does a victim stop being a victim? As Stephen Hyath so *un*-politically correctly stated, Clarice was free, white, and twenty-one. Theoretically she knew what she was doing and could have been held legally accountable for her actions, as could her father. Then again, she had been molested by him since childhood, suffering—besides innumerable physical indignities—the slow erosion of her moral values. This was the hidden side of incest, the side people rarely talked about because it made them more uncomfortable than the physical act itself.

Before Daddy gets into your pants, he convinces you it's all right. After a while, you even start believing that it is. You tell yourself that what Daddy's doing is all right and with that initial lie, that first ravage against your soul, other lies follow. From an early age, you learn to convince yourself that black is white, that self-interest is love, that pain is pleasure. Your ability to discern truth disintegrates. You may look the same to others on the outside, but inside, in your *heart,* you are rotting away.

I took a final swig from my water bottle and pulled back into traffic.

I needed to run.

I needed to sing the Corn Song.

I needed the world to be sane again.

Chapter 25

But I'm no fool.

The shooter, the person who had killed Clarice, was still out there, so I skipped my usual Papago Park run and turned the Jeep around. I drove north to Cave Creek, then turned off on the road that led to the old Hohokam ruins. The heat pressed against me as I chugged up the narrow path to the time-crumbled village, but I had worse demons to worry about.

Memories of harsh hands, of whispered excuses. Of lies, and lies, and lies.

Some of them my own.

The Baptists' bible had said we must not suffer a witch to live. Why didn't it say the same thing about warlocks? About the dark spells of those men whose passions corrupted young girls' souls and caused their hearts to shrivel? Why didn't it cry out against mothers who hated their daughters enough to kill them?

I wondered for a moment where my own mother was, if she was living her life somewhere content in the belief that I was dead.

Then I closed my mind against her. I would not walk that trail again.

The climb to the ruins took me longer than it should have, because every footstep was weighted by memory. More than a dozen times, I slipped on the shale and brushed my hands against the thorny spines of barrel cactus. By the time I reached the crest of the hill, my hands were drenched with blood and sweat but I welcomed the pain. It chased the memories away.

When I reached the courtyards where the Hohokam had walked and loved and slept before First World was destroyed by water, the air felt pure. With a red-tailed hawk sailing high above me, I stood on the stones of the past and looked out over the present.

And sang.

> *On Tecalote field, the corn was growing green.*
> *Growing green.*
> *I came down to the land and I saw.*
> *I saw the tassels waving in the wind.*
> *And I sang for joy.*

No tassels waved here. The Hohokam were gone, their forgotten fields reclaimed by sage, cactus, and coyote. They dreamed in the Underworld now with Earth Doctor.

The Pimas had taken their place.

As the white man had taken the Pimas' place.

When do sins stop?

I walked over to the edge of the cliff and looked down at the fallen bighorn, its picked-clean bones now gleaming in the sun. In the way of the desert, a few beetles—the tail end of the food chain—still scurried there dining on what tasty morsels still remained. It occurred to me that at the same time the bighorn had fed a small army of scavengers, Clarice's body lay decomposing in a lead-lined casket, protected from predators and benefiting no one, not even the grass growing on her grave.

Modern life made no sense.

Suddenly a wave of sorrow engulfed me for the woman I'd once considered a friend. I thought about the wounds she'd inflicted on others—on Magadalena Espinoza, Dulya Albundo, Cliffie, George Haozous, what she was about to do to her own mother, about to do to me. I thought about all these things, the actions of a soul-twisted woman who would ravage anyone's dreams for her own self-centered desires.

I thought about it as the beetles ran through the bighorn's ribcage, until the sun disappeared behind the mountain and darkness engulfed the valley. I thought about it until I finally figured out who'd killed Clarice.

Chapter 26

When I got home, I showered off the dust and nightmares. Then I poured myself a giant glass of iced tea and sat in front of Haozous's painting for hours, listening to Big Bill Broonzy wail the "I Got Up One Morning Blues," Elmore James crying out "Blues Before Sunrise," Jimmy Reed sliding through the incomparable "Bright Lights Big City."

Unlike so many people I knew, their pain was not self-inflicted. Instead, it arrived as clean, sharp, and clear as their stories. Their babies done left them, their jobs went bust, their lives weren't nuthin' but bowls of shit. Yet they sang on, creating a legacy of beauty that remained long after their own lives had ended.

Around midnight I finally staggered off to bed. To my surprise, I slept well.

Chapter 27

I got up at four a.m., climbed into the Jeep and headed north. Before I called Kryzinski, I needed to make sure that what I suspected—no, what I *knew*—could be proven in a court of law. For that, I had to hand Kryzinski an illegal entry. I'd do the deed in the darkness, tell him what I'd found, then he could get his own squeaky-clean search warrant. All it would take would be a "belated" memory from me, a little lie in service of a greater truth.

The construction trailer was dark, the parking lot empty. Dawn was at least an hour off. After driving the Jeep around to the back (just in case), I pulled my lock pick from my carryall, jimmied the lock, and went inside. The only light was from the soft glow of the button on cell phone, which was being charged again at the electrical outlet. The sculpture was where I'd seen it last, on the rosewood table in front of the sofa. I picked it up—*damn,* it was heavy!—snapped on my flashlight, and looked more carefully at the ground underneath the horse and rider.

There was the carved signature: *Frederick Remington, 1888.* As I continued to study it, I saw the crispness of the lines, the lack of the usual seam ridge left behind on cheap copies.

Because this *was* no cheap copy. The sculpture was an original casting made by the artist himself, a piece of priceless art the Remington-loving but alimony-paying Evan had told Gus to bring back when he'd sent him out to kill Clarice wearing a pair of Jay Kobe's old Nikes.

"I couldn't let him leave it there," Evan's voice said behind me. "What if one of those sticky-fingered cops took it home?"

I spun around, at the same time reaching for the gun in my bag.

But I wasn't fast enough. Something hard slammed into my head, light exploded all around me, and I began to fall.

Just before I lost consciousness, I heard Evan sob, "Why couldn't you just leave it alone? She wasn't worth it. She wasn't worth anybody's tears."

I came to in total darkness, my knees tucked under my chin. The air around me smelled like gasoline and burned rubber. Where was I? What was happening? Was I stuffed in a storage room somewhere about to be burned to death?

Frantically, I lifted my hands—mercifully untied—and began to feel around my small prison. I encountered a hard, metallic object and fumbled along it like a blind woman reading Braille. I found another object, this one larger and more rectangular, that appeared to be a tackle box or a tool kit. The soft, round mass in back of me felt like a pillow.

Then I noticed that the floor was moving, that I was being jostled back and forth. A soft purring, the hushed *urrrrrr-urrrrrr-urrrrrr* of a finely tuned engine, issued through the walls of my prison. When I raised my hands straight above me, I could touch the ceiling.

I was in the trunk of a car.

Being taken somewhere.

Then I understood that the thick metal object shoved up against my face was probably a jack, the rectangular thing the car's tool kit. The pillow was no doubt a car cover.

My fingers scrabbled through the trunk again, hoping to find my carryall with its fully loaded .38 still inside, but it wasn't there. Evan had probably dumped it someplace else, hoping it wouldn't be discovered with my body, hoping to put off identification as long as possible. I fingered the throbbing lump at the back of my head and felt something sticky. I was bleeding, but considering the thickness of the blood's texture, I estimated that the wound had already begun to coagulate. So far, so good. I cocked my head and listened carefully, but I couldn't hear other traffic sounds over the motor's murmur. The jouncing I was enduring was getting worse, sometimes flinging me all the way up against the trunk lid.

Evan was taking me off-road somewhere, probably to dump me in the desert. Just as he had done to Gus.

How stupid I had been! When I thought back, the signs had all been there. Evan was living in the trailer and just because he wasn't there when I arrived didn't mean he wouldn't come back. It was the tail end of Saturday night, for Pete's sake, and he'd probably been out yowling with all the other tomcats.

But it was too late for "I shouldda's." I needed to be thinking about the future—such as what I'd do the minute that car came to a stop and Evan unlocked the trunk to finish the job.

How hard did he think he'd hit me? Strong enough to kill? He probably thought he'd killed me, but I'd been turning, in motion, and the blow had been a glancing one. I could see a faint glimmer of hope in my situation. If Evan thought I was already dead, I would at least gain the element of surprise when he opened the car's trunk to dispose of my body.

My body.

I didn't like the way that sounded. Not at all. Then, for some reason, an odd question occurred to me…

Had Agnezia prayed for me last night?

Well, well. They say there were no atheists in foxholes and now I had proof that there were few atheists in car trunks, too. But not believing in miracles, I shook the thought out of my head. The only thing that would save me now would be my own actions.

A particularly severe lurch of the car threw me against the side of the trunk and smashed my nose against the jack. Stars again, a rush of hot liquid—blood, not tears. I was too terrified to cry. Trying not to injure myself further, I probed the bridge of my nose and found it misshapen. Another probe again—more stars—and to the accompaniment of a scraping sound, the bridge moved.

My nose was broken.

The car lurched again but I was able to brace my arms against the side of the trunk and keep my ruined face away from the jack.

The jack.

It wasn't my .38, but now I had a weapon. I only hoped that I'd get a chance to use it.

Was it still dark? I raised my head again and stared at the area where I thought the trunk lid might connect to the body of the car. A cat's whisker of light bled through the darkness. It was already growing uncomfortably hot in the trunk and I knew it would soon become an oven. How long had I been unconscious? Minutes? An hour? How long had Evan been off-road?

And *where* off-road?

I remembered Evan's car, an Infiniti I-30 sedan, not a vehicle known for its off-road capabilities. So he probably wouldn't be heading up a dirt track into the mountains.

Just out into the desert.

With difficulty, I smothered a hysterical laugh. *Just* the desert? With the last monsoon rain days in the past and daytime temperatures averaging around 115, I'd be lucky, even if I managed to escape from the car trunk, to survive a full day out there. Not unless…

I searched the floor of the trunk again, hoping to find that plastic jug of water most desert-savvy Arizona residents always carried in their trunks. No such luck. Evan had apparently not been a Boy Scout.

I lay there quietly with my fingers clutching the jack, and conserved my strength until I felt the car slow down. Then I lifted my head off the floor of the trunk and listened.

The up and down bumping motion I'd endured changed to a slow, sideways rocking. The purr of the Infiniti's motor lowered to a troubled growl.

We had to be in soft dirt. Or sand.

The river bottom, maybe?

I began to feel hope again. If we were in the river bottom, my chances might not be so bad. Water from the monsoons frequently collected in small pools and stayed there for days. Water might even be still running in some places. Then I remembered how low an Infiniti rode, how few inches of the undercarriage cleared the pavement. Nobody, not even poor ol', dumb ol', murdering ol' Evan, would be fool enough to drive an Infiniti down into the

Salt River bottom. With its low-slung carriage, it would be certain to belly out on the rocks that tumbled down from the mountains.

The Infiniti's growl changed to a whine as the car slowed even more. Within a few more seconds, the car stopped moving.

When I cocked my head, I could hear a muffled noise which sounded human. A curse? The engine's whine shrieked up the musical scale into a soprano's register as the car began to rock furiously backwards, then forwards, then backwards again. Evan must have gotten it mired in sand and now he was trying to rock it out. But he was doing it too quickly, too forcefully, and it was all I could do not to yell at him not to burn up the engine.

While the car continued its relentless back-and-forth, I took the opportunity to scrunch around in the trunk, to hunch over and get my feet under me. Even though I angled my body to the side to gain maximum space, my head still pressed painfully against the trunk's lid. My spine creaked, my heels jammed into my butt, my knees savaged my chin. But I was balanced on my toes, ready to spring.

If I only got the chance.

The Infiniti's rocking movement continued for a few more minutes until the engine's shriek became almost unbearable. Stop it! I wanted to call. Look at your tachometer!

The shrieking continued until I heard the Infiniti give a final desperate wail, then fall silent. I smelled the acrid, metallic odor of overheated metal.

The fool had burned up the Infiniti's engine.

"Fuck!" Evan's voice was quite clear, now.

The hair stood up on my arms as I heard a door slam and footsteps crunching around the side of the car towards me.

Showtime.

As a key scraped at the trunk lid, I tightened my grip on the heavy jack. Evan probably had a gun and I knew I'd have only one chance at him—and not a very good one at that. After all the time spent in the darkness of the trunk, the morning's light would probably blind me as soon as Evan lifted the trunk lid.

Then light exploded into the trunk and I exploded out. Totally blind, I swung the jack in a wide arc with all the strength left in my aching arms.

I connected.

I heard a crunch, a grunt. The sound of something big falling. A soft, bubbly moan.

Leaning down and aiming the jack in the direction of the moans, I swung again.

And again.

Soon all I could hear was the hot wind rushing through the mesquite.

Panting, I stood there, cramped muscles screaming. But I kept the jack at the ready until my retinas adjusted to the morning light. When I could finally see again, I stumbled over to Evan's crumpled form to discover a gaping wound on the left side of his head. He was bleeding profusely and the forehead just above his eye looked slightly misshapen. I pressed my fingers to the carotid artery under his jaw. His pulse was regular, but weak.

At least I hadn't killed him.

I tossed the jack back into the trunk and disentangled the gun from his limp fingers. It was a .45, probably the very .45 he'd shot me with from a rented Taurus. Then, the gun trained on him, I sank onto the sand and tucked my head between my knees. When the dizziness finally passed, I stood up and took a good look around.

I was surrounded by miles and miles of desert in every direction. Far to the east, under a hot sun which had only just begun its merciless ascent, stood a range of jagged peaks which looked like the western end of the White Tank Mountains. Evan had driven us at least seventy miles out into the desert from Phoenix. The Infiniti, its engine now probably residing in Infiniti heaven, was stuck up to its axles in sand. Even if I'd been able to crank the engine over, there'd still be no digging it out.

And the day was heating up.

In disgust, I glanced at Evan. *Here's another fine mess you've got us into, Ollie.* Then I got up, walked over to him, and—just in case—tied his hands behind him with his own belt, and his ankles with more strips of cloth from his shirt. The dilated pupil didn't bode well, but I'd seen people injured more severely get up and swing a tire iron at someone. I didn't want him trying to kill me again when I was busy trying to keep us both alive.

The knowledge of the severity of our plight made me want to vomit but I didn't dare. In the next few hours, I'd need all the liquid I could conserve.

But even if I could conserve the very sweat that dripped from my body, we might both be dead by sundown.

Chapter 28

But I wasn't dead yet.

Gun firmly in hand, I scrambled onto the Infiniti's hood, stood on tiptoe and looked around, hoping for a sight of a windmill or a water tank. Nothing. The dirt track Evan had driven the car down curled off to the horizon, passing nothing that looked even remotely man-made. Then I held still for a few moments, listening for any sounds of civilization: machinery, traffic, laughter. But all I heard was the whisper of the wind and a few peeps from cactus wrens.

Trying to walk out of the desert was a fatal mistake, the very mistake which killed so many tourists and even desert-dwellers every year. Without a survival kit and at least a gallon of water, I had no hope of surviving more than an hour or two out there. First would come the thirst. Then the stomach cramps. Then the hallucinations.

Next would come the buzzards.

The climbing sun sent waves of heat rising from the desert floor. I had to do something fast, find us some protection before it became too hot to move. I scanned the landscape again, this time for the presence of any wildlife which might indicate a local water source. I saw none, but my sinking heart lifted somewhat when I spied a patch of barrel cacti. After noting their location, I jumped carefully off the Infiniti. This was no time or place to sprain an ankle.

Now it was time to inventory the car, and after that, get Evan into some kind of shelter. I didn't like the sound of his breathing.

I found the car keys where Evan had dropped them when I'd bashed him in the head, but as I put them in my pocket, I realized how little good they'd do us. While the battery was probably still good, the car's air-conditioning would only run off it for a few minutes.

Then the battery, too, would die.

At this point, the Infiniti was of little more use than scrap metal.

And the few items I could scavenge from it.

The open trunk was empty except for the car cover, which was stuffed into a duffel bag; the tool kit; and a battered paperback by Tom Clancy. Still keeping an eye on Evan—head wounds frequently looked worse than they really were—I walked around to the passenger door and rummaged through the glove compartment. There wasn't much there to help me, either, just his car registration, a few Burger King coupons, and some women's telephone numbers written on bar napkins. Somehow it didn't surprise me to discover that Evan was a habitue of the Bourbon Street Circus, a strip club, and Babe's, a Scottsdale nudie bar. Already looking for wifey No. 4, I guessed.

"Evan, Evan," I said, though I was doubtful if he could hear me. "You've already been reduced to living in a trailer, eating at Burger King, and here you are, still thinking with your hormones."

He didn't reply. His eyes remained closed.

The Infiniti's back seat yielded Evan's laundry wrapped in a sheet of clear plastic upon the end of which was stamped in red letters, 24-HOUR LAUNDRY AND DRY-CLEANING, A VALLEY TRADITION FOR 32 YEARS. The thought that Evan had stopped off last night to get his laundry, and then proceeded to try and kill me seemed sicker than hell. But then again, he was a Hyath, wasn't he? Those people invented the word *sick*.

I hauled my treasures out of the Infiniti and put them in a pile by the trunk. Then I walked back to Evan. Calmer now, I noticed the largest wound I'd inflicted on him had stopped bleeding, and I thought his breathing was easier.

"Evan!" I shouted, prodding him with my foot. "Wake up!"

A moan.

I shouted at him some more and continued to prod him until his left eye opened. The pupil was dilated.

"Huh!" That was all he could manage.

Knowing the import of that dilated pupil, I realized that all the energy I'd expended tying him up had probably been wasted. My heart clutched with unwelcome pity as I squatted down beside him. "Evan, you've got to wake up. You've got a concussion and we're stranded out here on the desert. You've got to tell me exactly where we are, how far we are from the highway."

He began to mutter but his words were so slurred that at first I couldn't make out what he was saying, other than it was something about Clarice, a plea for her to do... to do...

To do what?

As he continued to mumble, his pleas became clearer. He thought I was Clarice and he was trying to talk me into signing the construction contract on the Hacienda Palms. He needed the money, he begged. His ex-wives had drained him and he was facing bankruptcy. If I didn't sign the contract, he'd have to kill me, so please, Clarice, please.

"Evan," I said patiently. "I'm not Clarice. Clarice is dead. I'm Lena Jones, remember? The detective?"

The other eyelid lifted slowly and he tried to focus. "Lena?"

"None other."

He gave me a loopy smile. "Head hurts. But I bet... I bet yours does, too."

"Sure does, you shithead. You tried to kill me."

One eye closed again, but the eye with the dilated pupil remained half open. He'd lost consciousness again.

I had to get him out of the blistering sun or he'd die.

Evan was a big man, well over six feet and probably topping two hundred and twenty-five pounds, so dragging him too far, over to that mesquite tree about thirty yards away, for instance, would be impossible. I'd have to bring the shade to him.

For that I needed more tools. After putting the .45 under the car for safety, but where I'd be able to reach it within seconds if I needed to, I began working on Evan. Being as gentle as possible, I fished through his pockets, found his wallet and threw it onto the pile by the car. In another pocket I found something more useful. A penknife. I hated what I had to do next but I did it anyway. I stripped off his shoes.

Then I returned to my pile of treasures and took inventory. Clean laundry. One pair of Nikes with shoelaces. A wallet. A knife. A Tom Clancy paperback. A few bar napkins. A car cover. A duffel bag. A tool kit. A jack.

Our chances for survival were looking up. They've have been even better if the fuck-up had thrown his damned old cell phone into the car, but you can't have everything, can you?

"Hey, Evan, I might be able to keep us alive for a full day!" I called to him.

He didn't reply.

Then I looked over at the Infiniti again and said, "No, two days. Maybe even three!"

Working slowly so as not to dehydrate myself too much, I stripped the Infiniti of everything I thought I would need. Using the heavy jack, I knocked off the rear view mirror and, with a screwdriver I found in the toolbox, pried away the Infiniti's hubcaps. I pulled the hood release and disconnected the radiator water reservoir and the container of windshield-washing fluid. They might not be potable, but the liquid was precious nonetheless. Reaching towards the motor, I pulled the dipstick out of the crank case. Evan, bless his murdering heart, had changed the oil recently and it sparkled golden and clear, so I touched my finger to the dipstick, lifted off a few drops, and smeared my lips with its soothing balm. My lips now protected from cracking, I dragged my treasures up the dirt track about twenty feet beyond Evan, as far away from the Infiniti as I dared. By noon, the sedan's sleek metal would be hot enough to cook on and staying in its immediate proximity wasn't a good idea.

I'd worked up a thirst scavenging the car in the warm morning sun but I couldn't worry about that now. I had too much to do before it got really hot. I untied Evan's feet, tucked them under my armpits, and inch by miserable inch, dragged the unconscious man further away from the car. As I worked, sweat ran into my eyes, stinging me, and I had to stop once to fashion a makeshift sweatband out of the hem of my T-shirt for my forehead. When

I'd finally dragged him about twenty feet from the car, I lowered his feet to the ground.

"Hurts," he muttered, having regained some semblance of consciousness during the torturous trip.

"I'm sorry."

He managed a feeble smile. "S'okay."

I smiled back, wondering why I felt pity for such a cold-blooded murderer. "We're going to make it, Evan. Just hang in there." I didn't bother re-tying his feet. He didn't look like he'd be able to do any traveling soon.

God, I was thirsty. The sweat I'd lost while dragging Evan had dehydrated me badly, but there was nothing that could be done about it now. I still had to get the sun's rays off Evan.

I rooted around on the desert floor, found a small stone, and popped it into my mouth to help with the dryness. Then I took Evan's pocket knife and cut three limbs off the mesquite. After checking on the angle of the sun, I got between Evan and the sun and drove two of the mesquite's limbs as deep into the earth as I could. Then I shook the car cover out of its duffel bag.

Taking the penknife, I slashed the hems of both the car cover and the bag and pulled out their drawstrings. Measuring carefully, I stretched the longest drawstrings from one mesquite limb to the next, creating a northeast to southwest line. Then I looped one end of the car cover over it, securing the car cover to the horizontal line with shoelaces from Evan's Nikes. Now I cut the other mesquite limb into eighths and, using a heavy wrench from the toolkit, hammered the mesquite stakes through the earth end of the car cover and into the ground so that the hot desert wind wouldn't blow it away.

It wasn't fancy, but the rough lean-to would protect us from the morning sun's assault. When the sun traveled towards the west, I would simply flip the car cover over to the other side and secure it again. As a bonus, the waterproof, reflective surface of the car-cover would provide additional protection.

I crawled into the lean-to and discovered that Evan had slipped into unconsciousness again.

"Evan? Evan! Wake up!"

Nothing.

He was still alive, though. I could hear him breathing, but it seemed to me that his breath was growing ragged. Alarmed, I felt the carotid artery. His pulse was uneven, too. Not a good sign at all. It occurred to me, then, that attempting to save the life of the man who'd three times tried to kill me was an odd way of spending what might be my own last day on earth, but I couldn't help myself.

Besides, Evan couldn't hurt me now, and it might be nice to have some company until Search and Rescue finally arrived.

If they ever did.

I had two more chores to perform before I was finished for the day, before the merciless sun climbed to its zenith and I'd be able to do no more than hunker down in the lean-to next to Evan.

During our many camping excursions, my Baptist foster parents had impressed upon me that water could be found in even the driest desert. All you had to do was look. Once they had even shown me how.

Using one of the Infiniti's hubcaps for a shovel, I dug a hole far enough away from the lean-to and the car to ensure the hole would stay in the sunlight. When the hole was about three feet across by two feet deep, I lined it with buffalo grass I'd harvested from the desert floor. After cutting off the top of the radiator overflow bottle, I wetted the grass down and placed the now-empty plastic container at the bottom of the hole. Now I cut the plastic cleaning bag in half and set one half aside for later use. I very loosely covered the hole with the other half, securing it to the top of the ground with several large rocks. I took a smooth rock with no jagged edges and set it carefully in the loose bottom of the plastic, creating an unopened funnel that ended just above the empty plastic container.

If this gadget worked the way the Baptists said it would, the sun shining through the plastic would evaporate the contaminated water I'd poured onto the buffalo grass. The evaporation would condense onto the sides of the plastic, then dribble down into my makeshift cup. I'd get only about one cup every eight hours, but as soon as it was dark, I'd dig another hole and use the remaining sheet of plastic.

I felt better already. The prospect of having water in about eight hours stilled the pocket of fear in my chest but I noticed that my thirst was increasing. In the desert, it was dangerous to let this go on too long, because by the time you realized you were dehydrating, it was already too late. I had to get a drink and I had to get a drink RIGHT NOW.

And I'd better try to get some liquid down Evan.

Ignoring the heat, I got busy again. My eye on the climbing sun, I used the heavy wrench to batter a hubcap into a scoop, then picked over Evan's clean laundry until I found a white cotton dress shirt. No polyester for the Hyaths, thank you very much. I took the tire iron, my scoop, and my second plastic container over to the nearest barrel cactus. Using the same vicious motion I'd used at Evan's head, I swung the jack at the top of the cactus. The top came off with a sickening crunch, not unlike the sound Evan's head had made when I connected. For a moment, my stomach heaved and bile rose to my throat. I choked it back down. Vomiting would cost me too much liquid.

I approached the cactus carefully, since there was no point in adding to increasing discomfort by getting stuck. Once I made certain that the liquid oozing from the severed head of the cactus was clear, I put a handful of sand into the plastic container. I scrubbed and scrubbed until I was certain that no remnants of denatured alcohol remained to poison me, then set it aside. I spent the next few minutes with my hubcap scoop, dumping moist cactus meat into Evan's clean shirt.

When I thought I had enough, I closed the shirt up and wrung it over the plastic container. Pure cactus juice dribbled out. I kept wringing until the juice stopped flowing, then tossed the pulp away. Hunger wasn't my enemy. In fact, the digestive process used up much of the body's water stores, so anyone stranded in the desert was wise to not eat at all.

Satisfied with my morning's work, I took my water over to the lean-to.

"Evan!" I nudged him with my foot. "Wake up!"

"Uh." One eye fluttered open again. It was his good eye, and I could tell that he saw me.

I stooped down, holding the plastic container up to his lips. "I brought you something to drink."

With my hand holding up his head, he managed to get some of it down. A few precious drops, though, dribbled to the earth.

I tried not to think about them, and drank the rest. Slowly. Sensuously.

I stayed in the lean-to with Evan the rest of the day, conserving my energy, taking care not to let panic lure me into a fruitless search for help. Hypothermia and dehydration were the desert's two most vicious weapons, and I wasn't about to give them the advantage. Who knows how long we'd be stuck out here? It was Sunday. Because he'd worked on Saturday, I'd told Jimmy to keep his butt out of the office until Tuesday. Dusty would be tied up with the ranch guests until Wednesday night, and might not even get a chance to call. And Kryzinski? He'd probably just think that I'd gotten too busy to sign my complaint about the shooter (about Evan, I reminded myself), and just put it down to my usual ditziness. Which meant that no one was going to miss me for at least forty-eight hours.

Time enough to die.

As I sat hunched in the shade of the shelter, the day heated up. I'd removed one of the pieces of cardboard inserted in Evan's shirts, and used that as a makeshift fan for us both. It helped some. Once a small dust devil whirled across the desert floor, picking up buffalo grass, dried mesquite leaves, and sand, flinging them towards us. As debris spun towards me, I wrapped Evan's head in another clean shirt for protection and tucked my own between my knees, hoping that the dust devil wouldn't destroy the shelter. I'd hate to have to build it all over again under the afternoon sun.

But we lucked out. After making life miserable for the tiny lizards that scampered in all directions from its path, the whirlwind danced away to the south, leaving the lean-to untouched.

"How you doin', Evan?" I asked, rearranging the shirt over his head. "You hanging in there?"

He didn't answer but I could tell by the slow rise and fall of his chest that he was still alive. And was it merely my imagination, or was his pulse stronger?

I threw a glance over at the Infiniti, making certain that a gopher hadn't scuttled off with the .45. To my relief, I saw that it was still there. If Evan regained his strength, as he appeared to be doing, I'd need to get to it in a hurry. I didn't kid myself that he'd be so grateful I'd taken care of him that he wouldn't try to murder me again. I'd already learned from the Hyaths that it was possible to like someone—love them, even—and still kill them.

Towards late afternoon, when the heat was on the verge of sucking the very breath out of my body, Evan woke up. "Lena?" The word was clear.

I turned towards him and saw that both eyes were open, but the pupil in the right eye looked even more dilated than it had before. Despite the heat, I shivered. I didn't want to share a lean-to with a dead man.

"How are you feeling?" I asked.

"Thirsty." His voice was faint but its earlier slur was gone. Maybe this was a good sign.

I patted him on the arm. "I'll get you something to drink."

On the way to the barrel cactus, I stopped at the car and scooped the gun out from under it. After tucking the .45 into the waistband of my jeans, I picked up the jack and attacked another barrel cactus. Soon I was back at the lean-to, giving Evan all my hard-won water.

"Tastes awful," he mumbled.

"Thanks ever so."

"Sorry." Evan sighed, closed his eyes again and for a while I thought he'd gone back to sleep. But after a few minutes, he spoke again. "I'm s-sorry, Lena. So sorry about so m-much."

"You should be." I looked at him more carefully and noticed a thin line of blood dribbling from his left ear. Knowing what that meant, I decided to untie his hands. I couldn't save him, but at least I could make him comfortable.

He smiled his gratitude and the handsomeness in his face briefly returned. "God, you are... you are one helluva w-woman. I wish... I wish I'd met you earlier."

I dabbed the blood away from his ear. New blood quickly replaced it. He was dying and I think he knew it, because he began to tell me everything.

When Clarice had refused to sign the development contract for the Hacienda Palms Golf Course, she had inadvertently signed her own death warrant. Evan had truly cared for Clarice, and the grief he'd displayed after her death had been genuine. But like his parents, he'd loved money even more than he loved anyone.

It was the Hyath family curse.

Once Evan made up his mind to kill her, he was smart enough to know that he'd be a prime suspect, unless he could point the finger at someone else. It hadn't taken him too long to realize that in Jay Kobe he had the perfect fall guy. All he'd needed to come up with then was the means and the opportunity.

Enter Gus Baylor. In the one true coincidence of the case, Baylor had applied for a job laying flagstones at Tudor Hills right around the time Evan, out of money and desperate, made up his mind to murder Clarice. No mean man with a computer himself, Evan checked Baylor's background and discovered the old murder conviction. The ex-con's subsequent behavior must have had Evan swooning in pre-murderous delight. Then, when Gus got into that high-profile fight at the Tudor Hills construction site, Evan decided it was time to strike.

"Gus…Gus hated women," Evan said, his voice made raspy by heat and dehydration. "I think he'd have killed Clarice for free, but…but the money I offered made him even more enthusiastic."

He'd told Gus to kill Clarice with one quick blow from the tire iron first, then beat her about the face so that it would look like she'd suffered another battering from Jay. There was no point in telling Evan that Gus hadn't exactly followed orders, that he'd slowly, lovingly, beaten Clarice half to death with his fists.

"Did you tell Gus to unlock the front door?" I asked.

Evan smiled. "I had to make s-sure her b-body would be discovered while I was…I was at dinner with Malik."

I'd been right there, too.

Evan wasn't done with his confession.

"The p-problem was...Gus was too nuts to trust. I knew I'd have to eventually get rid of him. I...I paid him fifty percent of his fee before he killed her and told him I'd pay the rest later." Here he smiled again. "He was as stupid as he was nuts. When I said I'd deliver the p-payoff in the desert outside of town, he didn't think twice. He...he was right on time. I paid him off, all...all right."

He'd talked too long and his voice began to fade. I gave him another sip of cactus juice and he rallied. Closing his eyes against the day's glare, he added, "I... I knew you were trouble the m-minute I saw you."

I remembered, then, his recognition of me the day I'd visited him at the construction site. *I recognize you from that time you were on TV. You'd proved some guy on Death Row was innocent.*

There was one more thing I needed to know before he passed out again, one more crime to lay at the feet of the Hyaths. When I asked him about it he nodded weakly.

Then he drifted back into unconsciousness.

I spent the rest of the day fanning poor Evan and staring out at the desert from the shelter of the lean-to, watching more dust devils suck up tumbleweeds and send them whirling into the air. The temperature continued to climb, and when the wind finally died down, I thought I could actually hear the heat sizzling up from the desert floor.

Succumbing to the stupor of the heat-stunned, I'd almost begun to doze off when I heard Evan's breathing change. Wide awake now I scrambled towards him, and he opened his eyes. The pupil in his left eye was totally dilated and a large pool of blood had collected under his left ear. His face was so swollen he looked like Alison Garwood the last time I'd seen her.

And I'd done that to him.

"Evan?" I whispered, cradling his head in my lap. "Don't worry. I'm here with you."

He smiled the guileless smile of a child and I knew he didn't recognize me. "Clarice? Clarice, honey, is that you?"

"Sure it's me," I said, lowering my voice so I'd sound more like her and stroking his hair while his ear bled onto my thighs.

"I'm sorry Clarice. I was wrong to hurt you. It was just that... It was just that without the money, no woman would ever love me again."

I leaned over him and put my lips to his ears. Still trying to sound like his sister, I said, "It's all right, Evan. I forgive you."

Evan turned his head, brushed his lips against my palm, and died.

Who knows when spirits leave their bodies? The Navajo believe they leave right away, sometimes hanging around the earth, though, to make trouble for the living. I didn't know what the Pima believed about death. If I lived through this, I'd ask Jimmy. Whatever the truth was, I wanted to make sure I'd covered all the bases for Evan. I let his head remain in my lap for a while and stroked his hair, murmuring, "There, there, Evan. There, there."

Eventually, though, I had to move him. I couldn't continue sharing the lean-to with a dead man. Not in this heat.

I looked over at the Infiniti, about twenty feet away. At the trunk, the opening of which was about three feet off the ground, at least. That solution was hopeless. So, whispering my own apology, I dragged Evan out as far into the desert as my failing strength would allow. But it wasn't far enough.

The buzzards found him just before sunset.

They circled down from the sky like pieces of black confetti. As one alighted, it looked back at me through glittering black eyes, reminding me of Eleanor Hyath. Repulsed, I turned my head away from their red eyes, their scabrous necks. They enjoyed Evan very much. They squawked and cawed over him, fought over the tastiest morsels.

Even covering my ears didn't keep out their happy chatter.

When twilight fell and the heat began to wane, I returned to the Infiniti, carefully keeping my eyes averted from the action in the brush. In addition to the buzzards, a few thousand blowflies were having themselves a high old time with Evan, but I tried to ignore them, along with the odor that wafted not-so-sweetly from their juicy banquet. I jumped on top of the car's hood again and looked around, hoping to see lights of any kind—cars, houses, maybe even lights from the Palo Verde Nuclear Plant, which had to be somewhere close by. But I saw nothing. The desert was devoured by shadows.

I jumped off the hood, opened it again, and smeared as much dirt-encrusted engine oil as I could onto one of Evan's socks. I closed the hood, and using the sock as a makeshift paintbrush, wrote *S-O-S* in letters so large they took up the entire hood. Even in the gloom, they stood out well on the Infiniti's metallic gold surface.

As a breeze started down from the mountains, I checked my hand-made water processing plant and found almost a half-pint of fresh water. Thanking the Baptists, I drank it down, not even minding the slightly plastic flavor. Now refreshed, I dug another hole and deposited the windshield-washing fluid container for my cup.

I made another visit to the cactus patch and this time used a curved hubcap as a water bowl. Then I took a piss, a good sign because it meant that my body was still a long way from dehydration.

My needs satisfied, I went back to the car and scraped Evan's clothing into a soft pillow. Then I slit the duffel bag down the side and lay down in the back seat, grateful for the soft, cushiony leather. Sleep crept up on me and I felt my eyes begin to close. Although the car's windows remained half-open (I had to be able to hear help if it arrived), I hardly noticed the hot, dry wind that swept down from the mountains. I was as snug as a bug in a rug.

I woke up during the night and stared at the mercilessly clear sky. Where was the monsoon when you needed it? At some point while I'd been dozing, the coyotes had found Evan. I could hear ripping sounds, along with a rubbery flopping as if something large was being repeatedly picked up and dropped.

Shuddering, I tried to sleep.

Awake before the sun even hinted at its presence, I checked both of my little water processing plants and was gratified to find two more half-filled containers of water. I drank them both down and then, with another of Evan's socks wrapped around my hand for protection, picked up the tool kit. I tried not to look in Evan's direction.

I chose a crescent wrench from the tool kit and slid under the car. My fumbling hands soon found the radiator release screw. After some grunting and knuckle-rapping, I managed to get it unscrewed and rusty water splattered down into my two plastic containers. As soon as they were full, I pressed the screw up to the radiator again, tightened it, and stopped the flow. Then I went back to my home-made wells and saturated the buffalo grass again, secure in the knowledge that I'd be able to harvest more water by noon.

I decided to wait until dawn before I attacked another barrel cactus. Directions and distances could be treacherous in the dark, and I didn't want to risk losing my bearings. Instead, I returned to the Infiniti and began hitting short taps on the horn every fifteen seconds. The sound carried well over the flat desert and hopefully would annoy some bad-tempered rancher who'd drive his truck over to complain that I'd interrupted his sleep.

At first, the noise chased the buzzards and coyotes away, but after they realized it held no threat, they returned and the ripping sounds began again.

I made myself think of Dusty's eyes. Jimmy's friendship.

I thought about the scar on my forehead and how much I had already survived. If my mother hadn't been able to kill me, how could the desert?

Then I remembered my moments of despair at Rocky Point, the temptation to swim out to sea and never return.

As a mockingbird began to trill the morning, what could possibly be my last morning, I at last realized how much I wanted to live.

The sun rose over the White Tanks, only hinting at its later excesses. The Infiniti's battery was a good one, and it was still going strong when the heat drove me out of the car. Before I took shelter again under my lean-to, I attacked another barrel cactus.

How long could I survive like this? My slim water rations wouldn't keep me alive forever. And I was beginning to experience symptoms that could indicate heat stroke—lightheadedness, clammy skin, stomach cramps. I had to stop moving and start resting.

So I curled up with the Tom Clancy novel and read about a submarine rushing through Arctic waters while the predators ravaged Evan's corpse in the hot sun. The irony was not lost on me. From time to time, I dabbed precious cactus juice on my face and fanned myself with a piece of cardboard. It didn't help all that much.

How long could I hold out?

I dozed on and off all day, emerging from my shelter only when the sun went down to harvest water and to savage another cactus. I noticed, now, that I had to hit the cactus several times before I could puncture its skin.

Either the cactus was getting tougher or I was getting weaker.

I spent the night in the Infiniti, staring out the windows and thinking about death.

The next day was hotter.

The sun rose, a malicious red ball that seared my skin. When the car began to heat up, I crawled back into my lean-to, spending the morning splashing cactus juice on my face. But nothing seemed to help. Once, in desperation, I even returned to the oven-like Infiniti and turned on the air-conditioning, but after a few minutes of life-lengthening cool blasts, the battery died.

Now I didn't even have the car horn to summon help.

Firing a few rounds from the gun wouldn't help, because anyone passing near enough to hear it would automatically think someone was out here hunting. Or practicing for a raid on the State Capitol.

As I returned to my lean-to, I didn't even bother looking over towards Evan. There probably wasn't much of him left.

Somehow I survived the morning.

Around noon, I began to feel woozy and as I looked out onto the desert's stark, minimalist beauty, I began to see shapes moving towards me through the wavery heat. I attempted to rise but fell back onto my pallet. No problem. The shapes got closer, closer, until I could see that there were Indians, a band of about six—men and women both—from a tribe I couldn't identify.

They were shorter than the Pima but taller than the Yaqui who lived near Phoenix. And their clothing...

I squinted my eyes as they grew nearer.

The women, burned deep brown by the desert sun, wore only rawhide skirts, leaving their breasts exposed. Like the men, who were clad only in short loincloths, they had painted zig-zag stripes on their bodies in red, yellow and white. Their long, unbound hair waved from their heads like pennants in the hot wind.

Hohokam.

"But you're all dead," I whispered, as they passed only ten feet from my lean-to. "You've been dead for centuries. You're with Earth Doctor now."

They ignored me and continued their silent journey eastward towards the Superstition Mountains.

I allowed myself another sip of cactus juice and sank back onto my pallet, aware that I had started hallucinating—the first step on my own long journey. But would it really be that bad? I'd lived near this desert all my life, listened to its hawks and its wind, breathed in its wildflowers and sage. If I died here, I'd simply become a part of it.

Would that be so bad? To nourish the soil or enter the coyote? There were crueler deaths, more wasteful graves.

That night, dreams came in short snatches, as if my unconscious mind was too weak to sustain them. Earth Doctor, Elder Brother, they all came to visit and offer their advice. The desert was a good and clean place, they said, but it took endurance to live there. I agreed with them and they were sucked up into a whirlwind. When the night was almost over, a red-haired young man with eyes the color of mine leaned over me and caressed my cheek. "There, there, Tina. There, there." I recognized his tender hands, his sweet smile.

"Daddy," I whispered.

Like a ghost, he dissolved into the air, but I wasn't alone for long. When dawn broke, a coyote approached with what appeared to be a smile on her bright blond face.

"I know you," I said. "We met at Papago Park."

She laughed and bared her long fangs. Then she stuck her nose into the lean-to and bit me on the ankle.

"Ouch!" I complained. "I'm not dead yet, dummy! You're supposed to let me die first."

She snarled and bit me again. I tried to go back to sleep, but every time I drifted off, she nipped me again. Finally she took hold of my jeans leg and began to tug, as if she was trying to drag me out into the sun.

"Stop that! It's hot out there!" My voice sounded like a bark.

But the coyote wouldn't leave me alone. She tugged and tugged. And every time I laid my head back down she gnawed on me some more.

She eventually made me so angry that I staggered to my feet, stumbled out of the lean-to, and took a swat at her with the Tom Clancy book.

She yelped, then pointed her muzzle skyward, as if demanding I follow her gaze.

I did. That's when I saw the plane.

The coyote grinned in triumph, then trotted off in the same direction the Hohokam had taken.

Finally roused from my stupor, I shuffled over to the Infiniti. With my last bit of strength, I grabbed the rearview mirror I'd pried off during my first day on the desert. As I stood there looking upwards, the blue-and-orange Cessna floated across the horizon, looking to my sun-dazzled eyes mighty like an angel. Capturing the sun in the Infiniti's mirror, I began to signal.

The Cessna floated on, oblivious.

Although I'd thought I was too dehydrated to cry, tears trickled down my cheeks.

"Pray for me, Agnezia!" I shouted.

I signaled again.

And the Cessna waggled its wings.

Chapter 29

I was a hero once more.

During my two-day hospital stay, the papers made me a celebrity, and I could already see new business rolling in for Desert Investigations. The headline on the *Scottsdale Journal* blared, SCOTTSDALE DETECTIVE SOLVES MURDER OF SOCIALITE, SURVIVES THREE DAYS IN DESERT! The only thing that annoyed me was the picture they had chosen. It was an old one from my Violent Crimes Unit days, which in itself was okay, but they had retouched it and my scar had vanished. I guess they thought they were being kind.

The story left out plenty, too. The reporter wrote only that Evan's body had been recovered by the Search and Rescue team radioed by the Cessna's pilot. He didn't mention how little of Evan remained, or the noisy protest the coyotes had set up as the Search and Rescue team dragged Evan's body away. Most of the Hyath family scandal had been expunged from the article, too, perhaps out of fear of a lawsuit. The story did note, however, that Clarice had filed a civil action against her father only to drop it mere days before her death. Other than my near-beatification, most of the article was about Clarice. Gus Baylor had been reduced to a mere afterthought, which I thought was fitting.

I also appreciated that the reporter took pains to point out the culpability of the proposed zoning change in Clarice's murder, and I hoped the Zoning Commission might have second thoughts.

Knowing Scottsdale as I did, though, I doubted it. The Hacienda Palms Golf Course was history.

When I turned to the jump on the second page, I saw an article recounting another death.

Finally understanding that the last night in the desert I'd dreamed only of the dead, I turned my face to the pillow and wept.

They let me out of the hospital the next day, saying that it was a miracle I had survived in the shape I had. My arms were so full of floral arrangements that I felt like the Queen of the May, but the object most precious to me I held in my right hand: a thirty-six ounce bottle of chilled Evian.

"God helps those who help themselves," I muttered as Dusty led me out front, where a pack of reporters and live TV cameras lay in wait.

"That's not what you said when I got to the hospital," Dusty said, as the media closed in. "I even remember you muttering something about prayer. And ghosts."

Ignoring him, I beamed at the reporters, then turned my scarred profile to the cameras.

They pressed in close and a live remote camera stuck itself right in my face. I started talking.

On what I was assured was a live feed, I told the press exactly why Clarice had filed that civil action against her father. I told them that her mother had always known about the molestation but refused to do anything about it because she might lose some money. I recounted almost verbatim the last conversation I'd had with both of the Hyaths and the damning contents of their pre-nupt.

When one of the reporters asked me if I wasn't afraid that the Hyaths would sue me, I shrugged. "After three days surviving in the Arizona desert, it's hard to be afraid of anything else."

Then I bid them good day and headed for Dusty's truck.

"Started a little firestorm back there, didn't you?" Dusty said, as he pulled out of the parking lot.

"The Hyaths can afford the fire-fighting equipment," I answered. Then I noticed that he had already turned down the street that led to my apartment above Desert Investigations, so I put a restraining hand on his arm. There were a couple of stops I wanted to make first, I told him.

He opened his mouth to argue then thought better of it and turned the truck around.

It took us only a few minutes to get to the cemetery. Clarice's grave had already taken on a look of neglect. A solitary bouquet of red roses nestled at the base of the headstone and as I leaned over, I saw that the card read, "From your loving father."

Loving? Perhaps that was the way he'd seen it. Only he and the Devil knew for sure.

I knelt down and carpeted Clarice's grave with my own flowers. My friend's face may have been false, but she'd cared as much for me as she could care for anyone, and for that I owed her roses.

Perhaps some day I would even learn to forgive her.

During my years as a detective with the Violent Crimes Unit, I had learned many ugly things about human behavior, chief among them the fact that evil always arrives with a bellyful of excuses. Those excuses were as false as Clarice's smiles. Yes, she had been sexually abused, emotionally abused, but it still didn't excuse her later behavior. She ruined Dulya Albundo's family, and indirectly, killed Dulya's mother. She had used George Haozous for her own purposes, and when she was through with him, tossed him out with the rest of the garbage. She was even preparing to ruin Cliffie, who had been her friend for years. God knows what damage she would have done to my life if she had lived.

The humiliations Clarice had suffered at the hands of her parents didn't excuse her later behavior; they didn't even explain it. Thousands, perhaps hundreds of thousands of children live through years of unimaginable hell, yet grow up to become decent, productive citizens.

Very few of us, and in truth I must include myself on the list of the abused, become killers.

Oh, yes. That too. Clarice was a killer, in intent, if not yet in action. Evan's answer to that final question I had asked him out on the desert had haunted me for days.

"Yes," he'd told me before he died. "Gus told me all about it. He thought it was hilarious."

Clarice had scheduled that meeting with Gus because she had also been in the audience at that infamous fight in Tudor Hills. Like Evan, she'd recognized a killer when she saw one.

And she'd wanted to hire him.

Clarice planned to kill her mother. With Mommy dead, there'd be more money for Daddy and Clarice.

The next grave I visited was more sorrowful. Other mourners joined me in laying armloads of flowers at the foot of the simple wooden cross. There were tears of regret, talk of yet another zoning change. Always alert to a photo op, the mayor was there. As reporters swarmed around her, she proposed a buffer zone to separate the reservation from the city, a buffer zone lined by a high fence, one too high for coyotes to climb.

As I looked down at the freshly dug grave of the blond-faced coyote shot on the way to her den by a gun-toting Scottsdale vigilante, I wept once more. The fool had shot the wrong coyote. That *my* coyote's pups would stay at a wildlife rescue organization until they were old enough to return to the wild only slightly eased my sorrow. I remembered their mother's wild smile as we faced each other across the Papago Buttes, the mark of the desert branded on her face.

She reminded me of me.

I bowed my head and wished her good hunting with Earth Doctor.

Then I turned around and went back to the truck where the man I no longer feared to love waited for me.

Epilogue

From the *Scottsdale Journal*:

SCOTTSDALE—Jay Kobe, widower of murdered socialite Clarice Kobe, was shot to death last night by his live-in girlfriend, Alison Garwood.

Neighbors reported hearing an altercation, then gunshots. They called 911.

When police arrived they found Garwood holding a gun and standing over Kobe's body. She was bleeding from a beating that Capt. Edgar Kryzinski, head of the Violent Crimes Unit, described as "savage."

"I loved him," Garwood reportedly told police. "But I just couldn't take it any more. Not after he killed our baby."

According to hospital sources, Garwood was referring to a miscarriage she'd suffered earlier in the month, allegedly caused by another beating.

Garwood is being treated for her injuries at Scottsdale Memorial Hospital. It is not yet known if she will be charged in Kobe's death.

To receive a free catalog of other Poisoned Pen Press titles, please contact us in one of the following ways:

Phone: 1-800-421-3976
Facsimile: 1-480-949-1707
Email: info@poisonedpenpress.com
Website: www.poisonedpenpress.com

Poisoned Pen Press
6962 E. First Ave. Ste 103
Scottsdale, AZ 85251